Disney

A DARK ASCENSION NOVEL

The Lost Ones

Published by Disney Press, an imprint of Buena Vista Books, Inc.
No part of this book may be reproduced or transmitted in any
form or by any means, electronic or mechanical, including
photocopying, recording, or by any information storage and
retrieval system, without written permission from the publisher.
For information address Disney Press, 1200 Grand Central Avenue,
Glendale, California 91201.

Printed in the United States of America

First Hardcover Edition, January 2024
First Paperback Edition, January 2025

1 3 5 7 9 10 8 6 4 2
FAC-004510-24298
Library of Congress Control Number: 2023933611
ISBN 978-1-368-10253-7

Designed by Soyoung Kim

Visit disneybooks.com

SUSTAINABLE
FORESTRY
INITIATIVE

Certified Sourcing

www.forests.org
SFI-01681

Logo Applies to Text Stock Only

DISNEP

A DARK ASCENSION NOVEL

The Lost Ones

New York Times best-selling author

LAUREN DESTEFANO

DISNEP **PRESS**

LOS ANGELES • NEW YORK

Prologue

James was born first. Marlene came three minutes later, quite unexpected and another mouth to feed.

"Twins?" their mother had murmured, dazed and exhausted.

"Twins," the doctor affirmed. He sounded rather pleased with himself. They were the first set he'd delivered, and, by effect, the first set the town had seen in decades.

Before she fell into a dreamless sleep, their mother stared at the rainwater dripping down from a pronounced crack in the bedroom ceiling, cursing her luck. There had been room for only one. One homemade crib in the modest nursery. One little window that faced the North Sea, and barely enough money for the roof over one child's head.

"What am I supposed to do with two of them?"

As it would turn out, everything about the twins was unexpected. While James inherited their father's quiet and contemplative nature, he did not inherit a love of the sea. The first time his father took James on his fishing boat—when James was just a week old—James cried as the cool salty air hit his face. He wailed as the mild waves swayed them, and he flinched at the calls of the gulls circling overhead.

For her part, Marlene was not the refined young lady her mother would have hoped for. While she had delicate features and the blue eyes of a fine porcelain doll, she was a restless and fidgety thing. If her twin brother wanted only to be left to lie in his crib and make sense of things, Marlene wanted to get out and explore. She pulled at the laces her mother sewed onto her sleeping gowns and writhed restlessly in her bassinet, grasping at the things she didn't yet have words for.

But even at the start, James and Marlene understood each other in a way that their own parents never could. Marlene learned to crawl first, but she stayed by James's side, waiting for him to be able to keep up with her. And James—ever observant—protected his sister by blocking her way when she reached for the fire in the woodstove without fear, or tried to toddle out to sea, dazzled as she was by the gleaming water.

It was a synchronicity that rarely required words. An instinct, as though each twin made up one half of an efficient machine.

"Marlene, can't you act like a lady?" their mother would sigh, scrubbing the dirt from her daughter's knees and cheeks after a morning of climbing trees.

"Look, son, look at how open the sea is," their father would say, hoisting James onto his shoulders. James would do his best not to turn as green as the water that swayed before him.

Their parents loved them, the twins knew. Despite their uncertainty at the additional financial burden an extra child brought, they adored both of their children and worked hard to offer them the best lives they could. But they still didn't know what to do with them.

And as they grew, both Marlene and James carried a collection of unspoken worries. Marlene feared for her brother's quiet, sensitive nature. She fought off schoolyard bullies, and grabbed his hand and tugged him along so that he wouldn't be swallowed up by the crowd on their outings in the city. He was so fixated on the finer details of things that he often missed what was right in front of him.

James, in turn, feared for his sister's relentless spirit. He worried that one day she would not stop and wait for him after she'd run ahead. He worried that her swimmer's legs and her boundless energy would one day carry her too far, to a place he couldn't follow, toward a danger he couldn't stop.

1

James and Marlene turned fifteen on the winter solstice in late December. It was the darkest day of the year, and, coincidentally, the coldest. James could feel it in his bones when he woke up that morning. The window was rattling in its pane.

As usual, Marlene's bed was empty by the time James opened his eyes. She would be downstairs already, boots on, waiting for him at the breakfast table. James liked to be punctual, but his sister made an art of being early for everything.

He took his time getting dressed in his gray tunic, which he had pressed the night before. He liked gray. It was neutral—neither exuberant nor dreary—and it hid the soot that spat out from the fireplace.

As expected, the gifts from their parents were already waiting at the center of the table when James descended the creaky wooden steps and entered the kitchen: one small bundle and a larger one beside it, both of them wrapped in burlap and held in twine. Both reeking faintly of the marina.

Marlene looked up at him as she sipped her morning tea. "I already had breakfast," she said, her light tone not quite matching the impatience on her face; wherever James went, Marlene always seemed to get there first with time to spare. "You'll have to make your own."

"Mother and Father aren't here?" James asked, though he already knew the answer.

"They were gone when I got up," she said. Her eyes landed on the gifts. "Shall we wait until tonight to open them?"

James shook his head. If they waited for both of their parents to be seated for a family meal at the same time, they would be waiting well into their next birthday.

"The big one's for me," Marlene said. "They labeled them."

James went to the kettle and poured himself a cup of tea. He could sense his sister's impatience at this, but he wouldn't be rushed. She got her way about so many things—she was confident, she had more friends, she could sing—and all he wanted was to take his time with breakfast on his birthday before walking to school in the freezing winter rain.

Marlene slid James's gift across the table as soon as he sat down. He didn't know why she was so eager. Their birthday had never produced anything grand—certainly nothing like the windfall that likely befell the children their mother nannied in London on their special days. Gold trinkets and tiered cakes stacked halfway to the ceiling. Spending so much money on a single day all seemed wasteful to James.

"Make your wish," Marlene said before James could move to open his gift.

James sighed. "Aren't we a little old for this?"

"It's tradition," she said, entirely immovable.

James rolled his eyes. *I wish to be left alone,* he thought, and reached for the twine.

Last year, Marlene had been gifted with a heart locket on a slender chain. The links had begun to tarnish and turn green. But his sister wore it anyway, its hard gleam making it the only shiny thing she owned. James had been given a knife meant for filleting fish. It had been sharp and clean. He sold it to a classmate for a handful of silver, which he put into his education fund in a jar under his bed.

James tugged at the twine that held his gift together. A small piece of metal fell away from the burlap folds and clattered against the table. His heart sank at the sound. Already he knew what it would be before he'd picked it up.

It was the only luxury his father owned: a small gold pin—real gold, unlike Marlene's locket—shaped like a sea bass with its mouth wide open, ocean waves rising up beneath it. The very same image was hand-painted on the side of his father's fishing boat, and on the facing of the small wooden cart where he sold his fish in the marketplace. The crest of the family business, passed down from James's grandfather to his father and now, apparently, to him.

Marlene glanced up and gave her brother a sympathetic smile. This was the year their father wanted James to start taking on the responsibilities of the family's fishing business. No more arguments. James would have to learn to swim, figure out how to gut a fish, and develop the biceps to haul the net out of the water.

It is not a gift, James thought, petulant despite himself. *It's a contract.*

Never mind that he hated the sea. He was a fisherman's son, and he had a responsibility to carry on the family business.

James had been rehearsing a rebuttal all his life. He'd drafted ten versions of his "I'd like to get an education and I'll pay for it" speech, but hadn't yet worked up the nerve to deliver it. As much as he resented his father's plans for him, James could see that his father loved him and that his fishing boat was the only thing he had to give. The idea of breaking his father's heart wounded James. But not so much as the thought of living a life he hated.

Their father had been hoping for a son to inherit the

fishing business. A son who loved the salty air and open waters as much as he did.

In the end, he wouldn't get his wish. James had been terrified of the water from the very start. All that deep dark openness frightened him, as though the sea would give a big yawn and swallow him up.

James had been a skittish yet self-sufficient child. He preferred things neat and orderly. His bed was always made, and his only cherished possessions—an abacus and a sketchbook— were displayed proudly on his shelf. When he looked out the bedroom window, he wasn't staring at the North Sea to the east. He was looking westward, over the rooftops of his little harbor town, for any glimpse he could get of London down the River Thames.

One day, James would live there, among those bustling city streets. He knew this to be true. He would wear a tailored suit with crisp, smart creases. He would carry a briefcase and work in a very tall building, inventing new machines. He would never again have to handle a dead fish or scrub newspaper ink from his fingers so long as he lived.

Across the table, Marlene appeared equally unhappy about her own gift. She was holding her new dress up by the shoulders, her face scrunched as though the fabric were made of rotted meat.

It was a pretty dress, sensible, its deep violet hue no doubt intended to offset Marlene's black curls. It surely cost more than they could afford. How many hours had their mother spent tending to a wealthy family's children to pay for it? How many nights had she come home long after her family was asleep, only to be up again before the sun to make the train back to London for another day?

"You hate it," James said.

"It's fine," Marlene responded, her tone short. "It just isn't me. That's all."

James understood the sentiment.

If James was a creature of routine, Marlene was anything but. She seemed to resent that she'd been born last, the burdensome spare child in a struggling family. She was not the son her father had wished for. And she was far too restless for her mother's attempts to turn her into a lady.

The unfortunate circumstances of Marlene's birth made her all the more determined to prove her worth. If her brother was always on time, she would be early. If her brother walked briskly to be somewhere, she would run ahead. If James feared the water, she would dive in headfirst. If he was the quiet one, she was magnanimous. Other children flocked around her. She filled up every corner of every room with her presence until she was impossible to ignore. Until her laughter could be heard from halfway across the sea.

It wasn't her brother Marlene was competing with, but rather with the opinions of those who presumed her brother to be the fastest and the brightest by virtue of being a boy, and of being the oldest—even if it was just by a short bit.

For his part, James saw them more as a team. Lost as he often was in his thoughts, he needed her to guide him back down sometimes. He found her competitiveness rather silly, but he didn't call her on it. He only reminded her, quite gently, and only when he thought she was open to reason, that the only opinion that should have mattered to her was her own.

Before they left for school, Marlene hung her dress neatly in the closet beside James's blazers, and James fastened the pin to his shirt.

The sky was overcast as they started their walk. For once, Marlene was the one dragging her feet. She seemed burdened with something, and she tugged at her coat to protect herself from the harsh sea air. The water was only yards from where they stood, and its chill was especially biting that morning.

"James," she began, her voice trailing. "Do you ever think that maybe we were born into the wrong family?"

"What are you talking about?" James asked. "We look just like Mother." And they did, with their black hair, fair skin, and blue eyes. So unlike their father, with his sun-bleached hair and skin that had become like leather from the endless hours spent out on the water.

"I don't mean it like that." Marlene waved one hand at him, impatient. "I know they're our parents. But sometimes it just feels like we were meant to be someplace else."

James looked over his shoulder. In the distance, he could just see the pale silhouette of tall buildings beyond the English smog. He didn't like when his sister spoke in abstracts, pondering over things she couldn't change. It made him anxious. Better to accept circumstances as they were and make a plan, sound and logical.

"Well, when we grow up," he reasoned, "we can go anywhere."

This seemed to cheer his sister a bit. She smiled and then kicked at a pebble. "True. But I wish we didn't have to grow up first to get there."

James was looking forward to growing up. But his sister lacked his patience. To her, it was taking an awfully long time to achieve the life that either of them wanted. He supposed that Marlene would sail off with a carnival somewhere and become a famous singer. Perhaps he could use his mathematics skills to manage her finances when she did. Either way, all they needed to do was finish school, and then they'd be in control of what happened next.

The sky growled with a loud clap of thunder, and all at once the clouds burst with rain. Blinding, cold, driving rain. Not uncommon at all for this time of year, but wholly unwelcome nonetheless.

"Hurry, James!" Marlene grabbed his wrist and started running.

James groaned as he dragged behind, thinking about the

careful work he'd made of his tunic the night before. School was two blocks away. Even if he could keep pace with Marlene, he was going to be soaked through by the time he got there.

Marlene moved faster than anyone he knew. She was like a flash of light when she had a mind to be. He did his best to keep pace but tripped on a gap in the cobblestones and tumbled right into a puddle.

The taste of blood filled his mouth. His palms ached where they'd scraped against the street.

"Oh, James," he heard Marlene sigh above the sound of the driving rain. She crouched beside him and offered him a hand. "It's my fault for rushing you."

"We would have still been on time if we'd just gone back home for an umbrella," James muttered, irritated. He'd noted the unsavory skies when they'd first departed for school, but Marlene had refused to wait for him to go back into their house and retrieve an umbrella, insisting they'd make it indoors before the rain hit.

He stood, and when he did, he felt immediately that something was off. There was just a tiny bit of weight missing—something that used to be there and was gone.

The pin was no longer on his shirt where he'd fastened it. For a moment, his heart lurched. Father was going to be devastated. Perhaps James had never wanted the pin, but he was willing to wear it for his father's sake.

Then he saw it—a tiny metallic gleam just two yards away,

at the water's edge. It must have skidded across the cobble-stones when he fell.

He ran to get it, only vaguely aware of the loud clap of thunder overhead. So much rain all of a sudden.

"James!" He heard his sister calling for him, felt her grab his arm.

"Would you be patient for once?" he grumbled.

But before he could turn to look at her, the world was swept out from under him.

It happened fast. Too fast for him to understand, at first, that he was underwater. The sea was cold and dark and end-less. A wave had come up and swept him clear off the ground, sending him tumbling blindly into infinite nothingness.

For one delirious moment, as his lungs filled up with water, James did not know that he was drowning. His mind trans-ported him to one of his comfort places: his desk. He was proud of his school desk. Although the wood had been old and scratched like all the other desks, he'd stayed late after class one day to refinish it with the stain his father used on his boat.

Somewhere at the front of the classroom, Marlene's dark curls were bouncing as she leaned forward to whisper with a friend. James raised the lid of his desk and was confused at the mess where his papers and ruler should have been. Instead, there was a tangle of seaweed, the smell of which caused an inexplicable pain in his chest. Water leaked out from the sides, trickling and then cascading all around him. No one noticed. He had the odd thought that he should scream, but when he tried, all that came out was water.

That was when he clenched his fist and felt the pin in his hand. The classroom, the faceless classmates, and Marlene's curls that shook like bells when she giggled all went dark. The pin was the only thing he could hold on to.

Panic overrode everything when James opened his eyes and realized he was in the ocean. He thrashed blindly, unsure which direction was up.

It made no sense. James thought this even as he was dying. Yes, he had been running close to the water. But he knew the parameters. He was always careful, because he knew his great weakness. But it was as though the water had reached out and grabbed him. Like it had come ashore to hunt him.

Something coiled around his arm. Marlene. He saw her heavy dark curls floating all around her head even through the murk of the water. She was pulling him, trying to get them both to the surface. How she would even find the surface, James had no idea. Later, he would look back at this moment and understand that he had not been transported to his classroom for a brief moment in time. That his immediate analysis of all these mundane details was a form of shock. And that if he had been alone—if his sister had gone ahead of him

to school, or if she'd never been born at all, as was expected—
he would be dead.

They both came spluttering to the surface of the water.
James raised his fist, still holding the pin, up over his head like
a flag of surrender.

Gasping and coughing, the pair of them crawled their way
to shore. Only then did they notice that they hadn't emerged
on the familiar cobblestone street from which they'd been
swept away. And it was no longer thundering. The English
winter wind was no longer blowing them about.

Instead, they were on a soft bed of warm sand. The sun
was shining, and some peculiar bird was singing a song neither of them had ever heard before. It sounded almost like the
crow of a rooster, but not quite. Something was off about it.

As he caught his breath, James sat upright, dizzy with
confusion. They were soaked to the bone and dripping onto
the sand.

Had they drowned? James was quite sure they hadn't.
Marlene had crawled up beside him, breathing hard. He
brought his fingers to his throat and felt his pulse.

"Where are we?" he rasped. Certainly not in England. It
was hot, the sun beating down so harshly that their clothes
were already starting to dry. "Are we dreaming?"

Marlene shook her head as though trying to awaken herself from a trance. She got to her feet and tugged James up by
the wrist. For once, James was grateful for her assertiveness.

"We must have . . ." she began, but then her voice trailed off. Still holding on to his wrist, she spun around to survey their surroundings. Open, sparkling waters to one side, and a thick wilderness at the sand's edge on the other.

Her brow furrowed. Marlene wasn't frightened—she rarely was—but she was confused. "Maybe we *are* dreaming," she said slowly. "I've dreamed of this place before."

"You have?" James blinked.

"Now and again," she said. "But usually when I do, it's more . . . foggy. Like I can't see it as clearly as I can now."

Although they were twins, they had never shared the usual benefits people expected twins to share. They couldn't read each other's thoughts. And they certainly hadn't ever dreamed the same things.

Still, they loved each other in a way that never needed to be said—and never was said. While Marlene made friends easily, James didn't have a single one. He had classmates who thought he was strange, stubborn, and stuck-up. Maybe they were right about some of those things, depending on the situation.

But James and Marlene would have been friends even if they weren't twins. Somehow, they both knew this. If they hadn't had the same parents, if they hadn't had the same eyes and the same single dimple in their right cheek, they would have found each other and become fast friends anyway. There was something at the core that bonded them. They needed each other. That was simply how it was meant to be.

The bird let out its unusual cry again, and Marlene's grip on James's wrist tightened. "I've heard that before," she whispered to him.

As though in response, the branches of a tree shook. The sound grew louder: a sharp, crowing call. And then, the figure of a boy tumbled from the foliage and shot up into the sky. James waited for him to fall, but he didn't.

Just like a bird, the boy flew straight toward them.

2

The boy was flying.

Flying.

Now James was sure they were dreaming. But Marlene wasn't shaken by this. She took a step forward, protecting him.

James hated how useless he felt when she did this. Last year, she'd grown taller than he was. As if she hadn't been bossy enough already, now he felt like she was trying to guide him along as though he were a sort of pet.

He shouldered his way beside her, ignoring the fact that he was rather frightened. Flying aside, he had never seen anyone dressed like this. The boy was dressed head to toe in green, with even a green cap fitted perfectly over his sandy brown hair. Even stranger were his ears—pointed at the tips like those of an elf in a child's storybook.

"What are you?" James asked at the same time as Marlene blurted out, "Where are we?"

Both were fair questions, James thought.

But the boy only threw his head back, and the sound of his laughter stirred up a breeze and made the forest rustle and stir. There were bright bits of light floating between the trees, and James wondered curiously if they were a bizarre type of insect.

There was someone else hiding in the trees. James saw a pair of eyes blink at him and then disappear into the shadows.

"There's nothing to be frightened of," the boy said. "You're lost, but that's okay. We all are."

"Lost?" Marlene looked skeptical. "We can't be lost. I've never been lost a day in my life."

The boy folded his arms and shrugged. "But you are. Everyone in Never Land is lost."

"Never Land?" James mumbled, more to himself than anyone. He was sure he'd not heard such a name. He knew all the cities and towns in England, and all the neighborhoods in London. He had studied the maps so intently that he was certain he could find his way to any street, even if he'd never been there before. He'd never come across a place called Never Land on any of his maps.

James spun to look at the sea and then at the strange

island. It was impossible. His heart thundered in his chest, and he forced himself to take deep, calming breaths. Panic would not help him. There had to be a logical explanation. One did not fall into the ocean in one's hometown and emerge on a strange island. This was a dream, or a hallucination. That was it. He had swallowed too much seawater. Soon he would wake with a clear head, and everything would be exactly as it had always been.

The boy was appraising Marlene with great interest. His brown eyes were fixed on her as he walked a circle around the pair of them. "How about that?" he said. "A human girl."

"As opposed to what?" Marlene fired back. "A female Dalmatian?"

The boy laughed again. But it was a warmer, gentler sound now. "Fairies. Mermaids. Plenty of them are girls. But to see a *human* girl? That's interesting."

The sea reached out and lapped at their ankles. It felt real—the warmth of the water, the wet clothes sticking to his legs—but James couldn't reconcile the idea he was really awake in this unusual place.

"I think . . ." The boy's voice trailed off. He leapt up in the air, so high that his silhouette disappeared against the blinding sunlight. He returned to the ground, his nose suddenly just a hair away from Marlene's, making her flinch. "It was you. You're the one that decided to come here. You wished for it." His face lit up.

"How could I have wished for this if I don't even know where we are?" Marlene asked, irritated. "For all I know, you're a figment of our imaginations."

James elbowed his sister. Hallucination or not, her sass was going to get them in trouble. This boy before them could be anyone. Positively *anyone*. And they were entirely at his mercy.

"'Figment,'" the boy echoed. He seemed to consider this. "What's a figment?"

"Not real," Marlene explained.

The boy reached forward and poked Marlene on the nose. She bristled, her anger palpable. James put a hand over her clenched fist. The gold pin pressed against his other palm told him that, contrary to what Marlene might think, this was all too real.

"I'm real," the boy said. "I'm Peter."

Peter. It seemed such a sensible name for such an absurd situation, James thought. He wouldn't have expected this boy to have a name at all but rather thought that he might answer to the bars of a melody, or the sound of birds all taking flight at once.

Behind him, the trees at the end of the beach began to rustle. James was sure he saw a crown of hair and a pair of eyes blinking at him from behind a large green leaf.

"A *girl*?" someone said from the trees.

If James had been braver, he would have charged toward

the woods and confronted that whispering voice. He would have protected his sister, and himself. But he was rooted in place, still hoping that this was all some sort of dream. Hoping that he would wake up in his own bed. Not for the first time, James wished he had more courage.

Marlene elbowed him. "James, look."

As though on cue, shadows began to shift and then emerge from the trees. There were boys huddled against one another in fright as though James and Marlene were the dangerous ones. Perhaps, James pondered, they were. He and his sister had washed ashore like kelp, with no explanation. There was nothing behind them but water. No boat; not even the distant shadow of land beyond.

"Come on over, boys, don't be shy!" Peter called to them.

Peter is the leader here, James thought. If he noted something in his head just once, he would remember it. He had a strong memory. Everyone thought so.

Under Peter's direction, the boys slowly came out of the shadows and into the sun. It was hard to determine their ages. The youngest-looking—a little boy who wore a matted skunk cap—was clearly a child. The other two seemed somewhere between his age and James and Marlene's—which, as of today, of course, was fifteen exactly.

"Slightly, Tootles, Sam—meet the outsiders," Peter said.

"We aren't outsiders," Marlene shot back, although they were.

James took in the sight of the boys. He could tell right away which one was Sam: the boy with sandy blond hair parted neatly on one side. Though the sea breeze still blew it jagged across his face, he looked reasonable, James thought. He looked like someone who would have a practical name like Sam.

The boys fell in line, and the youngest, Tootles, crawled toward them on all fours. He sniffed Marlene and James like a puppy.

"Are you really a girl?" Tootles asked in a small voice.

Marlene laughed. "I am, in fact."

"Why are you here?" the boy asked. His big eyes lit up. "Are you here to be our mother?"

"Don't be dumb, Tootles," Slightly said. "You wouldn't know a mother if one fell on your head."

"Would so!" Tootles protested, but then his face screwed up thoughtfully. He looked like he had more to say, but he couldn't quite work it out. "What does a mother do again?"

Marlene toed the boy's shoulder, pushing him away from where he crouched by her feet. "No, I'm not here to be your mother." She raised her chin. "I'm Marlene. This is James. And if we don't leave here right now, we'll be very late for school."

Instinctively, James felt for the satchel with his school supplies that he'd been wearing, but it was gone, and so was Marlene's. They must have fallen off in the struggle, he thought, and began to worry—despite everything—that all their homework was lost.

"School!" Peter laughed. He leapt into the sky again, nearly disappearing in the brightness of the sun.

"What is school?" Tootles asked.

"You don't know what school is, either?" James was so shocked for a moment that he forgot his fears and spoke up. "It's a place to learn. There are teachers, books, numbers—all of that?"

"I think I've seen a book once," Sam said. He spoke softly. "Maybe. I can't remember."

This served only to recharge James's worry. "We have to get out of here," James whispered to his sister. "They've never heard of books. Something is very wrong with this place."

If they didn't read, and they didn't go to school, what else was there? James couldn't fathom it. The boys were clean enough, but there was still a wildness to them that he couldn't place. The whole island was wild—bright flowers and thick green leaves making up the forest beyond the shore. It felt like an illusion.

When James had been small, his father had taught him how to bait a fishing hook. The worms were a treat that the fish couldn't resist, and James couldn't blame them. A delicious treat just appeared in the middle of the water, and they'd feel foolish to pass it by. But that was the thing—delicious treats and magical things *didn't* just appear. Not without a catch.

"Marlene," James whispered, his voice more urgent this time. She shushed him, but it wasn't her usual impatience, James knew. She was practical enough to see that something about this place was wrong.

Wasn't she?

"Very well, then," Peter said. He was circling the air above them like a paper plane. "Follow me. I'll show you how to get out of here."

The strange boy bolted forward before another word could be said. Marlene chased after him, with James—as always—stumbling to keep up with his sister.

"Wait up!" Marlene cried, though she was mostly talking to Peter's shadow as it darted between the trees and reemerged from the shady patches of moss.

"We're only getting lost," James gasped as he tried to keep pace beside her.

"We're already lost," she threw over her shoulder.

The boys chased after them, cheering and hollering as if this was a sort of game. Wherever Peter was leading them, the boys already knew the way. They swung from branches and coasted through brambles with ease, their earlier shyness forgotten.

The scenery blurred by so quickly that James nearly missed the splashes from the pond they were passing. But a figure caught the corner of his vision, and he skidded to a stop.

"James!" Marlene stopped when she realized he was no longer beside her. "What are you—"

"Shh." He held up a hand. "There's someone in there."

As though summoned, a head emerged from the pond's surface. A woman with big glittering eyes and golden hair. She giggled at them and then disappeared again. A red fin splashed water at them.

"What in the world . . ." James was blinking, rubbing his eyes.

"Haven't you ever seen a mermaid before?" Slightly asked. He was swinging by his knees from an overhead branch.

"Mermaids aren't real," Marlene said, but for once in her life she sounded uncertain.

"I didn't think human girls were real," Slightly countered.

James stared at the pond. The water had gone still, but he thought he could see shadows swimming about below the surface.

"Where did Peter go?" Marlene asked, looking around. There was no sign of the boy in green.

James whirled about. Nothing but forest surrounded them now. His heart rate quickened.

Marlene slipped her hand into his. It was a gesture of

comfort, offered frequently when they were children, though less so now that they were older. "Don't worry," she said. "He has to be somewhere."

"Up here!" Peter was overhead again, leaping from one branch to the next.

The twins took off after him, both giving chase to his shadow on the ground. He led them through the forest until the trees disappeared entirely and they found themselves at the edge of a jagged cliff. Marlene nearly tripped over the edge, intent as she was on tracking Peter, but James held her back.

They were high above the ocean. The water crashed into the rocks, frothy white and sparkling blue.

"Well?" Peter landed beside them, light as a feather. "Take a look. Can you see your home?"

There was nothing but sea and sky. James regarded Peter as though he were playing a prank on them. Maybe he was. "Of course we can't see our home from here," he said, his voice a grumble. "There's nothing out there."

"Really? That's a shame," Peter said. "This is the best view you'll get in Never Land. That is, unless you're a fairy. They can fly higher than anyone. If you can't see your home from here, though, it doesn't exist."

"Of course it exists," James said at the same time as Marlene said, "Fairies?"

"Oh, yes," Slightly piped up from James's other side.

"They can be nasty if they don't get their way, but if you're friendly, they'll sprinkle you with dust so you can fly."

Like Peter, these boys had a way of appearing out of nowhere. James pressed his palm to his temple and tried to think. It was still morning, and the sun had been to the east, opposite London. That meant the city's windows would be glinting as they reflected back the light. James squinted hard in the opposite direction, but there were no buildings. There was no city. There was only the harsh rebuke of the water as it crashed against the rocks.

"There must be other islands," James suggested. "A port. A train. Something."

"Not in Never Land," Peter told him. "This is the only island you'll find here."

Marlene approached the cliff, gnawing pensively on her lip.

Peter was studying her. The mischievous glint was gone from his brown eyes, and he turned oddly serious. "You hear it."

"Hear what?" James asked. Marlene didn't answer. He followed her gaze, but whatever had captured his sister's interest wasn't apparent to him.

"It's this place," Peter went on. "It's welcoming you."

A cold dread raced down James's spine. He didn't like whatever this look was in his sister's eyes, and he tugged at her arm. "Marlene. *Marlene.*"

She flinched, startling as though being awoken from a dream. "Hm?"

"We have to go home," James said.

"Oh." She looked at him. Something in her face had changed, but James couldn't identify what. "We can stay here for a little while, I think." She spread her arms wide, as though giving herself over to the call of the sea. "There's no harm in that."

3

Never Land was far bigger than Marlene could quantify. Each new portion of it seemed to manifest itself into existence as they arrived. There were weeping trees dripping with flowers and dew, deep dark pools of water teeming with creatures she'd never seen before, and then, in the clearings between the forest, a sky that was frightfully blue.

As Peter led them across the island, they were greeted by more boys, peeking out curiously from behind trees and cliff-side caverns. One by one, they introduced themselves: Cubby, Nibs, the Twins. Others who were all fascinated by these outsiders, but particularly by Marlene. They simply weren't used to seeing girls at all, let alone anyone as quick and confident and brimming with energy.

"Honestly," Marlene said when they started crowding her. "Don't any of you have mothers? Sisters?" But she was laughing now, less irritated and more charmed by their curiosity.

"What is it like where you come from?" Slightly asked her, circling her as she walked.

"Does it rain?" Cubby asked.

"Where do you find things like thimbles and buttons?" said Sam.

"Boys, let her breathe," Peter said. He shook a tree, and a bounty of apples rained down from the branches. The boys flocked happily to them. "There will be plenty of time to ask all your questions later."

For a while, she'd allowed the parade of Lost Boys to lead her through the forest. They spoke over one another and argued over whose turn it was to explain which flowers tasted like sugared candy, and which trees offered the best vantage points to spy on the others.

The more Marlene saw of Never Land, the more her thoughts of returning home melted away as though they had never existed. By the time the sun began to sink, Marlene had eaten five of the sweetest, juiciest pears she'd ever tasted. She'd met half a dozen mermaids—some of whom were not very friendly—and learned that the glowing yellow spheres she saw flitting about in the sky were fairies, not fireflies.

And Peter—he was especially proud of this place. Even though he could fly, he patiently walked beside her, shushing the boys whenever they became too excitable.

Marlene didn't remember being separated from her brother. She only realized, quite suddenly, that he wasn't there, and that he hadn't been for some time.

Time. How many hours had it been?

"Come on," Peter said, and took her hand.

Soon they sat atop a giant boulder that overlooked a tranquil pond. Marlene had grown up in a harbor town, but she'd never seen water so blue.

The sun was lower in the sky. Marlene could just barely see it through the dense trees. "What time is it?" she asked.

Peter shrugged. "I don't know. It doesn't matter." At Marlene's alarmed expression, he laughed. "What would be the point? Anywhere you need to be, you already are. Anything you have to do, you can stop what you're doing and just do it."

Marlene didn't have a counterargument for this. How did one argue with a boy who didn't believe in school or clocks or logic? Who just flew about like a bird gathering shiny things to build its nest?

Finally, she said, "My brother and I have to get back."

"Back to what?" Peter asked.

"Home," she said. "Our parents."

Peter wrinkled his nose. "Why would you want to do a thing like that?" he said.

Marlene opened her mouth to ask if he missed his own parents, but she thought better of it. Not everyone had a home to go back to, she supposed. Even so, although this enchanting island was fun enough, it didn't have the things one required: vendors from whom to buy food, ports at which to trade wares, shops in which to purchase things like fabric and furniture—and money with which to purchase them.

It seemed so obvious, and yet she couldn't form a rational argument. Why *did* she need food vendors when she could just reach up and pluck a delicious plum from its branch? Why purchase fabric for new clothes when she could be in a place where there were no mirrors to see them? What was the use of furniture when she could rest in a bed of soft moss, or squish her bare toes in the warm sand, or perch atop a boulder?

As though he could read her thoughts, Peter was smiling at her.

She shook her head. No. She couldn't stay here.

"James," she said. "He'll be worried about me." As ever, the thought of her brother brought logic back into her mind. James would be able to remind her why they had to go home. Why they needed clocks and tables and chairs.

Peter bristled, and for just a second, Marlene detected something unusual in his demeanor. He seemed less like the magical boy who seemed to rule this place and more like an ordinary schoolboy who had tasted something sour.

A moment later, the expression was gone. "Let's go find him," Peter said.

Again, Peter walked beside her instead of flying. He smelled of a cedarwood fire and the first fragrant burst of spring. He was an island of his own, mysterious and inviting. She'd never met such a human, never would have believed someone like him could exist, except for in her books.

Marlene heard the laughter before she saw her brother. When Peter led her into a clearing, there was James, staring in wonder as a sphere of yellow light orbited his head.

"There. See? He's fine," Peter said. "Better than fine."

Marlene could scarcely believe it. One of the boys—Sam, if she was remembering correctly—grabbed James's hand and tugged him down an embankment to show him some sort of lizard. And James, who hated mud, who despised getting even the least bit sweaty, who had never made a friend in his life, was enjoying himself.

It stunned Marlene to silence, and she didn't call out to him. She didn't remind him that they had somewhere to be, or that their parents would be worried. All of that seemed to fade away until there was only the strange new feeling of joy. And a very small, very distant notion that they could stay here forever.

4

It was only when the sun was melting on the horizon that James began to remember that tricky little word that had eluded him since earlier in the day: *home*.

He looked over to his sister, who was knee-deep in a tranquil pond looking for some fish to cook for supper per Peter's instructions. Her hair was falling out of its ponytail, sending thick springing curls bouncing all around her face. James recalled that it had looked much more sensible this morning, tightly wound back. Her skirt, much like James's trousers, was damp with mud and river water. Their school clothes were positively ruined.

School, James thought. They had forgotten all about school.

He dropped the fruit he'd been eating, went over to his sister, and grabbed her hand, pulling. "James, what—" She stumbled out of the water. The boys who had remained with them—Peter's having taken his leave to attend to other matters, it appeared—all stared in surprise, but James didn't care. For once, he was the one taking charge and Marlene was the one to follow.

Mermaids. Fairies. Pink iguanas and fruit that tasted like peppermints. And not an adult in sight. None of it could possibly be real. They had to have been dreaming, or stuck in some sort of trance. Perhaps this was all a shared hallucination as their bodies were left floating out at sea somewhere. How could he have forgotten how strange this all was?

He stomped down a dirt path, past the thickest part of the forest, until they reached the cliff that overlooked the frothing sea.

"Look!" he cried, gesturing wildly to the water. "Look out at the horizon. What do you see?"

"James, what in the world is the matter with you?" Marlene's eyes were wide. It wasn't like James to panic or to take charge like this. He was ordinarily the quiet one. As twins, they had very much fallen into a sort of unspoken partnership. A balance. Marlene decided when it was time to go anywhere, and how long they should stay. James offered observations and numbers and quiet suggestions. He never took off running first. He never made demands.

"What do you see, Marlene?" James persisted.

Marlene blinked. "The sunset, I suppose. What's so strange about that?"

"The sun is setting," James echoed. "The day is over. We missed school. We missed lunch. How many hours must we have spent here?"

Now Marlene's expression turned grave, the importance of what James was saying at last taking root. "Father must be home by now. Mother, too, if she isn't staying in the city for the night."

"We have to go home, Marlene." He was staring at her hard, as though the words could pierce straight through her heart. "We can't stay in this strange place."

Her brows furrowed. "But how?" she said. "I can't remember how we got here."

The only thing to answer was the water, sloshing angrily against the rocks far below.

"It was something to do with the water," James said, though he wasn't entirely certain. The morning seemed to be a lifetime ago. Only vaguely could he recall trying to keep pace with his sister on the way to school. Then being underwater, and then, somehow, suddenly washing up on this island.

His hand moved to his chest, where he felt the weight of the gold pin. At present, it was the only indication he had that there was a world outside of Never Land. That he belonged somewhere other than this strange place.

"There's nowhere for us to go . . ." Marlene said, her voice trailing thoughtfully. Even now, she didn't panic. She rarely ever did. "Not unless we have a boat."

"A boat would do no good." James shook his head. "Where would we paddle off to? There's no land on the other side."

The twins peered over the edge of the cliff and stared down at the churning tide. "Maybe the way out isn't *across* the water," Marlene said, "but *through* it. Maybe if we jump—"

"Are you thinking properly?" James asked. His grip tightened on the pin.

Marlene shook her head. "I think that's how we got here. We fell in one side of the water and came through the other side. We didn't get in a boat and sail over, so of course we can't go back that way."

James felt an anxious knot in his chest. What his sister was saying was absurd, but in another, stranger way, it was the only thing that made sense.

She slipped her hand into his and gripped down tight. "It'll be all right if we don't let go of each other. I think we should try, James. I think this is the way home."

Home. Their humble, practical seaside town. Their sensible clothing and the smell of salt and seawater. Neatly made beds and mathematics books and puzzles stacked in the corner of the closet.

Their home was a simple little place that James had often resented, favoring instead thoughts of being in London, of smelling like ink and paper, not fish and ashes from the wood-stove. But it had never occurred to him that his home could be lost to him forever, and in that moment he wanted desperately to return to it and hold on tight.

"We could die," he said. In contrast to the rest of Never Land, the water below was loud and churning.

"I can't explain it," Marlene insisted, "but I just know that it's the way home. I can feel it."

All James could feel was dread. But he nodded.

The air around them was quiet and still. Far off, they could hear the giggles of the strange boys who accompanied them everywhere they went. They were friendly, even if Peter was a bit unnerving in a way that James couldn't identify. But James was still fearful of them. Fearful of how easy it was to get lost in their games, fearful of how quickly and unnoticeably the hours had passed. Fearful that if he joined them, he would never see his home again.

As unreal as it seemed, the water was the only way.

"Ready?" Marlene squeezed his hand.

James held his breath. Nodded.

They didn't need to count to three. When it came to certain things, the twins knew each other too well for that.

Moving in tandem, they stepped back and then charged toward the end of the cliff. Although every instinct within James shouted for him to stop, he kept running until there was no longer any ground beneath his feet.

The sea swallowed them as soon as their bodies tore through its surface.

The water all at once was dark and unforgiving and vast. Never Land disappeared, taking its vivid sunset with it. Panic surged through James's limbs as he and his sister tumbled, powerless, aimless, into uncertain depths.

His lungs burned and his mouth filled with water. This—this—was why he had always hated the sea. He'd always known somehow that it would be the death of him.

What a strange and terrible dream, he thought, as his mind began to cloud over.

Then, just when he was sure he was about to die, oxygen filled his lungs again.

He was the first to surface this time. Marlene was still floundering in the water beside him, and he reeled her up like a caught fish. Spluttering and coughing, they trudged through the shallow water and onto the jagged rocks and sand.

"Are we home?" Marlene asked.

James knew, even before his vision fully cleared, that they were. He could smell the familiar salty air and discern the familiar gray morning fog.

Morning? How could it be morning? he thought. He was certain they hadn't tumbled through the water all night.

"Come on." He helped Marlene, who had doubled over to retch out a mouthful of kelp. "It's already morning. Mother and Father will be beside themselves."

It was strange to be back home. As they trudged through the same familiar street, it was as though they had never left at all. *Don't you understand?* James wanted to shout at a passerby who regarded his and his sister's drenched clothes with confusion. *Don't you get that there's another world out there, filled with fairies and mermaids and a boy who knows how to fly?*

A cold breeze made him shiver. Marlene sneezed.

The twins returned home still thrumming with magic. James felt it in his breath and in his bones. He felt as though he were half-awake, still grappling with a dream that had been both frightening and beautiful.

He was the one who reached for the doorknob. He couldn't guess at what his parents would say. He and Marlene had never been gone for so long before.

"Hello?" Marlene went down the hallway ahead of her brother. "Mother? Father? We're so sorry we—"

She stopped when she reached the kitchen. When James caught up to her he could see that the chairs were still where they'd left them—Marlene's slightly askew; the wrapping from their birthday presents still on the table, twine trailing over one edge.

He looked to the clock above the stove. 9:00 a.m. sharp. They'd left home only an hour ago.

"That can't be right," he whispered. But if they'd been gone longer than a single day, their parents would be home and frantic. The police would have been called.

Marlene was equally dumbfounded. She rubbed her eyes as though the world might change when she gave it a fresher look. "It's still the same morning that we left."

After toweling their hair and changing into dry clothes, the matter of school long forgotten, Marlene and James sat on their bedroom floor for hours with a sea of papers spread out between them. Like pieces of a puzzle, they drew each piece of Never Land they could remember and tried to fashion them into a sort of map.

James was a meticulous illustrator. He used his ruler to draw a map of Never Land as close to scale as he could manage.

"This is where we washed ashore," James said, pointing to a spot he'd drawn. "And here, all the way on the other side"— he ran his finger across the pages, tracing the route they'd taken—"is where we jumped."

Marlene stared in puzzlement. "We were gone for hours. Hours. How is it that time here scarcely passed at all?"

James grabbed the box of tacks from the desk drawer and began pinning the pages on the wall. There were big pieces missing. Black rectangles of places they hadn't seen or that their minds couldn't recall.

He stared at the piece of paper on which he had drawn the shore where they first met Peter and the boys. "There must be a sort of door in the water," he tried to reason. "And when we fell into the water here . . . it somehow . . ." He trailed off, his finger lost on their makeshift map. He knew that he sounded unreasonable; ridiculous, even. All he could think to add was "But how?"

When he turned to face Marlene, he saw the contrition on her face. It was very unlike her. "Marlene. What is it?"

"There isn't a door, James," she blurted. "What Peter said—I think he was right. *I'm* the reason we ended up there." She pushed herself up off the floor and began to pace in agitation. "For days before, I felt it calling to me."

"Calling?" James asked.

"Like a song, but very far away. The way that the water sometimes sounds like human voices, you know?" James didn't, but Marlene didn't seem to be focused on his answer. She was staring through the tiny window between their beds now. A beam of late morning sun caught her curls, drying springier than usual with seawater, and she looked wild to James in that moment, unrecognizable. "I can't explain it. And then this morning, when we made our birthday wishes, I wished . . ."

James followed her gaze. But all he saw was the same dull gray town he always saw, the water bleary and pale green beyond. What the water could have to say to him, he couldn't imagine.

Marlene detected James's puzzlement and sighed, bending to pick up the last piece of paper and pinning it into place.

It was a drawing of the mermaid pond, with a level of detail James found impressive. His own drawings were lifeless and jagged, but his sister had an artistic side. She was able to conjure up stories and pictures from blank pages, as though they had always been hiding there waiting to be found.

"I mean that we just don't belong."

Marlene was frightening her brother. He had always known that he didn't fit in with their parents' plans, but the solution—as he saw it—was a simple one. "One day we'll get out of this town—"

"Yes, yes, when we grow up," Marlene interrupted, already knowing what he was about to say. "I can't wait that long."

"So, you want to do what, exactly?" James snapped. "Swim around with mermaids and play with a group of flying boys?"

"Maybe." She was getting irritated. "They were nice, weren't they? And it was pretty. We could be like them."

"Like them," James echoed caustically. "Prancing around in the forest all day eating fruit and having no idea what time it is."

"Time," Marlene cried. "Time! Why do you care so much about time? Schedules, and calendars, and what all the numbers add up to. It's insufferable sometimes!"

"Why do you only care about acting like a child?" James said. He was angry now.

Something flashed across Marlene's eyes. She'd never been so frustrated—so desperate. Her shoulders were tensed, and James braced himself for whatever she was going to shout back at him.

But suddenly she deflated, and all she said was "You don't understand." Her tone was one of disappointment rather than rage, and that stung James all the more.

She turned for the door, and James wanted to stop her, but he didn't know what he could possibly say to make her see reason. So he followed her down to the kitchen, and together, wordlessly, they began preparing dinner, the way they had done a thousand times before.

5

The sun was beginning to go down, the rainy afternoon giving way to a cloudy, starless night.

The twins' mother was the first to arrive home. She burst through the door, shaking out her umbrella and mumbling to herself about the downpour. She smelled of the city. Of the trains and steam and perfume she wore especially for work.

She was a tall woman, slender and graceful with a young face and soft skin that she ritualistically doused in fragranced lotion. She stood in stark contrast to the aged wooden walls of their modest home, never quite fitting in. She was like a glamorous aunt who visited them on occasion, rather than the very woman who had raised them. Both of the twins often thought this, though they'd never said it aloud to each other.

"Marlene, darling, you aren't wearing your new dress," she said by way of greeting when she entered the kitchen. "Don't you like it?"

Marlene could barely hide how despondent she felt. Just that morning, she'd been in the most beautiful world she could ever imagine, and now she was here, stirring a pot of salmon stew.

"Of course I do, Mother," Marlene said. "I just didn't want to get it dirty."

James stood beside his sister, cutting potatoes into neat quarters. He tried to ignore her obvious misery, but it seeped into him like a chill after being caught outside in the rain.

How long had she been unhappy? He thought back. At school, their classmates flocked to her. She was easy to get on with—and James knew this better than anyone, because he'd shared a small room with her since he could remember. Marlene was all sunshine and light, the breath of air flowing through the small, close rooms of their home. They rarely even argued, which was why today's fight about Never Land felt especially ugly to him.

Fairies.

He sliced another potato.

Mermaids.

He dropped the quarters into the stew.

Nonsense. All of it.

Their father arrived shortly thereafter, bringing the overwhelming stench of fish and rain. He clashed entirely with the London image their mother tried so desperately to maintain.

As a birthday present, their mother had brought a small cake she'd managed to bake while minding her charges in the city. It was strawberry, which was Marlene's favorite. James had never much cared for it, but he always pretended it was his favorite, too. The same way that Marlene pretended to be seasick when she knew James was too frightened to go on their father's fishing boat and she didn't want him to be left behind by himself.

Once the birthday wishes had been doled out and the family sat down to warm stew and leftover, crusty bread, James and Marlene's parents chattered so eagerly about their respective days that they didn't notice how quiet the twins were.

After she had finished eating, Marlene quietly excused herself from the table and went outside.

I shouldn't go after her, James thought. It wouldn't accomplish anything. But then he stared at his parents, their earlier buoyancy giving way to a more contemplative quiet as they sipped their after-supper tea, and he wondered if either of them was truly happy. His mother spent long hours caring for the children of a wealthy family in the city, and his father spent more time on water than on land.

Their mother seemed more content to nanny the polished and well-to-do children she cared for. She didn't know what to do with a daughter who had no interest in being the dulcet, sensible young lady she ought to be. Their father was older, exhausted by the hard labor of his profession, and he didn't know what to do with a son who had no interest in taking over the family business so that he could retire.

It wasn't very strange that Marlene was unhappy here, when he thought about it like that. None of them was happy here.

For a week, James and Marlene considered what to do. They argued, mostly, about whether to go back or to treat Never Land like a strange dream and never speak of it again.

After dinner, seven days after their return exactly, James found his sister outside, high up in the tree adjacent to their bedroom window. The day's rain had let up and the clouds had cleared away, revealing a moon that was full and vibrant. They hadn't spoken all evening after she'd threatened to return to Never Land alone and James had called her a stubborn child.

She peered down at him. "What do you want?"

"It's cold," James said. "You should at least wear your coat."

This was his awkward way of making amends. Marlene sighed and extended her hand down to him. He took it, allowing his sister to hoist him up to the fat branch that she considered to be her thinking place.

"I'm sorry I called you a child," James said once he'd more

or less found his footing, clutching the branch so tightly his knuckles were turning white. He hated heights nearly as much as he hated water.

"It's all right," Marlene said with a wan smile. "I suppose I am."

From where the twins were perched, they could see the ocean glittering in the moonlight. And now that they knew what hid beneath it, James could still feel a bit of that strange magic stirring in his ribs. A rebirth of sorts.

"I've been thinking," Marlene continued. "All those boys—even Peter—don't seem to remember where they've come from. But they have to have come from somewhere. There are no adults on the island—how would they have been born there?" She put her chin in her hands. "I think Never Land makes them forget."

"We forgot, too, for a minute," James murmured.

"More than a minute," Marlene said. "The whole day slipped away before we knew what had happened."

James didn't want to admit it aloud, but before his natural reason and panic had taken over, it had been a brilliant feeling, forgetting. Nothing to worry about, nowhere to be. He had felt peaceful playing by the mermaid ponds.

Marlene stayed quiet for a moment, then spoke. "Suppose we go back," she said. Before her brother could interrupt her, she charged on. "We'll bring a pocket watch. You have one, don't you? That way, we'll keep an eye on the time."

Their father had gifted James with a pocket watch three years ago, on James's twelfth birthday. It was secondhand and had required some repairs, but it was all their family could afford, and James treasured it. He understood his father's concession that he had a son who loved numbers and order and schedules, rather than the sea.

James kept it polished and safe in his drawer, wrapped in a cloth, so that it wouldn't be stolen or broken by his schoolyard bullies.

"It doesn't matter if we have a watch," James said, already shaking his head. "It isn't safe."

"It's the safest place there is!" Marlene countered. "We jumped off a cliff into the sea and weren't even hurt."

"Suppose we can't get back?" James said. "Suppose next time we drown."

"We won't."

"How can you possibly know that?"

"I just do," Marlene answered through gritted teeth. She was frustrated again, which in turn frustrated James.

"Because you can just feel it," James replied, not hiding his sarcasm.

Marlene groaned. "All right, fine, I'll make a deal with you," she said. "We'll flip a coin. Heads, we go back one last time. Tails, we take the drawings off the wall and go to bed and forget this ever happened."

"How long have you been planning this one?" James asked.

Marlene fished a coin from her skirt pocket and smirked. "I took this from your piggy bank before I came out here."

She offered the coin to her brother. James turned it in his palm. This was a bad idea. That was what he should have said. And this was his coin, besides. Part of his Christmas money. Marlene had spent all of hers on chocolates, of course, because she was Marlene, impulsive and reckless, and she needed him for balance.

He ought to have taken the coin, put it in his pocket, and told her that she was being foolish. They both were. But there was some sort of pull. Perhaps it was the same one that called to his sister.

He gave Marlene a grin and tossed the coin into the air.

Clumsily, he missed the catch and it fell, spiraling, toward the ground.

"You dropped it on purpose!" Marlene cried.

"I did not!"

"Did you see where it fell?"

James struggled down the body of the tree, legs shaking. Marlene shinnied down after him, on his heels, doing nothing to ease his anxiety. "For heaven's sake, James, go faster. You aren't going to fall."

She leapt past him, landing in the wet grass and fanning her arms out for balance. Before James had even reached the ground, she was already crawling around looking for the coin.

James saw its metal glint just a yard away from his sister,

and he hesitated. He could go over there and grab it before she saw. He could put the coin away and never look at the result. This silly coin did not have to decide anything for him.

There was something about this one night, peculiar in its moonlit magic, that made him abandon his sense of reason.

"It's there." He pointed, and Marlene crouched down in front of the coin.

After a beat, he knelt beside her.

Heads.

?

It isn't sensible, James thought as they approached the schoolhouse the following morning.

The coin flip had decided it, though, and fair was fair.

Marlene was unusually quiet beside him. They didn't race each other to the schoolyard but walked in perfect step at the same pace. Her pensiveness unsettled James, not just because it was so unlike her, but because it had an air of sadness to it.

They had agreed to return to Never Land. But they couldn't decide on when, or how long they would stay.

"I've done the arithmetic," James whispered to her as they reached the wooden fence around the schoolyard. "A full day in Never Land is only an hour here—ninety minutes at the most."

"Marlene!" A girl with blond braids waved with one hand

Chapter 5

as she twirled a jump rope in the other. She, the girl holding
the other end of the rope, and a third girl who had been jumping all abandoned their game to run toward the twins.

"Where were you before the holiday break?"

"You've never been absent."

"We were so worried!"

Marlene gave them an easy smile, her eyes bright. "Our
parents took us to London for our birthday," she said, and
clasped her hands together. "It was marvelous."

The girls huddled together as Marlene spun a story about
a mysterious park—a hidden one that one could visit only
upon invitation, for it was behind a very esteemed building.

James listened as his sister described Never Land, and a
crowd of curious classmates surrounded them. She delivered
the story with a flair for the dramatic, but he knew all the
while that what she was saying was true.

"I've been to London, and I've never heard of a garden
like that," a boy said, scowling. "You made that up."

"She did not," the girl in the braids said.

Before the argument could continue, their teacher came
to the front steps and tugged the rope to ring the bell. And
James watched sister as he walked a step behind her.

The truth was that he liked Never Land, but the thought
of returning frightened him in a way he couldn't put words to.
It was dangerous for a place to be so beautiful, and for time to
drip away so easily.

He couldn't concentrate on his work. His eyes kept flitting to Marlene, who stared at her work as though everything were in a foreign language she couldn't decipher. At lunchtime, she avoided him as if she knew he would only continue to try to talk her out of her plans. Instead, she immediately immersed herself in a cloud of her friends, all of whom wanted to hear more about this mysterious garden.

"I can't tell you any more than I already have," James heard her say from where he sat alone on a bench with his mathematics book. "Really, I've said too much. I promised to keep it a secret." This seemed to devastate them.

At the end of the day, Marlene gathered her two closest friends—the girl in the braids and another girl with freckles and dark hair—into a tight hug. "I'll see you soon," she told them, and ran to catch up to James.

"I wish I didn't tell them," she said. "It's like I let them in on the secret."

"Marlene," James began, his tone grave.

She stopped walking. "James," she said firmly. "You're not going back on your word. We agreed. We said we'd do what the coin says."

In that moment, James could see how sad his sister was, and he recalled how happy she'd been when she told the story to her friends.

He sighed. "Never Land means that much to you?"

"Please, James." At once, her voice was small. She never

asked for things. There was so little in this town that she wanted, and so little that James or their parents could do to make her feel like she belonged here, besides. "Please," she said again. "I can't go without you."

They weren't the same, and at the same time they were tethered by their twinness, that unspoken thing no one else understood about them. He couldn't let her go alone. He would dive into a volcano if she went in ahead of him. He would follow her to the moon, because they weren't complete or safe unless they were together. The world simply wouldn't make sense if they were apart.

"After we finish our chores," he said. "And we only spend one day. We're back before Mother and Father come home."

Marlene launched herself into his arms, sending him toppling backward and nearly falling into the street. "Thank you!" she cried. "I knew you'd keep your word. I knew you would."

James understood then that if he went back on his promise, if he chose to stay here in the world of clocks and logic, Marlene wouldn't be brave enough to go without him. Never Land was the first thing that was bigger than her own courage.

He would do this for her. And he could only hope he wouldn't come to regret it.

6

"Whatever you do, don't let go of my hand," Marlene said.

It was after supper and night had descended on their little seaside town. When their parents turned in for the night, James felt a pang of guilt that they weren't saying goodbye. But it was no matter, he told himself. Based on how their journey had gone last time, even if they stayed in Never Land for days, they'd be back home before morning. No one would have to know they'd left.

Now, he held Marlene's hand in a vise grip, and she gave it a reassuring squeeze. "I promise I won't let you drown," she said.

James snorted at that. "I'll haunt you if you're wrong."

Marlene laughed, but her expression betrayed the same nervous energy James felt. No one was out on the streets at this hour. If something did go wrong, there would be no one to save them.

"You're sure this is where I fell in the water the last time?" James asked.

"Fairly certain," she said. And before James could challenge her, she began to count. "Three . . . two . . . one . . . Go!"

They ran, and James felt the cold water slam into him the instant he jumped. He opened his mouth—to cry out, to shout that he'd changed his mind, that this was a horrible, horrible mistake.

And then—the cold and ink-black water became something bright blue and warm. James emerged from the surface, gasping and spluttering, as Marlene hauled him to his feet. They had made it to the shallows somehow.

It was a bright and clear morning. The first thing James heard was the peaceful twittering of birds, and then a voice crying out, "They've come back!"

"Only for a little while," James said to Tootles, who was bounding down the sand dunes like the little skunk he often pretended to be.

Tootles grabbed Marlene's hand and began tugging her toward the forest. "I was the lookout," he said excitedly. "Nobody believed you'd come back, but I knew that if I waited, you would. I was in the highest tree. You can see almost everything from up there."

"How long were you waiting?" Marlene asked. Back at home, only a week had passed, but in Never Land, a single moment seemed like an eternity.

"I don't know," Tootles said. "Come on—I'll race you back home."

Before either of the twins could ask where home was, he took off running. Marlene bounded after him, laughing. And as ever, James struggled to keep up with his sister. Though it seemed Marlene had finally met her match in this little boy in the skunk-skin cap. So fast were the two of them that they didn't notice when James doubled over to catch his breath.

He leaned against the bark of a giant tree whose roots emerged from the mossy ground. He reached for the pocket watch he'd brought along, which was still ticking even after being doused by the sea. It read 10:00, the current time in London. He and Marlene had been expected to turn out the lights and go to sleep an hour ago.

Peculiar that it still worked, James thought. He had been unsure when Marlene had first proposed the idea, but he was relieved to see that this time they would be able to tell how many hours had passed.

The sun was brighter here. Sharper. And the air was peculiar. It tasted sweet, like a batch of fresh cookies was perpetually baking somewhere off in the distance.

Far away, someone was shrieking with laughter.

Marlene had disappeared off into the horizon somewhere, and for once, he didn't feel as though he was being dragged after her. The relief was surprising to James, who was beginning to feel a sense of curiosity about this place. The tree currently shading him had the greenest, sharpest leaves he'd ever seen. The sunlight candied them with brightness. James leaned in closer to inspect the foliage.

The branches were thick and frequent, and before he could talk himself out of it, he began to climb. His arms trembled as he made his way up the first branch, and then the next. But he didn't look down. If he was able to jump off a cliffside without being harmed, this tree was nothing he couldn't manage.

By the time he reached the top, his heart was pounding. He emerged through a curtain of branches and found himself in a beam of sun. Never Land was spread out before him like a living map.

His anxiety turned to breathless wonder. This island was the heart of Never Land, and James could see that more clearly now. On all sides, water. A glittering and waving sea that was nothing like the water back home.

"What are you doing up there?" A voice made James flinch and startle. He hugged the trunk so he wouldn't fall, his fingers rooting themselves in the soft bark.

When he finally had the courage to look down, he saw

Sam—the only boy with a sensible name—staring up at him.

Similar to James, Sam was small in stature. He had a nervous, fiddling energy. Every time James saw him, his hands were in constant motion, tugging at the hem of his shirt or knitting blades of grass into satchels.

"Just having a look," James said. He did his best to sound brave. His eyes fixed on something in the distance. A dark shadow interrupted the smooth horizon. "What's that over there?"

"I can't see anything from down here," Sam said, sensible as ever. "What does it look like?"

James squinted. "I'm not sure yet. Come and see for yourself."

Sam hesitated, then began a slow, wobbly ascent up the branches. It wasn't every day James encountered someone as careful or shy as himself, and it made him feel strangely braver. "You're all right," James encouraged. "Look, you're already most of the way up."

Sam ventured a cautious glance up at James, who extended his arm. Who was this boy, James wondered, and how had he ended up in a place like Never Land? Sam took his hand and clung to it for dear life, and James reeled him up, the same way Marlene had always done for him when he went clambering after her.

All the boys in Never Land had an odd sense about them, as though they'd come to life from the pages of an enchanted novel. But Sam—Sam was practical. He spoke softly, and the first time James and Marlene had visited Never Land, he'd heard Sam worrying over what needed to be mended, or tidied, or cooked. And as he crawled onto the branch beside James and hugged the body of the tree, James suspected that they could be friends.

James could make out the object he had seen as a ship. By now, it had veered eastward, and James could see that Never Land also contained another island far in the distance, faint and purple, like a scar.

"I thought Peter said there are no other islands out here," James said. "But that ship is heading right toward one."

Beside him, Sam went pale. "Oh," he said. "That place. We don't talk about that."

"Whyever not?" James said. "They've got a ship! They can probably take us to all sorts of places—"

Sam clapped his hand over James's mouth. Stunned, James stared at him in wide-eyed silence.

"Listen," Sam said, very softly. "If you see any ships out there, you have to pretend that you've seen something else. A seagull, or a mermaid, or nothing at all."

James shifted his gaze back to the sea, and a pit of dread churned in his stomach. He didn't like being told what to do, especially when there was no logic behind it. Order, structure, rules—these he could follow. But there was no sense to be made of pretending an entire ship didn't exist.

Something strange came over him. Perhaps it was this place. Magical and bright. It gave him the feeling that he was invincible. After all, he had plunged himself into the depths of the sea and emerged on these shores without a scratch. He was braver than the boy he had been just that morning.

He pried Sam's hand away from his mouth. "Tell me who's piloting that ship," he demanded. "Tell me right now, or I'll go to the cliffside and scream for the captain to come over here."

Sam was sweating. Blond hair stuck to his forehead, and his cheeks were flushed. "P-please," he stammered. "You don't want to do that."

"Very well. I'll find out for myself." James moved to descend the tree, and Sam grasped his shirt.

"Okay!" Sam cried. And then he whispered, "Okay. I'll tell you." He huddled close, and James could feel the warmth and the nerves radiating out of him. "Never Land used to be one big island. Peter has always been in charge, in a way. He took us all in when we got here. He makes sure there's enough food, and that nothing bad happens to us."

Bad. The word struck James like a lingering chord from a tightly strung guitar. He had forgotten such a word existed until just now.

"One of the boys decided he didn't want Peter to be in charge. Thought he could do a better job," Sam went on. "He conspired with some others who felt the same way, and they staged a coup. One night, they tried to kill Peter in his sleep." He held his finger against James's throat as though it were the blade of a sword. "Tried to gut him like a fish. But the fairies saw it happen and they split the island in two, pushed the second half across the water. All the traitors went to their island, and the rest of us stayed here with Peter. The island is *just* out of sight, right to the very inch. But sometimes—" Sam's eyes were wide. "Sometimes, if I think about it and I remember it's there, I'll see it."

"I don't get it," James said. "Why give them their own island? Why not just kill them?"

"Nobody dies in Never Land," Sam said, as though it were the most reasonable thing in the world. "That's Peter's only rule."

Marlene saw the ship making its way toward a landmass on the other side of the sea, and she skidded to a stop.

Tootles was far ahead of her before he noticed her absence, and he scampered back to her side.

"What's that?" Marlene asked. "I see—is it an island?"

"Come on." Tootles tugged her hand. "The others have been waiting for you."

He took off at a run again, and for once in her life, Marlene wasn't in a hurry to be the fastest. She couldn't know that, at the same moment, her brother was on the other side of the island with the exact same pit in his own stomach.

Marlene hopped onto the branch of a nearby tree and hoisted herself up for a better view. The ship was far away, growing farther by the second. But she could see the faint landmass on the other side.

Peter lied to us, she thought. He had told them that his island was the only one in Never Land. But why?

She wished she'd thought to bring James's telescope. Or the binoculars their mother used to watch for birds in the springtime. They hadn't brought anything with them but James's pocket watch, and she was suddenly realizing how silly that had been. Even if they were planning on being in Never Land only a few days, she should have known to be more prepared.

By the time she reached the top branch of the tree, the sky had turned cloudy. A cool ocean breeze pushed through her dark curls.

A flutter. A rush. And suddenly Peter was hovering in front of her with his hands on his hips.

Marlene's focus shattered. Her thoughts dissolved. She clung to the trunk so that she wouldn't fall. "You startled me," she snapped.

"You're back!" Peter said, seemingly oblivious to her annoyance. He looked down at the ground and whistled. "You really like heights, don't you? I haven't met many kids who like heights."

Marlene scrunched her nose. "You hadn't met me."

Peter hovered in front of her, blocking her view of the boat and the island across the sea. Marlene didn't ask him what was out there, or why he had lied. Something told her not to.

"What if I told you that you could fly like the rest of us?" Peter said.

"It wouldn't be the strangest thing I've learned in this place," Marlene replied.

"Tink—hey, Tink, over here." Peter darted across the sky as though stroking through water. In his absence, Marlene looked back to the skyline, but the ship was gone. Swallowed up by the glittering water and the beaming sun.

Peter returned, flanked by a floating sphere of yellow light. He had introduced Marlene to the fairies, but only vaguely, gesturing to them as though such a thing should be perfectly ordinary. But this was the first time Marlene was close enough to have a proper look. There in the sphere of light was a lady who would have been able to sit in the palm of Marlene's hand, with delicate, phosphorescent wings.

Marlene leaned closer for a better look, and she could have sworn the woman was scowling suspiciously at her.

"Marlene," Peter said with what sounded like a hint of

tenderness in his voice, "meet Tinker Bell. The most beautiful fairy in Never Land."

Tink blushed at this, but there was a distrustful gleam in her eye.

With a flourish, Tink spiraled through the air, spilling bits of light and dust around Marlene. They hit her like a burst of heat, and then, at once, a summer wind. The light entered through her skin, warming her.

Peter hovered beside her. "Close your eyes," he said softly, and she did. "Think of something happy. Tremendously, frightfully happy."

For Marlene to think of what made her happy, she first had to think of what made her miserable. Dreary, cloudy skies and a closet full of dresses she never wore. But especially, she thought about James's expression when they'd jumped into Never Land for the second time. She was worried that she had been unfair to drag him along. He had only done it because he loved her, she knew. Was she taking advantage of their bond? Would she have done the same for him?

Deep down, in a part of her mind she would never admit to having, she envied him, and that envy made her bitter with herself. James was tidy and smart and practical, and one day he would have a sensible job as an inventor in London. He had always been sure of this, and Marlene had always been jealous of him for that. No matter how she tried to best him at everything, it didn't matter. He had the one thing that she didn't. He didn't belong in their ramshackle little seaside town any more than she did, but at least he belonged *somewhere*.

Where did she belong?

There weren't words for the images that flooded her just then. A bright and melting sun. Birds rushing up and up in formation. The sweet smell of flowers with sharp petals, insects buzzing with song. It was a place she had never been but always sensed. She'd read dozens upon dozens of fantasy books, searching through fictional worlds for anything resembling this feeling she imagined, but it seemed to exist only inside of her.

"Look." There was quiet laughter in Peter's voice. Marlene opened her eyes and realized that she had let go of the tree trunk. She had drifted up, up, beyond the top of the tree, whose branches were vibrant and filled with sun.

She brought a hand before her face, and a smatter of glittering dust fell away from her.

"I'm floating?"

"You're flying," Peter corrected her. "Here. Look." He swam backward in the air, exaggerating his movements.

Marlene chased after him, and she felt so light. So impossibly light that it made her burst out laughing.

She was distantly aware of Tink, still scowling and fluttering after her. It worried Marlene that she was at the mercy of this unpredictable fairy and this unusual boy, but she propelled herself forward all the same. Her body dipped and rose erratically, like a fly caught in a spider's web.

Think of the light and the smells and the wind, she told herself. She leaned forward and spread out her arms, and she flew.

A gust of wind came and she rode it like a ship on a wave.

"There you go, you've got it," Peter called to her. "Follow me and I'll show you where to find the best view."

He darted forward faster than the wind could carry Marlene, and she swam clumsily in the air to keep up with him. "Hey! Wait!"

It was not a thing she'd ever said, as accustomed as she was to being the fastest.

Peter looked over his shoulder and laughed, but he didn't slow his pace by so much as a beat.

Think of something happy.

The wind. The sun. The fact that her hometown was far, far away, and she would never have to eat fish stew again. Where she wouldn't fall asleep listening to the ticking of the clock and wake up to the map of London that James hung over the dresser. Never going back.

Fly.

She soared ahead until she was at Peter's side. She grabbed the hat from his head and placed it over her tangle of curls. The shock in his eyes made her triumphant. If Peter was the fastest one in Never Land, she would learn to be faster.

They were racing each other now. Peter stayed at her side only to humor her and then take satisfaction each time he zipped ahead, showing off with somersaults and barrel rolls.

By the time Marlene had gotten the hang of it, they had already flown beyond any piece of Never Land that she had ever seen. Peter led her to a cliffside that curled and bowed high above the rest of the island. Right at the edge stood a giant tree with thick branches that reached out over the water.

Peter sat on the farthest branch, in a place that would have been too daring even for Marlene to climb to if she hadn't just learned how to fly. But now she joined him with a curious and suspicious interest in this strange boy and this strange world that held him.

Marlene could almost believe she was dreaming. Flying wasn't possible, after all, and neither was anything else about Never Land. But here Never Land was regardless, pushing summer wind against her face.

As she sat beside Peter, he stared at her face as though she was the wonder. His eyes were wide, mouth slightly parted. The faintest glint of sweat dotted his forehead. His cheeks were ripe with pale freckles.

Marlene reached forward and pressed two fingertips against his throat, probing until she found the dull thud of his pulse.

"What are you doing?" he asked her.

"Making sure that you're real."

It would be foolish to trust him, Marlene knew, and so she didn't. But he still fascinated her.

He pressed his fingers to her throat in the same spot. They stared at each other, in perfect parallel. Their hearts thudded against each other's skin to confirm that they were both alive.

7

James couldn't understand what Sam had told him. Nobody died in Never Land? But how could that be? Someone couldn't just make a rule and live forever. That wasn't how the world worked. But perhaps Never Land was different.

"Well, technically they *can* die," Sam clarified. "But we're not allowed to kill them. And it's not like we'll die of old age."

"You're not allowed to kill people anyway," James said. "Not where I come from, at least."

Sam looked at him, his eyes big and curious. "But does it ever happen?"

"Sometimes," James admitted, suddenly feeling uncomfortable. "I'm sure it does."

Sam nodded off to a volcano, made purple by the distance. "Peter threatens to toss us in there if we break the rules," he said. "But he's only kidding. He would never."

"Lovely." James hopped down from the tree, gaining confidence. "We'll need a saw," he told Sam, changing the topic.

"What for?" Sam's legs trembled as he clambered his way down the final branches.

"To make a raft," James said. "My father taught me how to do it. I've been crafting them since I was a baby, practically." He might have been a terrible swimmer, but James was an exceptional crafter. Anything that required measurements, he could assemble.

The memory of his father was strangely fuzzy. He couldn't remember the shape of his face, or what color his eyes and hair were. Odd, James thought.

"Why would we need a raft?" Sam asked.

"Don't be dense." James grabbed the boy's arm and helped him down the final branch. "We're going to sail out to that island."

"We can't!" Sam cried. "Peter wouldn't want us to."

"What's Peter going to do about it?" James plodded forward. If he couldn't find a saw, he would need branches that were thick enough to form a raft, but pliable enough to be snapped. "He may control *your* every move, but I'm not one of his Lost Boys."

Who made Peter the boss of this place anyway? He must

have had a terribly large ego, James thought, if he believed he could set so many rules.

James was reveling in this newfound sense of bravery. It was entirely alien to him. And Sam followed in his footsteps, seemingly mesmerized by James and his authority.

"Tell me more things," Sam said, after they had been gathering large twigs for a while in companionable silence.

"What sorts of things?" James asked. He knelt beside a large rock that was rooted into the dirt. "Hand me that sharp rock over there. I think we can cut these twigs now."

Sam obliged. He sat in the dirt beside the pile of twigs and watched as James struck them between the two rocks to cut them into uniform sizes. "More things about your father. What else did he teach you?"

James shrugged. "Things that don't matter, mostly. How to catch a fish."

"Fish are delicious," Sam said, his tone wistful. "But I'm terrible at catching them. They always get away."

James looked up, briefly appraising him. He had never seen Sam cast a line, but he could guess that he was too soft to follow through. He probably drew back the bait when he saw the fish coming, and he seemed too skittish to even impale the worm on the hook.

"Anyway, didn't your father ever teach you how to do anything?" James said.

"I don't have parents," Sam said without emotion.

James chopped the edge of a twig with clean precision. He beamed proudly at his handiwork. "Everyone has parents."

"Not Peter," Sam said. "Not any of us."

"Then who gave you your name?" James asked.

"Nobody," Sam answered. But he seemed unsure. "I don't know. I've just always had it."

No wonder Marlene liked Never Land so much, James thought. It was filled with delusional people just like her.

Not that it mattered. After today, they would go home and never come back. He'd agreed to abide by the coin flip, but this place was too strange, and he wouldn't agree to do such a thing again.

"Go grab some of those purple vines if you want to make yourself useful," James said. "We can use them like ropes to tie everything together."

At least, James hoped as much. He had never seen vines like these before. Or flowers and trees like these, for that matter. Never Land was vast and green, with bright pops of vivid colors. Each breeze carried a different sweetness than the last, evoking some strange memory James couldn't quite form before it faded away again. It was like waking from a dream he could no longer remember, and not understanding what it was that had made him so happy.

But he had a sense that he would get answers on the other side of the sea, where Peter's enemies lived. Perhaps, he thought, they would be able to tell James of a more sensible way home so that he and Marlene wouldn't have to nearly drown themselves again. His need for logic fueled him. Peter wasn't being truthful, James thought. How could it be that none of these boys remembered how they'd gotten here, or who they'd been before? Why was there no clear bridge between this place and his hometown?

Then James began to think that if there *was* a logical explanation, one that made it safe to travel back and forth, then Marlene's wanderlust could be satisfied. She could traipse back and forth the same way their mother did to London. He wouldn't have to worry about her so much, and she would be happy.

"Tie them like this," James said as Sam watched him work the vines around the twigs. "This will secure them so that they don't untie. You don't want your raft to fall apart when you're in the middle of the sea."

"Could we go anywhere with a raft like this?" Sam asked. He struggled to unfurl a vine, and it slapped him in the cheek.

"A raft like this will do in a pinch," James said. "But it won't get us very far. Not to someplace like France or America."

"What are those?" Sam asked.

"Countries." James appraised him again. "Haven't you ever been to school?"

"Of course," Sam was quick to say. "I've been there all the time. I find it quite nice." James could tell that Sam was trying to adopt his inflections as he puffed his chest out in a show of confidence. It only made him seem all the more like a child.

"You have no idea what school is, do you?" James said. Sam deflated and shook his head, and James continued, "It's where you go to learn about things. Like mathematics. Mathematics is especially important when measuring parts. That's how I was able to build this raft."

It wasn't often that James had such a captive audience as Sam, and he was enjoying it. Back at home, Marlene was the one who drew the crowds. Everyone liked her. They fed on her stories and jokes and shared their candy with her on the schoolyard while James lingered shyly in her shadow.

Besides, James was coming to like Sam. He was down-to-earth, if a bit doe-eyed.

They carried the raft over an embankment, flanked by dragonflies and bright pink moths that seemed to be following them. The air was a bit colder when they reached the beach. Up close, the water was not as bright and sparkling as it had been from atop the cliffs.

"All right, I'll get on the raft and use this stick to paddle. You push it away from the shore and then climb up." James hoped his haughty tone could mask his fear.

Sam had gone pale again, and he took a step back.

"What is it?" James asked.

"N-no." There was a stammer when he said it. "I—I just don't think this is a very good idea."

Grumbling to himself, James climbed on the raft. If Sam insisted on being useless, he would have to do it himself. He wielded the stick that he'd fashioned into an oar and pushed it against the shore.

James hoped that his panic did not show as the raft began drifting out. His palms turned clammy and his heart thudded in his ears.

Never Land is different, he told himself.

"Wait!" Just as the first wave drew the raft farther from the shore, Sam waded in after it. He broke into a swim, and James was astonished at how skillfully this awkward, clumsy boy could move through the water.

Sam climbed over the edge of the raft, and James snared him by the collar to pull him the rest of the way up, secretly relieved to have a companion for the journey after all.

The water was clear and calm, and for the first time in his life, James felt something like ease as he drifted on its surface. Peter's island within Never Land grew smaller against the horizon, and the enemy island began to come into view.

"James?" Sam balanced himself beside him. "Aren't you worried that they'll try to kill us, the way they tried to kill Peter?"

"If that happens, I suppose we'll have to kill them first," James replied, but he wasn't certain he knew how.

"You can't kill them," Sam insisted. "It's the one thing that's forbidden."

"But some things in life are worth the risk, Sam. Like figuring this place out. They have a ship and Peter doesn't. That means they can go farther out. Maybe they've visited the rest of Never Land."

"We've never needed a ship," Sam pointed out. "We can fly."

James cocked an eyebrow as he took this in. "The boys on this other island don't fly?"

Sam shook his head. "To fly, you need pixie dust from the fairies, and the fairies never go there."

Interesting, James thought, but didn't say aloud.

Thunder roared and a sudden bolt of lightning split the sky. James flinched. Sam huddled against him like a whimpering puppy.

"There's nothing to worry about," James said reassuringly. Surely storms in Never Land were much calmer than what he was used to in England—despite the lightning and thunder, the sun was still shining on the fringes of the storm clouds, and the air was calm. The tide wasn't rising even an inch.

The next clap of thunder was so loud that it left a hollow ringing in James's ear. Suddenly he thought of Marlene, who had run ahead of him into the wilds of this strange place. What had she gotten up to, he wondered, and did she even notice that he was no longer following her?

An inexplicable dread hardened in his chest. He couldn't justify it. Marlene could handle herself, and she had never minded a good storm. But the air smelled different now—salty, faintly perfumed and sour—and the clouds darkened overhead, blocking out the sun that had seemed so strong only moments before.

The island was close. James paddled with renewed fervor.

By the time the next bolt of lightning struck, the world had darkened, and the water began to stir like restless bodies trapped beneath an infinite blanket of pale blues and greens.

"James!" Sam cried out in warning, a moment before a wave crashed forward and capsized their raft.

The island disappeared, the sky, Sam, Never Land—its terrible beauty and sharp, radiating magic—all swallowed up by the unforgiving sea. James grasped the first thing he could find, which was a tuft of Sam's shirt. The pair of them tumbled, thrashing aimlessly underwater, before Sam found his bearings and began to swim upward, somehow pulling James along with him.

James squeezed his eyes shut and waited to surface back on the familiar shore of his hometown, the way he had when he'd jumped from the cliff with Marlene.

With surprising strength, Sam pulled him to the surface. They came up gasping, clawing at the edge of the raft, which was still floating nearby.

The world had gone turbulent, so dark that James could no longer see the islands on either side. Sam was shouting something at him, but he couldn't hear the words over the roaring water.

His heart thudded. James's eyes streamed with tears and his body trembled. He hated himself for all of this, the way that water turned him into a useless child. Paralyzed as he was with fear, he couldn't bring himself to climb back onto the raft. Perhaps he should just let himself sink into the ocean and let it take him back to his small town like it had before, but something stopped him. He still wanted answers. He just needed to gather the courage to find them.

Another shout broke through the noise, but this time it wasn't Sam. When James managed to raise his head, he saw the unreal glow of what seemed to be hundreds of spheres of light coming from Peter's island. He'd seen them floating about as he and his sister meandered through Never Land's brambles on their first visit.

Fairies.

The fairies were surrounding James and Sam now, and James dared to feel a small sense of relief. No one could die in Never Land. That was Peter's rule, and the fairies had come to rescue them.

He reached out a hand, and a dozen fairies grabbed hold of his wrist, pulling him up. With his other hand, he kept his grip on Sam. They would need to be rescued together, he thought. It was the least he could do after dragging that poor skittish boy along on his own excursion.

The fairies weren't holding on to him with their bodies, he realized, but with something resembling strands of hair made entirely of golden light. The light wrapped around his other wrist, and then his ankles, coiling so tightly that he yelped out in pain.

There was a jingling sound, like a bell ringing. And as James got closer, he realized that it was coming from the fairies. It must have been their form of speech. One word rang out clearly, even above the riotous thunder. Sam translated, looking scared.

"Traitor."

8

Marlene felt the knot in her chest the moment she heard the first clap of thunder.

Peter floated up from the branch and raised his head. His nostrils flared, like a prey animal that sensed danger on the horizon.

"What is it?" She flew after him and stumbled in midair as her body tried to remember how it went. The fairy magic seemed to surround her, like motes of dust caught in the light. Peter told her that it would linger for as long as she allowed it, and Marlene was not about to give it up anytime soon.

"The storm . . ." Peter's voice trailed.

"Doesn't it rain in Never Land?" Marlene asked, confused

by Peter's reaction. The droplets were starting to fall now, lazy and fat and sparse. The sun lit up the clouds in roils of gold and gray.

"Only when the fairies are up to something," Peter said. He grabbed her hand. "Come on."

He flew off so quickly that Marlene didn't have a chance to be startled by the force of his grip. No one but James ever led her anywhere, and even that happened rarely as it was usually her doing the leading. They had always reached for each other the way that vines coil around branches and climb for the sunlight, and having someone else in James's place was disconcerting.

The storm quickly turned violent as they flew. The cold air stung at Marlene's face, and it felt as though there were an electric current moving through her.

Where was James? She remembered all at once that he had been behind her, and that she had left him. It infuriated her how easy it was to lose things in Never Land. Time, thoughts, reason, and now her own brother.

The rain hit her body with heavy plunks and reverberated like syllables in her head. *James. Home. James. Home.*

She and Peter stopped at the water's edge, and through the murk, Marlene saw the island she'd glimpsed much earlier when a mysterious ship had been sailing toward it. Now she saw the glow of fairy lights out in the distance, and the silhouette of two Lost Boys struggling in their grasp.

The knot in her chest went heavy. No. That was not a Lost Boy.

"James!" She flew forward, but Peter pulled her back. She threw him violently off her.

"What are they doing to my brother?" she demanded.

Peter's expression was defensive. "That depends on what he's done to them." He sounded a little uncertain, but ready to believe the worst of James. A web of lightning reflected in his bright brown eyes. Reflected, too, was the ramshackle raft that floated unmanned at the water's surface.

Peter was not the prey that sensed danger, Marlene realized. He was the predator about to strike.

Traitor, traitor, traitor, the fairies jingled. James was dangling helplessly by his ankles now. Beside him, Sam had broken into tears and was sobbing out an apology.

"We didn't mean to," Sam was telling them. "We're sorry." But it was no use. The fairies had no intention of listening.

James writhed, but the constraints that kept him upside down only tightened. He heard something splash and hoped it wasn't his pocket watch—the only way he could truly tell time in this strange place. The fairies were in possession of endless vines. Ordinary tree vines, enchanted by some sort of magical glow.

There was a crack of lightning. Then a sharp whistling sound, and one of his ankles broke free of its restraints. James was so startled by the motion that it took him a moment to realize it had been an arrow. Then another, and one of Sam's constraints broke loose.

A bit of light spiraled down through the air. One of the fairies had been hit by an arrow. A tiny winged body floated on the water's surface, and the light was snuffed as the fairy sank. James's stomach lurched at the sight.

"What happens when you kill a fairy?" he rasped.

"I don't know," Sam managed to choke out. He'd gone pale with fear. "Something bad, I think. Something very, very bad."

More arrows rained toward them, and James—still dangling by one ankle—saw the ship looming closer.

Peter's enemies had arrived, but they weren't shooting at James and Sam, or even at Peter. They were shooting at the fairies.

The fairies' jingles grew higher in pitch—a fragile song of a cry—as many of them were impaled. Whatever Peter's enemies wanted with him, it wasn't nearly as terrifying as these cursed little things that had captured him. He would rather face the wrath of boys than of fairies.

Suddenly Peter flew overhead, and Sam called out to him for help.

"No, you idiot," James said. "Can't you see he'll never let us go to the other island if he drags us back?"

James wasn't sure what waited for him at the enemy island, but something told him that after displeasing Peter, going back to where they had come from would be much worse.

"I don't want to leave Peter's island," Sam sobbed. "I never did. This is all your fault."

James twisted and tried to sort himself upright. The blood was still rushing to his head, making his ears throb, and before he could argue with Sam, he saw the figure that was suspended in the air beside Peter. A bolt of lightning illuminated her face.

"Marlene?" he whispered. For an instant James was sure he was dreaming. His sister was in flight! He could scarcely believe it, and then, in the next moment, he realized that she looked more like herself than he'd ever seen. All fire and strength, her jaw clenched and eyes bright. It was as though she was always meant to be this way.

The next arrow severed the last of their restraints. Before James and Sam had a chance to hit the water again, they were ensnared in the web of a fishing net being reeled toward the enemy ship.

"Stop crying, stop it," James hissed at Sam, who was clinging to the ropes. "You'll get us both killed. We can't look weak." But James did feel weak, and scared, despite his own words.

The remaining fairies retreated, and only then did James see the look on Peter's face as he hovered above them, watching the scene unfold. His eyes were ablaze, fists clenched at his sides.

"James!" Marlene raced toward him, intent on rescuing him the way she always had.

"Don't!" James called out over the next clap of thunder. Her outstretched fingers snared the net, and she fumbled for his hand. For once, he didn't take it. His mind filled with terrible images—Marlene, impaled by an arrow. Drowned at sea. Tortured by these unknown enemy boys for reasons James couldn't yet fathom. All his life, his sister had protected him, and for once, he knew that she would be in danger if he didn't push her away.

"James, grab my hand. If I pull you away, I think I can take the net out of their grasp." She met his eyes with a wild, bewildered gaze.

"No," James shouted. "Go home! Get away from Peter. Get out of this wretched place while you still can!"

"James, you idiot." She tugged at the rope, bracing her feet in the air as though she could gain leverage. "What have you gotten us into?"

James could hear the boys on the enemy ship laughing.

An arrow flew toward her, and Marlene just dodged it. But the threat of death wasn't enough to deter her. She drew a deep breath and dunked herself underwater. James could hear the confused shouts of the enemy boys as they struggled with where to aim their arrows.

"What's wrong with your sister?" Sam asked, his hysterics momentarily forgotten in exchange for awe at what Marlene was doing. James only growled with frustration.

After several seconds, Marlene broke through the surface with a gasp. She was brandishing a piece of red coral that looked almost like a heart, sharp at its point. "The rope is strong, but I can saw through it with this."

"Kill her!" someone yelled from the enemy ship.

Marlene took another deep breath and disappeared underwater again. James struggled to reach through the holes in the net. The next time his sister came up for air, he grabbed her wrist to stop her from going under again. "You've lost your mind," he shouted.

"And you've lost yours! What were you thinking coming out here?"

Even as the rope was drawn backward, ever closer to the enemy ship, Marlene grasped James's arm with both hands and pulled. For the first time since he could recall, James saw desperation in her eyes. When their gazes locked, they shared the same cold rush through their blood, and James understood that she was every bit as frightened as he was. Somewhere in the distance, Peter was hovering above them, shouting commands at the fairies and demanding that the enemy boys surrender.

"Come on," Marlene said through gritted teeth. "Work with me, James. We can't let them take you." She propelled herself up into the air again. The net lifted with her ascent, pulled between her and the boys on the ship.

The next arrow sailed past her head, and she barely dodged it.

"Get out of here!" James tried to pry her fingers off him, but she wouldn't ease up. Nobody was supposed to die in Never Land—that was the only rule—but these boys were exiled because they made their own rules. They had tried to cut Peter's throat while he was sleeping, and they would think nothing of impaling the heart of a silly girl who interfered with their plans.

Marlene screamed, frustrated. Her legs thrashed in the air as she tried to pull him to safety. In a frenzied, delirious moment, James thought his sister was just enraged enough to do it. But even she was no match for a net secured to a ship.

Before the next arrow could hit her, a shadow darted out across the sea and grabbed her. Through the gloom, James saw the unmistakable green of the shadow's clothing.

Peter.

He tore Marlene away with such force that her grasp on James was severed. James and Sam wheeled back, swinging helplessly in the net.

"Let go of me!" Marlene was kicking at Peter, jabbing her elbows into his ribs.

"They'll kill you, too," James heard Peter say to her. "We tried, but you have to let them go. They're lost to us."

Peter cast one final sad, torn look toward Sam before he flew back for his island, a still-thrashing Marlene in tow. James watched their shapes getting smaller, his sister's protests growing fainter, as the distance between them grew.

James was probably going to die. He realized that now. Peter's enemies were not going to give him any answers. They would fill him with arrows the way they had tried to do to Marlene.

Sam was still crying as he coiled himself around James's arm, but James couldn't concentrate on anything but his sister, slowly disappearing on the horizon.

He felt as though it was the last time he would ever see her.

9

Marlene had become something feral.

She spat at Peter as he dragged her to the cliffside. He didn't flinch, not even when she landed a firm kick on his shin. Peter wasn't much to look at—a twig of a boy—but he was solid, and his strong grip easily overpowered her. When they landed, he stood somberly as she screamed and tried to fly out of his arms.

"If you don't care about my brother, don't you at least care about Sam?" she pleaded. "He's one of *your* boys."

"I do care," Peter said, and Marlene could hear a trace of sorrow in his voice. "Sam is always so cautious. He would never venture out that far on his own." His eyes darkened. "Your brother had a hand in this."

Marlene wanted to argue, but she knew that Peter was right. She had seen the abandoned raft coasting on the waves, and she'd recognized her brother's handiwork. It wasn't like him at all. Practical, orderly James who loved rules and hated the water would never have done a thing like this back home. What had made him so reckless?

"It's my fault." She realized the words as she said them aloud. Her limbs went slack. "He didn't want to come back here. I forced him. I forced him with that stupid coin toss."

"Marlene, listen to me." Peter moved his grasp to her shoulders, and he spun her gently to face him. "Sam and James are gone. I'm sorry, but we can never go back there. Those boys would cheerfully kill us all."

Marlene heaved a steadying breath as she stared out across the sea. The ship that had captured her brother was just large enough yet for her to see from where they stood.

The storm had settled now. The fairies who'd survived the melee were drifting toward them. Tears stung the corners of Marlene's eyes, and she clenched her jaw. In tearing her away from her brother, Peter did not understand what he had done. She couldn't leave her brother as easily as Peter apparently could abandon one of his Lost Boys.

"Maybe you're happy to let them die, but I'm not," she

said. She lunged over the edge of the cliff. But rather than taking flight, her body turned heavy and plummeted downward. A cluster of fairies grasped her arms with small sharp tendrils of light and hoisted her back up.

"You won't be able to fly if you're so filled with hatred," Peter said. His voice was eerily even. "The magic won't work."

"Put me down," Marlene demanded of the fairies. Their grasp was painful, like she was being held by thin hot coils of wire.

With a nod from Peter, the fairies dropped her to the ground, and she fell in a heap, an awkward tangle of limbs.

"Don't be angry with her," Peter told the fairies. "It isn't her fault so many of you died. We have James and Sam to thank for that."

Marlene turned her head sharply to Peter. Despite the flat tone of his voice, she saw the pain in his eyes.

"Sam?" A soft voice made Peter and Marlene turn their heads to the brambles. Tootles peeked back at them, Slightly at his side. "What's happened to Sam?" At the sight of the tears that streaked down Marlene's cheeks, Tootles's lip began to quiver.

"Sam betrayed us," Peter said. His expression darkened. His proud stance did nothing to mask his misery as he said the words. "He and James sailed to the enemy side."

"Sam wouldn't do that," Slightly said.

"The fairies tried to bring them back to us," Peter said. "But the enemies killed them."

Tootles shook his head frantically. He ran to the edge of the cliff and stared out, as though he could see what was happening across the water. Marlene turned to follow his gaze. But it was as though the enemy island had disappeared, leaving nothing but dissipating storm clouds.

The other boys were coming now, all of them drawn by Peter's strange magnetism. Even Marlene felt it. The soul of this boy was everywhere, a beating pulse that kept Never Land alive. Because Peter grieved for the lost fairies—and a Lost Boy—the entire island grieved with him. The flowers— normally bright and fragrant—wilted and hung their heads. The fairies sobbed in chorus like the gentle patter of rain.

Peter stood beside Marlene, and she shivered at the strange and overwhelming presence he wielded. He leaned in close. "I'd like to trust you," he murmured. "But your brother betrayed me, and you'll have to prove that you're not the same."

Before Marlene could ask what he meant, Peter called out to the fairies, "Detain her."

The storm dissolved all at once, and Never Land was filled with an ethereal glow. But as the ship moved closer to the enemy island, with James and Sam dangling from the net that held them, already James could see that it was different from Peter's island. The flowers were bolder, larger, all of them with sharp thorns. The shore was a mass of rocks, rather than a soft bed of pale sand.

James was quiet and stoic. His heart had stopped pounding, and he'd settled into a haunting sort of calm. He didn't want to die—not now, and especially not here—but his one solace was that Peter had taken Marlene to safety. She wouldn't pay for his stupidity.

It just figured, James was thinking, that the one time in his life he decided to be brave would end like this.

Still, all hope wasn't lost. He had underestimated the violence of the enemy boys—that was true—but he and Sam weren't dead yet.

"Listen to me," James whispered to Sam, who had been reduced to quiet sniffles. "You and I are both more rational than the other Lost Boys. I could tell that about you right away."

Sam looked at him with big, watery eyes. "W-we are?"

"Yes," James said. "And if there's one thing I know, it's that diplomacy works." He tried to make his voice sound reassuring. "Follow my lead."

The ship was brought to shore, and it rumbled as the anchor lowered. James's stomach dropped with it. He had heard that one's life flashed before one's eyes right before near-certain death, but in that moment he was thinking only about this new island that lay before him, slowly illuminating itself as the sunlight spread out from the clouds. It was lush with deep purples and bloody reds, and houses high up in the trees were connected by vines that appeared to serve as zip lines.

As the ship came to shore, a lookout called to them. James caught a glimpse of his freckled face peering down from a tree house directly above. "You bagged some Lost Boys?"

"Looks like it," another boy said, hopping down from the ship. "Caught them trying to invade us. The fairies kicked up a storm something awful to stop us, but we got 'em."

James stuck out his chest. So long as he pretended not to be terrified, he would be able to speak clearly. It was a trick he'd picked up in the schoolyard. He directed his words to the boy coming down from the ship. This boy was clearly the oldest and the most commanding, with a broad stride and a captain's hat that had been fashioned out of leather stitched with twine. He was obviously in charge, and if James was to survive, he would have to appeal to this boy's graces.

"We aren't invaders," James said. "And I'm not a Lost Boy."

"What are you doing?" Sam moaned, curling into a ball.

"Shush," James whispered sternly. He grasped at the net and projected his voice again. "I was coming to your island to get answers and to find another way out of Never Land."

One that didn't involve nearly drowning himself, preferably. And one that offered some degree of logic. England existed, and Never Land existed, and therefore it stood to reason that one could take a train or a boat from one and arrive at the other.

One of the boys nocked an arrow and aimed it at James and Sam, turning to the boy in the captain's hat. "You want me to kill 'em, Cassius?"

The captain tapped his lower lip. "There is no way out of Never Land," he said.

"But there is," James said eagerly. "I've done it."

There was a chorus of laughter from the boys as they hopped down from the boat and joined their captain. There were seven in total, including the lookout in the tree. The captain—Cassius—wasn't the tallest, but he gave off an aura that was not unlike Peter's. At his hip hung a straight ivory sword that glinted in the sunlight.

Ivory, James thought. For there to be ivory in Never Land, there had to be some large, tusked creature, and he was sure he'd seen nothing of the sort on Peter's island.

"You've left Never Land?" the captain called out to James. "I see what's happening—you drank too much seawater, and now you've lost it."

James looked at the boy still aiming an arrow at them and gulped. "I'm not sick," he insisted, and worked to force down his panic. All his life, he'd resented that Marlene always stepped in to save him, and now for once Marlene wasn't here. Wasn't this what he had wanted—a chance to prove himself without being coddled by her?

Cassius tilted his head. "I remember you," he said, pointing at Sam. "You're the one who couldn't fly no matter how much pixie dust the fairies threw at you. But you"—he nodded to James—"I've never seen you."

"Wh-what he says is true," Sam piped up at last. He was trembling. "He really did leave. I saw it. He jumped off the cliffs and disappeared, and then he came back."

James looked at him, surprised. He had been so certain that nobody had followed him and Marlene that day. He'd listened for footsteps and even watched for Peter's shadow on the ground in case he was flying overhead. And yet someone had been watching them the whole time, and they'd been none the wiser. It appeared Sam—this clumsy, nervous little thing—was cleverer than James had anticipated.

"Don't lower your weapon, Bluejay," Cassius said to the boy with the arrow. "Shoot them if they try to run." He waved one of the other boys over and said, "Lower the rope."

As the pulley began to churn and the net drew closer to the sand, James felt that old familiar panic surging within him. He cursed the coin toss that had returned them to Never Land, and more than that, he cursed himself for letting something so stupid determine his fate. He should have stood up to

Marlene, told her to go on without him if she was so adamant about returning to this wretched place.

And now, soggy with seawater and under the watchful eye of a boy with a weapon, he wasn't certain that he'd survive the day, much less make it home.

As they were lowered to the rocks, James forced himself to stand upright. He grabbed Sam under the arm so that he wouldn't drop under the weight of the net.

There were no fairies here, that much was clear. James heard the buzzing of cicadas and saw the colorful bursts of butterflies, but this island lacked the magical, otherworldly pull he'd felt on the other side of Never Land.

He would have to prove useful to them, or else they would kill him. He understood that much.

At Cassius's command, three boys removed the net and quickly secured James's and Sam's hands behind their backs with a length of twine. Water lapped up onto the rocks and James felt a brand-new surge of panic. Poor swimmer or not, he would have no chance of surviving if he went underwater while in these restraints.

Another boy jabbed Sam in the back with a stick, and Sam yelped.

"March," Cassius instructed. "Both of you."

As Sam walked beside him on wobbly legs, James began to understand why his sister always rushed to protect him from schoolyard bullies. James had never met anyone more skittish than himself, and he felt a sense of responsibility for this boy despite their short acquaintance. He wanted to protect Sam, even now as he was unsure whether the pair of them could be saved.

As they marched down a dirt trail and into the lush wilderness of this enemy island, James looked more closely at the ragtag group of boys who surrounded them. They could very well have been among Peter's Lost Boys, save for the fact that they were all carrying weapons. Bluejay kept an arrow trained at them, while the others wore swords and daggers made of ivory or steel at their hips. The rhythm of their tandem marching reverberated in his bones.

Peter was the only one among his Lost Boys to have a sword, James remembered. A straight, slender golden blade at his hip. But he didn't need it—his Lost Boys did whatever he said. In fact, the whole island seemed to bow to Peter's commands; even the magical fairies did his bidding. So who—or what—was in charge on this island?

Okay, he thought. *These boys are only as strong as I am— otherwise they wouldn't need weapons . . . and, like Sam said, they can't fly, either, or they wouldn't have lookout posts.* James didn't have a sword, and he wasn't particularly strong, but he was armed with wits and logic, something that was sure to be in short supply among these boys if they were anything like Peter's.

"Are you going to kill us?" Sam blurted out. James could

have kicked him. They would have to approach the situation carefully and appeal to the boys' sense of reason, and here was Sam feeding them awful ideas.

"That all depends on you," Cassius replied, seeming not at all surprised by the question.

James heard the rush of water before he saw it. One final turn down the path and they emerged into a small area surrounded by waterfalls. The little bit of bravado James had mustered dropped to his feet. There were four waterfalls running over rocky cliffs, all of them pouring into a lake several yards below. The pool at the center was blue and black at its depths.

"All right, untie them," Cassius told one of the boys. He moved to stand before James and Sam, a smug grin at his lips. "This is the deepest pool in Never Land," he said. "None of us have ever been able to swim to the bottom of it. If what you say is true, you'll be able to swim right through from here to your precious home."

James stared down the funnel of waterfalls and felt himself go dizzy. His stomach churned.

There were piles of bones in the caverns carved into the rocks on the way down, and it took James a moment to realize that they were human. His stomach lurched.

"They all thought they could escape, too, one way or another," Cassius said. "And now? I don't even remember their names. Do you, boys?"

The enemy boys responded with a chorus of "nope" and "nuh-uh."

"What are you waiting for?" Cassius said. Bluejay nudged James in the back with the arrow. "Jump. Go on home."

In his periphery, James could feel Sam staring at him expectantly, his eyes round with fear.

Home.

His sensible, comfortable bed. The chime of the village clock tower. His father's muddy and calloused hands hooking bait onto the line. His mother's blossoming perfumes.

He wanted badly to go back to England—that was true. He wanted to grow up and move to London and invent new marvels. This future was the life that flashed before him, rather than the life he'd lived up until that moment.

Jump. All he had to do was jump and he could have it back.

But his legs wouldn't move. Why wouldn't they move?

"Yeah," Cassius said from behind him, voice dripping with satisfaction. "That's what I thought."

10

It was the first time Marlene had seen Never Land at night. The darkness was twisted with shades of burgundy, pink, and vivid blue, the sky erratic in its brightness. The stars were beaming and winking playfully at one another.

She saw all this through the bars of a wooden cage that hung suspended from a giant oak.

From here, she could just barely see the enemy island on the horizon, and her heart was sick to think what must be happening to James. Was he even still alive? She had to believe that he was. Whenever James was nearby, she sensed it. Before she'd hear the door creak open, or before the staircase groaned under his steps, she just knew that he was somewhere close.

If he were dead, she supposed that she would feel it. She would know.

Never Land was silent now, save for the lingering chirps of night bugs and the occasional flutter of a bird moving through the trees. The Lost Boys were sleeping, but Marlene was wide awake. Her body thrummed with the outrage of it all.

Peter had ordered her to be locked away like a pet parakeet, though to what end she still couldn't be certain, as he hadn't so much as looked at her once the boys had dragged her away from the cliffside. Away from her brother. Away from the water that could take her home.

They'd left her a bunch of grapes and half a papaya for her troubles. Grudgingly, she'd eaten all of it, gnawing hunger overwhelming her stubbornness. If she was going to find a way out of here, she would need all the strength she could get.

Nibs and Cubby had been keeping vigil below her cage for most of the evening. They each carried a giant twig to serve as a makeshift weapon. Nibs brandished a skeleton key on a large ring. It was old and rusted, much like the lock on Marlene's cage.

Now Marlene could see from her perch that Cubby kept nodding off and Nibs kept pinching him on the cheek. They whispered to each other, and Marlene could rarely hear what they were saying. But they kept staring up at her, which made plotting an escape difficult.

"You ask her," Cubby whispered.

"No, you," Nibs said back.

Marlene gripped the bars of her wooden prison and peered down at them. "Ask me what?"

The boys huddled together skittishly. It was as though they'd never met an outsider before, and Marlene wondered about that. Had Peter been the first Lost Boy in Never Land? He certainly seemed to be the one who knew the most about this place. Had the others all joined him at the same time? Marlene had tried to ask them earlier about where they had come from and where their parents were, but no matter how hard she pressed, the boys had insisted that they didn't have parents and that they had always been in Never Land. Marlene suspected neither of those things was entirely true, but she had eventually given up.

"Come on, then," she told them. "I won't bite."

Nibs canted his head all the way up to face her. "Do you really have parents?"

"Parents?" Marlene balked. "Yes. A mother and a father."

"You're lying," Cubby said.

"Peter has told us about mothers and fathers," Nibs said. "They are the ones who read you stories at bedtime and never, ever get angry."

It took everything within Marlene not to laugh at this. Her mother fluttered to and fro in their small house like a bird that had gotten trapped inside and was desperate to find its way out. She was beautiful with a dulcet tone of voice, and she spent all of her time nannying the children of a wealthy family in the city. When she regarded Marlene at all, it was with a weary sigh. *Why can't you dress like a lady?* she would say. *Don't you want people to find you beautiful?* She certainly became angry, and often. Her father didn't, but he also never read them stories. In some ways, he was as practical as James.

"Peter doesn't know everything," she told them.

"He does so," Nibs fired back. "He flies outside of Never Land all the time. He can go anywhere he wants. He's seen the whole world, and he tells us stories you couldn't even imagine."

Marlene hid her surprise. Peter left Never Land?

She thought about the strange pull she'd been feeling in the weeks leading up to her birthday. The dreams about flying, and of beautiful orbs of rainbowed light. She hadn't told James about any of it—he wouldn't understand. When they were small, he used to roll his eyes whenever she told him about the fantastic adventures in the books she was reading.

She felt that same magic around Peter, even now that she was furious with him. Peter wasn't just a boy who inhabited Never Land. He *was* Never Land, and he had called her here.

Her worry for James flared anew. She had to find him, and they had to leave this place before they became like all the other Lost Boys and forgot that time was passing at all.

"How long do I have to stay in this cage?" Marlene asked.

"Until Peter says," Nibs told her. "Probably a hundred years. He's mad. I've never seen him like this before."

The bushes rustled, and Marlene saw the furry outline of Tootles's skunk cap.

"Oh, good," Cubby said. "Guard switch. Now we can go to bed." He thrust the stick into Tootles's hands. "Just poke her if she gives you any lip."

"Yeah." Nibs tossed the skeleton key at Tootles. "Try not to let her kill you."

The pair of boys shoved Tootles as they left, and Tootles scowled after them.

Once she was sure they were alone, Marlene said, "They aren't very nice to you, are they?"

"No," Tootles said with a resigned, long-suffering sigh. "It's because they're so much bigger. They never let me play with them unless we're playing capture the thief and I'm the thief. They tie me up for hours."

"That's awful," Marlene said. But she felt hope now that Tootles was her guard. He was sweet, but more important, he was naive, and he liked her.

Tootles kicked at a pebble and then sat on the fallen log previously occupied by Cubby and Nibs.

Marlene considered her next move carefully. Without James's pocket watch, it was impossible to know how much time had passed. Tootles was the only Lost Boy who hadn't kept guard before now, which meant that there was nobody left but Peter.

Marlene didn't want to be here when Peter came back.

Though Peter hadn't confided in her, his rage at being forced to leave Sam behind due to James's carelessness was tangible. She felt it even now, like the lingering sting after a slap.

If she saw a boy like Tootles back home in England, she would kneel down and ask him if he'd lost his mother. He seemed too young to be out by himself. But this wasn't England. Everyone was lost here, and everyone bowed to the whims and fancies of this unusual island.

Still, a boy as young as Tootles must have felt a longing to be protected. To have someone read him bedtime stories and make him feel safe. He must have wanted a mother or father like the ones Peter had told all the Lost Boys about.

Marlene thought about her own parents and tried to remember what it had been like to be so small. A memory came to her. She held one of her mother's hands and James held the other. Marlene was wearing a bright red wool coat with a fur collar, and it had worried her to own something so beautiful and easy to destroy. But they were going to London so that her mother could apply for a nannying job, and she'd wanted Marlene and James to look their absolute best. She wanted the wealthy London family to see how caring and attentive she was with children.

It was their first time on a train. It was cold and crowded. The floor rumbled loudly as they moved, and James started to cry.

A woman standing across from them smiled at James. She

began to sing—a lovely, high sound that rang out even among the noise and chatter of the train car. Old and faded as the memory was, Marlene still remembered the melody.

Marlene began to hum. As the tune grew louder, she could swear that the Never Land stars themselves were listening. They throbbed in their sky and seemed to shift, as though drawing closer.

By the time the song was over, Marlene noticed that Tootles's eyes had grown sleepy, his face relaxed and dreamy. "Where did you learn that?" he asked.

"From my mother," Marlene lied. "She's always singing, and telling bedtime stories, and baking—"

"Bedtime stories?" Tootles piped up. "Really?"

Marlene nodded.

Tootles's face fell. "I wish I had a mother or father."

Marlene hesitated. She'd always hated being deceitful— it made her stomach hurt. *This isn't home,* she had to remind herself. *This is Never Land.* If she wanted to get out of here and save her brother, she would have to play by Never Land's odd and ever-changing whims.

"Have you ever seen what a mother and father look like?"

Tootles shook his head.

Marlene reached for the locket that hung at her neck. It was cheap and tarnished, but even so she liked it. It was, in fact, the only gift from her mother that she liked wearing.

"I've got a photo of my parents," she said. "I can show you."

Tootles hesitated. "I'm supposed to stay down here," he said. "Slightly says we can't trust you. He says if you're anything like your brother, you'll kill us all in our sleep."

"That's nonsense," Marlene scoffed. "I'm nothing like James." That, at least, was true.

Tootles looked around to be sure that they were alone, and hope fluttered in Marlene's stomach. He heaved a deep breath, crouched low, and leapt into flight. He brought himself up, up, until he was hovering before her. "Okay," he said. "Let me see."

Before he approached, he hung the key on the branch of an adjacent tree, where Marlene couldn't reach it. He wasn't as naive as she would have suspected.

He was still cautious, and Marlene could see that the other Lost Boys underestimated him. He was younger, smaller, but that only meant he had to be that much more clever.

She tugged the chain of her necklace as far as it would reach so that he could see her locket. He hesitated but flew closer, bracing his feet on the rim of the cage and grasping the bars.

Marlene snapped the latch with her thumbnail, and the locket opened into a pair of twin hearts with a photo on either side. To the left was her father, looking nothing like the hardened, coarse fisherman she knew now. As a young newlywed, when the portrait was taken, he'd been regal and soft-featured, with sparkling eyes. And to the right was her mother, also young, but with a sterner expression. Her dark hair had been pressed straight and smooth and pulled back into an elaborate bun. Even then, her mother had dressed for the lavish life she'd wanted but ultimately never found.

Marlene rarely looked at these photos, but when she did, she was startled by how much her own parents looked like strangers. It frightened her to think that they were once so young and filled with promise, and that they'd ended up living such an ordinary and dissatisfying life. She worried, also, that she resembled her mother so closely. When she looked at her mother now, Marlene could see her own face reflected back in her mother's aging and tired visage, eyes filled with regret.

She did not want to go back home and become that disappointed woman, old far before her time. But after dragging James into this mess, the least she could do was rescue him so that they could decide what to do next, together.

"Wow," Tootles rasped. "The mother is so beautiful. I wish I could meet her."

Marlene's smile was genuine. "Perhaps I can introduce you."

Tootles's expression fell. "Oh," he said. "But there aren't any grown-ups in Never Land."

"Well, there will be someday," Marlene said. "When you all grow up."

Tootles laughed at that, and his giggle echoed beneath the calm night sky. "We don't grow up, silly."

Marlene was startled, although this made about as much sense as anything else in Never Land. After all, the first day they had ever spent in Never Land had taken up only an hour back home.

She had estimated Peter to be almost her own age by the sight of him, but when she thought about it—really, truly thought about it—he was far more cunning than any of the children she knew back home. He could be a hundred years old. A thousand. He could have been here since the dawn of time itself.

"Tootles," she said, "you've been around twins like James and me. So you must know how special it is."

"Of course," Tootles said, puffing his chest haughtily. But then his expression went uncertain. "Why?"

"Well, we were born at the same time," Marlene said. "It means we know things about each other that nobody else does. Like we can read each other's minds."

This was half-true, at least. She *could* read her brother's mind, but only because he was so predictable. But there were days when James scarcely knew her at all; she talked about her books or her ideas, or how much she loved the sea, and he regarded her as though she had sprouted a third ear.

"Really?" Tootles beamed with curiosity. "Can you tell what James is thinking right now?"

"Not exactly," Marlene said. "But I know that he's still alive. I can feel it." She pressed her fist to her chest. "Because we're twins."

It was true that she sensed James was still alive—or perhaps it was only wishful thinking. James had always been there. They'd slept shoulder to shoulder in a crib meant to hold a single baby, and they shared a tiny room meant to hold a single child. As the unexpected twins in a poor family, they'd adapted to taking up space meant for one. No matter where one of them went, the other was always nearby.

One could call it a twin connection if one liked, but however it had happened, Marlene and James could sense the other's presence, like the aroma of autumn arriving on a late summer breeze.

In this way, Marlene knew that her brother wasn't dead, and that he was frightened.

"What about Sam?" Tootles asked, a cautious measure of hope in his voice. "If James is alive, do you suppose Sam will be, too?"

"Probably," Marlene said. "But not for long if we don't rescue them."

She saw the desperation on Tootles's face, and she hated herself for taking advantage of the boy's kindness. But she had hopes of her own, too. She couldn't live by Peter's rules. Not if it meant leaving her brother to die.

"Tootles, listen to me." She reached through the bars and cupped her hand over his. "We can save them. Just the two of us. I know it sounds scary, but you're much braver than Peter gives you credit for."

Tootles gnawed on his lip. "I am brave," he said. "I'm not even scared of the dark. They make me go out and investigate strange noises at night."

"There. See?" Marlene squeezed his hand. "I knew that about you right away."

"But I can't betray Peter," he said, shaking his head. "It's his island. He might kick me off."

"No, no, he won't do that," Marlene insisted. "Once he sees that we've brought Sam and James back, you'll be a hero. He'll finally see how great you really are."

Tootles broke free of her grasp. He flew backward, light as a bird. "I can't," he said. "Peter said we can't trust you. He said you might betray us, too."

Maybe you shouldn't trust Peter. Did you ever think of that? Marlene thought with a vibrant flare of anger. Peter and these Lost Boys didn't care one bit about time. They had so much of it. An endless supply of sunsets and stars. But as long as James was a prisoner, his hours were numbered.

"Aren't you worried about what they'll do to Sam if we don't rescue him?" Marlene asked.

Tootles curled up on the branch of an adjacent tree. He covered his ears, but Marlene went on. "There isn't a lot of time, Tootles. They could kill him. Do you want that on your conscience?"

"It won't be for long," Tootles whimpered.

"What do you mean by that?" Marlene asked.

"We'll forget about him. That's why Peter let them go." His lip was quivering now. A thick tear rolled down his cheek. "That's what happens in Never Land. Things go away, and you forget them. Good and bad."

Marlene grasped at the bars. Her knuckles were white from the strain. "What else have you forgotten?"

"Lots of things." Tootles wiped his wrist across his eyes. "I don't know."

A shock of understanding jolted through Marlene like lightning. None of the boys could recall their lives before Never Land—but they'd forgotten things from their time here, as well.

None of them *remembered*.

Furiously, Marlene thought of home. Of the crack in her bedroom window where the cold whistled through on snowy nights. Of her father's steady hands teaching her how to cast a line. Of the brick school to which she and James walked every morning. She could see it all clearly—now. But how could she be certain that there wasn't more? How would she ever know if something precious slipped out of her memories while she was frittering the hours away in this absurd place—something like James?

"Tootles!" Worry clouded her judgment all at once. She shook the bars, and her cage swung from the motion. "You have to let me out! You just have to!"

"I can't," Tootles said, and he looked down guiltily. "I'll be in trouble."

"You said the other boys pick on you," Marlene said, switching tactics. She made her voice gentle. "Because you're so much smaller."

"Not hardly!" Tootles snapped, but then his shoulders fell. "Well. Maybe sometimes."

Marlene reached through the bars, straining until her fingers were just able to wipe at the tears streaming down Tootles's face. "If you let me out, we can form our own alliance," she said. "I'll make sure no one picks on you ever again."

"You'll be my mother?" Tootles perked up.

"Your friend," Marlene said, her voice tight. "But only if you let me out."

11

After James's failure to jump into the waterfall, the boys led him to their campsite. They were Peter's enemies, which already endeared them to James, in a way— even if he couldn't trust what they would do to him. Arrows were pointed at James and Sam from all sides as they sat beside a roaring fire. The sun was disappearing now, and the trees were thick and noisy with night creatures.

James hated himself for how frightened he was. How worried he was for Marlene, and how angry he was that she had dragged them back to Never Land.

Even as he thought it, he knew he wasn't being entirely fair. They *had* agreed. And Marlene humored him far more than he had ever done for her, which was why he'd come along despite his sense that something wasn't right about this place.

How long had he been here? Minutes? Hours? For one absurd moment, James could have sworn he'd been in this new camp forever. Peter and his Lost Boys seemed as though they'd happened a lifetime ago. If Sam hadn't still been there quaking beside him, James could have convinced himself he'd simply dreamed it all up. Part of him was tempted to check his pocket watch, but he knew better than to make any sudden movements with so many arrows on him.

Cassius paced back and forth. His sword gleamed with authority. "You're liars, both of you," he said.

"Me?" Sam squeaked. "I haven't said anything."

Bluejay drew back his arrow, and Sam closed his gaping mouth.

"Since I've never seen you before," Cassius went on, drawing his sword and pointing it at James, "you must be a spy for Peter."

James had never been particularly adept at courage, but he thought he was holding up quite well, given the circumstances. He rose to his feet.

Behind him, Sam gasped. "James," he whispered.

"I'm not a spy," James said, and canted his chin upward so he could meet the taller Cassius's gaze. "I hate Peter. He has my sister."

"Sister?" Cassius laughed, and then his eyes widened

slightly in recognition. "You mean that girl with the black hair chasing after our boat is your sister?"

"Peter is holding her hostage," James said, impressed with himself for crafting such a quick and easy lie. If they perceived Marlene as an enemy, her life would be in danger just as his life was now. Perhaps there was just enough truth to it, anyway. Peter did have an odd effect on Marlene that James detested. The way he stared at her a beat too long. The way he crooned and spoke softly when he was addressing her. The way he leaned in and breathed the same air as her.

"Liar," Bluejay said from beyond the shaft of his arrow. "I bet you're Peter's best friend. I bet you'd follow him right over the edge of Never Land if he told you to."

"I'll do anything to prove it." James shook his head, feeling braver with every word. "I'm not here to spy on you. All I want is to get my sister out of his grip and go home."

Cassius considered this. He gestured to one of the enemy boys and said, "Get this boy a sword. We'll see what sort of fighter he is." He turned to James again. "We'll duel, and if I win, you'll stay here as our servant."

"Yeah, and you'll clean up after the elephants," Bluejay said with a cackle.

"If *you* win," Cassius went on, "you can be my bodyguard. We'll go and get your sister, and *she* can be our servant."

James gritted his teeth. Servant. Bodyguard. Marlene washing clothes and cooking meals over a fire. The thought would have made him laugh if it all hadn't been quite so dire.

Either way, it seemed he and Marlene would be trapped here forever. That wouldn't do.

An enemy boy stepped forward and, at Cassius's directive, placed the hilt of a sword in James's hand. It was smaller, cruder, than the one Cassius wielded. James had never seen a sword up close before, much less held one. But as his fingers tightened around the hilt, he replayed every moment of his life when he'd wanted to be more and had somehow failed.

Crying because he'd scraped his knee on the schoolyard.

Inconsolable as he mourned the death of a goldfish he'd kept in a bowl in his room.

Wheezing for air as he raced after his sister.

Shrinking away from the water when his father tried to take him fishing for the first time.

As the memories flooded through him, James knew that he wasn't in this duel simply to defeat Cassius. He was in the fight of his life against the old James—the weak, cowardly boy he'd been back in England. If he had any hope of surviving Never Land, he would have to pierce the old James clean through the heart.

Cassius smirked. The enemy boys began to chant his name. A whisper at first, and then a crescendo.

Cas-si-us, Cas-si-us.

James's heart thrummed in his ears. He raised the blade

with a trembling arm. One of the boys snorted in laughter at his unpracticed form.

Cassius charged forward with a primal shout, his blade aimed at James's throat. Stumbling, James just managed to dodge it.

The ocean. The pocket watch ticking against his chest. Marlene. Home.

He couldn't die here, or worse, become indentured to these feral boys of Never Land.

Desperation made him brave. Grabbing Sam—who was standing nearby watching the scene with wide eyes—by the wrist, he ran past Cassius. Together they shoved through the circle of chanting boys and bolted into the thick of the forest.

"Come on, Sam," he snarled through gritted teeth. The boy could barely keep up, frightened and confused as he was.

"Get them!" Bluejay cried.

James darted to the left, tugging Sam along. They ran until they came upon an embankment with a shallow river sparkling at its seam.

"Here," James whispered.

"I can't believe you did that," Sam rasped.

"Shh!"

It was dark now, and the dense trees blotted out much of the stars. He could hear the enemy boys tromping through the undergrowth of the forest, marching off in search of them. James held his breath and started to make a plan.

This island was much smaller than Peter's. James knew as much because he'd gotten a good look at it as they were being captured. *Okay,* he thought. *Okay.* As long as he was on land, he could find his way anywhere. The water was the only place where he felt truly lost—all of that blue nothingness stretching on forever. But land was just a series of paths, valleys, and streams. He and Sam would wait here until he was sure the enemy boys were off his trail, and they would then follow the stream back to the sea. He would take Sam back to England by jumping into the waters as he'd done with Marlene. Then he would come back, emerge on Peter's island, and retrieve his sister.

The notion sounded far-fetched even as he thought of it. But most things about Never Land were far-fetched, and the alternative was to take his chances with these enemy boys.

Something rustled in the trees, and his blood went cold. They had found them already? He clutched the hilt of the sword still in his hand.

"James. *James.*"

He whipped around at the sound of that familiar voice, and as he did, a figure descended gracefully, soundlessly, from the sky. Marlene.

She had been flying. He could sense the magic on her. Bits of glowing fairy dust fell from her messy curls.

James staggered to his feet, scarcely believing what he

saw, for it was too good to be true. In the next beat he was running to her.

"I knew you were still alive," she said, and threw her arms around him.

When they embraced, James's mind flashed with a burst of memories that had gone dull but were suddenly bright and sharp. Opening presents by the fire. Reading by lantern light long after they should have been asleep. Crawling in the sand looking for shells. Seaweed crowns.

The longer he stayed in Never Land, the more his memories of home faded. But Marlene's nearness made him remember. Was that why the Lost Boys had all forgotten? Because they didn't have anyone from their own homes to remind them?

Never Land—and the world that surrounded it—had a way of making home seem far away and dim, but Marlene brought it back.

"How did you get here?" he asked.

"I flew, clearly," she said with an air of practicality, as though she were answering an arithmetic question.

"We have to hurry," Sam said with urgency. "They're after us."

Marlene drew back so that she could have a better look at the pair of them. She saw the sword in James's hand, cloth-ing gone ragged from snagging on the brambles of the forest, mud covering his shoes and legs from where he'd crouched along the stream.

Before she could open her mouth to comment, the sound of a twig snapping drew all of their attention. A shadow of a boy emerged from the trees behind her. Moonlight glinted in his bright green eyes, making them glow ethereal and menacing.

Bluejay.

In one broad stride, he was upon them, his arm hooked around Marlene's shoulders and the sharp point of his arrow aimed at her neck.

She scowled. "Let go, you silly child."

Marlene was fearless to a fault, but as much as he'd found himself longing for her presence since he and Sam had been captured, in that moment, James hated this part of her, wished it away altogether. She didn't know these boys. Didn't realize that they weren't benign and soft like the ones on Peter's island. She couldn't fathom what they might do to her. To all three of them. But James had seen the skeletons tossed in their shallow graves, and he understood that being captive here was not an option.

Bluejay opened his mouth and shouted, "Over here!"

Time seemed to slow to a stop. Never Land, awful and pretty and strange. London's high-reaching towers and bell chimes. A future filled with papers and briefcases and train whistles. Heaps of bones lost forever behind the thin curtain of a waterfall.

Marlene pulling him from the water. Marlene picking him up by the arm when he fell. Fending off schoolyard bullies. Mending his buttons. Flying across the sea to rescue him from this awful place.

All those times she had saved him, and for once it was his turn to save her.

He raised his sword, ran forward, and stabbed Bluejay through the ribs. Bluejay's hold on Marlene broke as he gasped and stumbled backward, clutching the spot where the blade had gone through. James saw the red spread out from beneath Bluejay's hands, and he thought he might get sick.

But then Marlene grabbed him and Sam under the arms, and before James knew what was happening, they were flying away.

More accurately, Marlene was flying while James and Sam dangled helplessly in her grasp.

James made the sour mistake of looking down. Bluejay was on his back, convulsing. Blood, dark as ink in the moonlight, spilled from his side and his mouth.

"Damn it, James," Marlene rasped. "I could have handled him. Why did you do that?"

James was too stunned to reply. But if he could have found the words to speak, he would have told Marlene that she was wrong this time and that he had done it to save them both.

But he couldn't speak. He could only stare behind him in horror at what he had done.

From farther and farther away, James saw Cassius scream as he broke through the foliage and witnessed Bluejay dying in the shallows of the stream. Cassius grabbed Bluejay's face and looked for whatever life was still left in the boy's eyes.

Cassius looked up just in time to see the faraway figures of Marlene and James and Sam, lit by the fragile glow of fairy dust, before they flew out to sea.

Halfway between the two islands, James began to hyperventilate in Marlene's arms, seeing Bluejay's surprised face as he stumbled backward over and over again. Never Land spun, sea and sky blurring in his vision. His hands shook.

"Not now," Marlene pleaded. "You can't panic on me." But he couldn't help it.

As soon as they'd landed back on Peter's island and all three of them were on their feet, Marlene grasped her brother by the shoulders. "Stop it." Her grip was a vise. "Listen to me. No one can know what you've done. It didn't happen. Do you understand me?"

Her tone was so sobering that even the blubbering Sam was quiet. James swallowed the lump of fear in his throat.

"I just risked my neck to get you out of there." Marlene started pacing back and forth. "If Peter finds out what you've done, I don't know what he'll do. Peter said he will tolerate *no one* dying in Never Land, not even his enemies."

"Why are you so concerned about Peter?" James demanded, snapping back to reality. "Peter this, Peter that. We have much bigger problems, Marlene!"

"We do now, thanks to you!" she cried.

"Maybe he's still alive," Sam piped up, trying to stop their mounting argument. "You only got him in the ribs. I saw it."

Marlene closed her eyes and pressed her palm to her temple. James had never seen her so worked up, so furious. It was as though something—or someone—was influencing her reaction. It took her a moment to compose herself, and James began to wonder if they were being watched. If not by the Lost Boys, then by the fairies. Those elusive little spies who were so loyal to Peter. What did Marlene think Peter would do to them?

"Okay." Marlene drew in a deep breath. "James hasn't hurt anyone," she said calmly. "Nothing bad happened. I flew over to the other side and I pulled the two of you back with me. Nobody saw us. Nobody died." She uttered that last word with a snarl so faint that only James knew her well enough to recognize it.

Sam was staring at her. At this strange creature, this girl who possessed as much authority and ferocity as Peter. Maybe even more.

There was something about Sam's expression that James didn't like, although he couldn't pinpoint what it was exactly.

"Sam!" Tootles cried, popping up from the copse of trees that bordered the cliffside where they'd landed. James startled. He hated this place. There was always someone materializing through the trees like a bloody apparition.

"You did it, Marlene! You really brought them back like you promised!" Tootles raced to Sam, nearly bowling him over with the force of his embrace.

Sam's pallid face regained a bit of color, and his expression lost some of its edge.

At the commotion, the floating spheres of fairy light began orbiting toward them. Footsteps and voices moved between the trees as the Lost Boys awoke.

Maybe it really would be like Cassius had said, James thought, with an irrational spate of hope. Maybe in Never Land, it wasn't that no one died, but rather that the dead were easily forgotten, and by morning it would be as though nothing had ever happened.

The Lost Boys flocked to Sam, patting him on the shoulder and begging for stories of all the horrors he must have encountered on the enemy island. Sam's chest puffed with uncharacteristic pride.

But when Peter finally emerged, gliding downward from the sky, everyone went quiet.

Peter landed first on his left foot, and then the right. He

walked as though on a tightrope, approaching Sam without making a sound.

The color left Sam's cheeks again. Slightly, who was standing beside him, said, "Come on, Peter. Don't be too hard on him."

Slightly, James observed, was one of the more trusted boys. He could read Peter's expression easily, stony and blank as it was just then.

If James had still been on the fence about whether or not to like Peter, Peter's coldness in that moment, with one of his own returned to him, would have cemented it. Peter stared at Sam for a moment, unblinking.

Then his gaze went to Marlene.

But Marlene was not one of Peter's boys. She stood tall, her chin canted, her eyes every bit as defiant and angry as his. It was as though she could read Peter's mind when she said, "I was able to get them back after all."

"You had no right," Peter finally spat out. "You've only just gotten here. You don't know anything about Never Land, and you have no idea what trouble you could have caused for all of us."

"Don't talk to my sister like that," James snapped. "You may be in charge of this island, but we don't belong to you." At that, he saw the surprise on Marlene's face. She expected the cowering brother she'd always known—the one who fell apart in the face of conflict. But this place was changing him in leaps and bounds. He had sailed a makeshift raft into enemy waters in search of answers. He'd possibly killed a boy to save them all from imprisonment. He was something he had never been before, and he realized now that he would have to become even more ruthless if he was going to survive.

Peter stared at him. Back home in England, Peter wouldn't have been much. He wouldn't have been the strongest, nor the fastest. He might have even been a victim of schoolyard bullying.

But here, in his mysterious way, he was a king. Palm fronds bowed before him. Fairies circled his orbit in shimmers of gold and white. If his heart were to stop beating, perhaps this entire place would disappear. Shrivel up to nothing and turn black.

"I'm sorry, Peter," Sam said, a tremor in his voice. "It's all my fault. I should have tried to stop him from going out there. He didn't know any better—"

"Stop that," James interrupted. "You don't have to explain anything to him." He turned to the boy that he'd come to feel so protective of. "You could come back with us, you know, Sam," he said, his tone softening. "You could have a good life back in England. You're smart. You could be a banker one day. Maybe an architect."

"Is that so?" Peter said. He crossed his arms over his chest. "Why don't you go on and try it, then. Leave Never Land. Grow up. Watch your hands turn wrinkly like prunes and let all of your hair fall out. Turn old and die like all of those sorry folks out there."

Sam turned away from James and shook his head furiously. "No, Peter. Don't make me leave Never Land. I don't want to grow old. I'll never go behind your back again. I promise!"

Had Peter really just said that nobody had to grow up in Never Land? James tried to hide his surprise, though he couldn't understand what these boys thought was so bad about growing up. What good was childhood if it never ended? Games and fairy tales were fun for a time, but there was a whole world out there. Buildings to be mended and clocks to wind and inventions to be made.

Marlene moved to stand beside James, and her hand slid easily into his. "Let's just go home," she murmured to him.

James nodded. *Home.* In a land filled with magic and mystery, such a practical word was fragile and precious.

"How far away is home?" Tootles ran to Marlene and coiled himself around her waist. "Will you ever come back?"

Even in Never Land, even among these strange boys, Marlene had found a devoted friend.

"Tootles, come back here." Peter held out an arm. Tootles looked at him, pouting. "Let them leave."

"No!" Tootles gripped harder at Marlene's shirt. She was still wearing her flannel pajamas—white with pale pink stripes. A tiny rose embroidered at the collar. In this world, it made her stick out like a beacon. "I don't want you to grow old! I don't want all of your hair to fall out."

Marlene patted his head. "It won't happen for a very, very long time," she said.

"It doesn't have to happen at all," Tootles whimpered. "You can stay with us forever."

Marlene gave him the same warm, sad smile that their father wore whenever he looked at the sea. "We all have to grow up," she said. "Otherwise, how can we learn what our purpose is?"

Tootles only clung to her, and Peter grew impatient. He stepped forward and grabbed Tootles by the arm. "Let her go," he said. "Let them both go."

Even Sam made his way back over to Peter and the other boys, no matter the repercussions that might befall him for his perceived disloyalty. James knew he couldn't fault Sam, or any of them, for staying put. This place was all they knew.

James tugged Marlene toward the cliffside before she could change her mind, Peter and the Lost Boys hanging back farther behind them. "We'll go on three," he said.

She nodded. "One."

"Two."

"Three!"

James squeezed his eyes shut when they jumped. The water hit him like a slap. The sky and the ground disappeared, and he tumbled helplessly in the ether of it until something pulled him to the surface.

He gasped as he broke through, and for once, he didn't thrash and panic. He managed to keep himself afloat. Rather than fear, he couldn't believe his excitement to be back in England and to have put all of this behind him.

But when he opened his eyes, he didn't smell the salty, fishy air. He didn't see the modest houses clustered together between shops, or the shadowy city beyond the River Thames.

He saw Never Land.

Marlene and James stared up at the cliffside from which they'd jumped. Peter was staring down at them, his arms crossed. His figure was glowing in the moonlight.

"What's the matter?" he called down to them. "I thought you were going home?"

"What have you done?" Marlene shouted back.

Not now. Not now, James thought as his panic began to surge again. He only wanted to go home. Wanted it more than he had ever wanted anything.

In answer, Peter spread his arms and sailed over the ledge. He flew in circles around them, like a shark. "I haven't done a thing," he said. He was looking only at Marlene, and James could have burst from all his hatred. "But I knew you wouldn't leave."

"Whyever not?" Marlene said.

"Because Never Land knows your heart's deepest desires. That's the only way you can ever get here in the first place. Not the ocean. The ocean just happens to be how you fell in, but you would have found some other way." He flicked his finger, sprinkling her nose with pixie dust. "You're here because you don't want to grow up."

Marlene gave Peter a murderous look, and James wondered if Peter was lying to them. But it made sense, in the way that some things could make sense only in a place like Never Land. If Marlene couldn't leave, that meant James wouldn't be able to, either. James wanted to return home, but more than that, deep down, he wanted his sister to come home with him. Just as she hadn't been brave enough to return to Never Land without him, he couldn't leave her here now. They always went together. It was simply how it had to be.

Casting one final glare up at Peter, Marlene turned around and swam for the shore, James keeping up beside her. If nothing else, he'd finally learned how to stay afloat.

"Okay, don't panic," she said as she and James crawled up on the rocks and sand. "There's another way out of here. There has to be. And we'll find it."

"Is it true what he said?" James asked. "Do you want to stay in Never Land?"

"Of course not. Don't be dumb."

But James could no longer be sure what to think. Marlene wouldn't meet his eyes.

12

It took hours, but Marlene finally fell into a thin, miserable sleep. Even then, she felt the presence of the Lost Boys keeping watch over her and James as they lay in the soft moss, still shivering from the aftereffects of the water.

She dreamed of her brother drowning, and of losing him in crowds. It was all her fault every time she lost him. *You chose this,* Peter's voice whispered, over and again.

"No," she tried to reply, but her words were heavy and muffled. She wanted to go home. "No."

Her own voice woke her. When she opened her eyes, she saw James curled in the giant palm frond he was using as a bed. In sleep, his face was troubled and pale.

How much time had passed back home? Marlene couldn't venture a guess. As each hour of Never Land crept past, it disappeared into an endless river of moments, days, memories, all being carried away. She studied her brother's face — so very much like her own — and tried to remember if they looked more like their mother, or their father. She tried to recall what their house smelled like, or whether she could see the full moon from her bedroom window.

These things were starting to grow soft at the outline.

The life Marlene had always known back in England felt pale and dim. In contrast, Peter's magic was bright. She knew, even without being able to see him, that he was nearby.

Marlene turned restlessly, the light from the fairies pinging against her closed eyes. Peter had realized that his own Lost Boys didn't make for the best guards after Tootles set Marlene free, and Peter was angry about it. So he'd wised up and employed the fairies to keep an eye on them.

The fairies, much unlike the boys, spoke only in jingles. They communicated with gestures and actions, and therefore ingratiating herself to them in exchange for freedom seemed rather unlikely. Besides, their loyalty to Peter ran so deep as to seem almost like something tangible. They kept watch over the siblings like a dome of stars. The flutter of their wings was the only indication that they were awake and watching as they hovered in place.

Marlene rolled onto her back and scowled up at them. Fairies. They were nothing like the ones in the stories she'd read. Rather than dainty and ethereal, they were conniving and mischievous. She was certain that one of them had spat on her as she slept. When they hovered before her face, Marlene saw how cross they were with her.

It was quite clear that they didn't enjoy having her on their island. Perhaps they could sense that she could see right through their glowing halos and knew that they were not to be trusted. Not one bit.

Peter strode up from the shadows, silent as a feather hitting the earth. He stood over Marlene, and they stared at each other. His anger was gone now, and he almost reminded her of James hours after they'd had an argument. Of the way James would stand in the doorway of their bedroom at a distance and ask, *Can we both be reasonable now?*

"Do you ever sleep?" she asked Peter.

"Not very much," he replied. "Look what happens when I do."

Marlene propped herself up on her elbows. "You understand that James and Sam would have died needlessly if I hadn't gotten them. You should be thanking me."

He held out a hand to pull her up. "Come on. I want to show you something."

Marlene looked back at James. He was still asleep, his lips and brow twitching as he dreamed.

"I won't have him hurt," Peter said, seeming to read her mind. "You have my word."

A fat lot that means, she thought. But she got up anyway. However she felt about Peter, he held the keys to his kingdom. She would get much further if he liked her. God knew James wouldn't be able to earn them any favor with this boy. When her brother despised someone, it was obvious. But Marlene had learned how to hold her tongue. At any given time, she knew exactly what she was thinking, and she felt the full weight of her anger or her joy or her anguish. She had learned that the power in knowing her own mind was not in how accurately she acknowledged the emotions she felt, but in how well she could keep them a secret until it came time to use them to her advantage.

As though on command, a fairy sprinkled her anew with dust. Tink. Tink might share her fellow fairies' dislike of Marlene, but she would do Peter's bidding, no questions asked.

Peter dove upward in flight, and Marlene followed him.

He led her over the forest and back toward that giant tree where they'd felt each other's heart beating. He landed gracefully on a branch, and Marlene stood beside him, cautious. She didn't know why he had brought her here, and she didn't trust this supplication of his to be authentic.

How could anything be real in a place like Never Land?

"Contrary to what you believe, I'm not angry with you for saving them," Peter said. "I would rather have them alive. *Both* of them," he added at her skeptical look. "You have to understand something, Marlene. Where you're from, people are what they seem," Peter went on. "But those boys, the ones across the sea—they're enemies. The whole lot of them. They've made their decision. And as long as we stay on our side, they stay on theirs."

"You have all the fairies on your side," Marlene said. "I didn't see any when I went over there. Can't the fairies protect us?"

He smiled grimly at her. "Thanks to your brother and Sam, dozens of them died because they flew over enemy waters."

Marlene remembered then, saw them sinking, heavy with the weight of enemy arrows. Their tiny bodies disappeared and went dim in the murk of the sea. But she'd been preoccupied by James and that silly, blubbering boy Sam. It had only seemed practical to focus on the living.

But each fairy meant something to Peter. He loved them as much as she loved her brother.

"I'm sorry," she said, and found that she meant it.

"You and your brother have made trouble for us," Peter went on. "Everything was fine and peaceful before you arrived."

"Then let us go," Marlene said, clenching her fists at her sides. "We'll be out of your hair—you'll never have to think about us again."

Peter turned to her. This close, Marlene could see the freckles on his cheeks. The slight chapping on his bottom lip. "I'm not the one who's keeping you here. Don't you understand that yet?"

"That's nonsense and we both know it," Marlene said. "I may read a lot of fairy tales, but I know how impractical they are. I'm not some silly child like your Lost Boys."

"No," Peter agreed. "You aren't like them. The other boys found their way to this place because they needed it, in a way. They don't remember where they came from now, but I do." Peter stared out at the woods where his Lost Boys were all safe and sleeping. "Abandoned or forgotten. Alone. Never Land tells me where they are and I go to them. I save them."

"You can't just take them," Marlene said, aghast. "Think of their families."

The sadness in Peter's eyes was palpable. "I do."

Marlene felt a chill at that. Maybe she'd misread Peter. At a glance, he seemed every bit as whimsical and lighthearted as the other boys here. But maybe he knew more than he let on, and, in this land of magic, that knowledge was his curse.

"Everyone else forgets," Marlene said, "but you remember."

Peter nodded.

"Why?"

"I don't know." He shrugged. "It's just always been that way."

"What about me and James, then?" she pressed. "You didn't come and collect us. There would be no reason to. We were perfectly fine where we were." She wasn't lying, she reminded herself. Being a bit bored and restless with her life in England was not a tragedy.

"You came tearing right into Never Land all on your own, in a way that few have," Peter said. "James I suspect only came along out of love for you. But you're here because you needed this place, Marlene, whether or not you're willing to admit that to yourself."

Marlene hated and loved the way that he said her name. With a flourish, like a song. She hated that he could make her feel so beautiful and so important.

"I have to go back," she said, forcing herself to be practical. Forcing herself not to be lost in what Peter was telling her. "Mother and Father will worry. I'll miss school."

"Have you ever thought about what it all leads to?" Peter asked. "Everything you do out there is just to get you to the end. You'll go to school so that you can get a job. Get married. Pay bills. Work until you're old and tired and sick. And then you'll die. You'll be buried, and time will pass, and it will be as though you never existed."

How did he know? How did he put into words the exact fear that she had carried since she was a child? She'd never voiced such a thing, not even to her brother. Especially not to him.

"You know a lot about adulthood for someone who never leaves this place," Marlene remarked.

"Well," he said. "It wasn't always this way."

She studied his face, curious. "Who were you before you came here?"

Peter shrugged. "I don't remember."

"Liar."

Peter grabbed her hands, drawing her toward him. She slipped, flew, and floated in the air before landing back on the branch.

"You can live forever here," he rasped. "Never Land is a gift. It saw something in you. It called you."

Forever, in Never Land. A place without rules, without itchy dresses or people telling her to sit still, to concentrate. A place where her mother would never again sigh in exasperation and say, *When will you stop climbing trees and start acting sensible?*

James, Marlene reminded herself. *Think of James.* He was miserable here, and the only reason he couldn't return home was because he was tethered to her.

But that was just the thing. She always thought about James. She slowed her pace when he couldn't keep up. She protected him when their classmates were cruel. She would grow up alongside him, and she would never be far from him, because he needed her.

But when had he ever asked what *she* needed? When had she ever been permitted to do anything for herself?

The thought frightened her, and she couldn't be sure what to believe. Home seemed so far away and small. England seemed so unappealing.

"I . . ." she began. *I want to stay here. You're right. I don't want to go home. I don't want to grow up.*

She tore her hands out of Peter's and jumped backward into the sky. "I have to get back to James," she said. He could make sense of this. He could remind her of what was real.

"Wait—" Peter flew after her. But both of them stopped when they saw the glimmer of distant lanterns floating in the darkness.

The enemy ship was on the horizon.

13

James awoke to his sister tugging on his arm.

"Come on, James," she whispered, urgent. Before James could even clear the sleep from his eyes, they were up in the air. She flew as he dangled under her arm, all dead weight.

"Try to think of something happy," she said, shaking a bit of pixie dust out of her hair onto him. "Then you'll be able to fly."

"Have you lost your mind?" he cried. "Whatever happened to walking? Where are we going?"

"We're under attack," she said, in such a way that James couldn't be sure whether she was serious. Marlene groaned at his weight as she pulled him along. "Really, James, can't you at least try to make yourself fly?"

James wondered if he was dreaming. His sister was acting so strange, even for her.

Fairy light illuminated the way forward, and when James saw that Peter was flying ahead of them at a faster clip, he remembered that everything was strange in Never Land. Of course they were under attack on an isolated island. Of course they were flying. Why would they ever have a normal problem with a normal solution?

But then James thought, *Isolated except for one enemy, across the water.*

"They're coming for us!" Sam was shouting. James looked down and saw the boy running below his ankles. "They're going to attack!"

Before Sam could say another word, Slightly swooped from the darkness and hoisted him up, like a hawk carrying its prey.

By the time James regained his bearings, Marlene was setting him on his feet. They were at the mouth of a cavern at the base of a hill. One by one, all the Lost Boys gathered— all of them still hovering midair but for Sam, who clearly wasn't able.

"Go inside, hurry, hurry!" Peter was shoving all of them into the cavern.

James, at the rear, resisted. "I'm not going in there," he said. "Not until I know what's going on."

"What's going *on* is that we're under attack, thanks to you," Slightly snapped.

"Me?" James spluttered.

"James, don't be difficult," Marlene pleaded.

"Difficult?" James advanced on her. "Difficult! That's brazen, even for you. First you drag us to this place, and then—"

Peter snared James by the arm, pulling him just clear of the arrow that whizzed past and embedded itself in the body of a tree.

Sam yelped from the darkness of the cavern.

When the next arrow came, it was on fire.

Slightly stood at the mouth of the cavern, the other boys standing behind him. He addressed Peter like a seasoned soldier well versed in battle. "What do you need?" he asked.

A horde of fairies descended on the burning arrow, extinguishing it with clots of dirt.

"Keep everyone inside," Peter said. "I'm going to face them, see what they want."

"Wait!" Slightly grabbed his wrist before he could take flight. "You shouldn't go alone."

"It's all right," Peter said. "They won't kill me. They know it won't end well for them if they try. Remember what happened last time."

Still, Slightly's words seemed to give Peter pause. He

turned to Marlene and James, standing beside each other, and considered them.

James's jaw swelled with hatred. It was Peter's fault that they were here, and Peter's fault that they couldn't go home. Marlene tried to be sensible, James knew, but she was vulnerable to her own imagination. Held hostage by daydreams. Peter fed into all of this, and as long as this boy was in the way, Marlene would never see reason.

But when Marlene leapt into flight just then, it wasn't because of anything Peter had said.

"Marlene, what are you doing?" The frustration in Peter's voice was something with which James could greatly empathize.

"I'm going with you," she said.

Peter flew up beside her. "It's too dangerous."

James was irritated beyond reason that he couldn't fly. Marlene had told him to think of something happy, as though such a thing were possible.

Another arrow sailed through the air, and Peter shouted, "All of you, take cover in the cavern!" He grabbed Marlene's arm, but she jerked angrily away.

"I'm going," she said. Before another word could be uttered, she was in flight.

James ran after her. As ever. As always. "Marlene!"

"I'll be right back," she called down to him.

James's feet pounded against the dirt as he tried to give

chase. But if Marlene was always ahead of him on foot, she was twice as fast in flight. He doubled over to catch his breath, lost in the thick of the Never Land wilderness. When he raised his head back toward the sky, she was gone.

A moment later, Sam emerged behind him, wheezing. "W-we have to take cover," he stammered, tugging on James's arm.

Arrows flew through the air, whistling before they crashed into trees. A giant oak erupted into flame, and in the maddened frenzy, James was sure he heard the tree cry out in pain.

Sam was still pulling him back toward the cavern, but James, having caught his breath, began to run after his sister once more. He knew it was futile. He knew that he wouldn't catch her this time, but he had to try.

Fear surged through his chest. Not for himself, but for her. He remembered the peculiar fire in her eyes when she'd tried to free him from the enemy net, and how fearless she'd been when Bluejay snared her in a chokehold. She was too brave for her own good. She needed him. She needed someone practical and cautious to rein her in before she carried herself too far.

Sam was running after him, shouting something that James couldn't quite make out. His lungs burned and his muscles ached. All he could think of was Marlene and whatever irreversible thing she was about to do.

By the time he made it to the edge of the woods, he smelled the smoke. Ash and soot clouded the air, and he looked back to realize he had run through a wilderness that was now on fire.

Gasping, he turned to the sea. He saw Marlene and Peter, lit by the glow of fairies that served to keep them safe. It seemed impossible that such tiny, fragile things could wield any sort of power.

The enemy ship was below them, Cassius at the helm. Arrows spiked through the air, speeding toward the island with unreal force. Perhaps the enemy boys possessed a magic of their own, after all.

"Marlene!" James's voice was lost to the distance between them. He cupped his hands around his mouth and bellowed her name again and again, but it was no use.

When Sam finally caught up, breathing hard, James turned on him. "Why the hell can't you fly?" he demanded. If only Sam could carry him out there, he could reach his sister. But with all the magic in Never Land, James had been saddled with the most useless boy this place had to offer.

"I—I don't know," Sam said. "I just can't."

Happy thoughts. Marlene said all it took was happy thoughts. James clenched his eyes shut and tried desperately to think. Cotton candy. Summer. The whistle of the evening train.

He jumped, only to land heavily back on his feet.

It was useless. He would spend eternity here if he waited to learn how to fly.

"I need to build another raft," he said.

"Now?" Sam spluttered.

"I have to get to her, Sam." James jumped up and grabbed a bowed branch, trying to break it with his weight. "If you had anyone to love in this infernal place, you would understand."

Sam veered back, injured by the words. His mouth pressed tight.

Trying to build a raft in time was futile and James knew it. There was no way to reach his sister, or to stop her, and he knew that, too. Frustrated, he abandoned his plan.

Peter had been impressed with how quickly Marlene learned to fly. He'd told her that all of the Lost Boys had been quite clumsy at first, dropping like dead flies whenever their concentration broke for even an instant. But flying had come easily to Marlene. She had considered it, and what she realized was that Never Land made her happier than she cared to admit. She knew that she couldn't live here forever, and that she would have to go home eventually. But still, she was good at pretending she could be here for the rest of time. For millions of years. Billions. Until the sun itself went cold and the stars turned to graves in their infinite galaxy. She would be one of the very last living things, and she would see the world end, and she would die only when there was no time left to squander.

When she imagined this, it made her happier than any book she had read, any song she had heard trickling out from London cafés on bustling afternoons.

The happiness didn't go away, even when all of her other thoughts turned dark and frightful. Even as she flew over the sea with Peter calling after her.

"You!" Cassius roared when he saw her. He stood up on the ship's railing. "You're the reason all of this is happening."

"You're the one who kidnapped my brother," she said.

Peter flew up beside her and snared her arm. "I'm the one you want," he told Cassius. "Stop attacking my island. Take me as your prisoner."

Marlene whipped around to face him, stunned. "Don't do that," she said. "Don't fight my battle for me."

"This isn't your battle," Peter snapped. "This island is *my* responsibility. I told you, you just make more trouble."

She was startled by his sudden peevishness. It changed the entire construct of his face. Never Land itself seemed uglier for it.

"Enough!" Cassius shouted. His fist clenched around the

bow at his side. "I want the one who stabbed Bluejay. An eye for an eye."

James, Marlene thought but didn't dare say. The only brave thing he'd ever done in his life was attack that boy, and it had been for her.

Her brother could never endure whatever hell these enemy boys might make him face for such a crime. But Marlene could survive them. She was certain about that.

She grabbed Peter by the wrist. His eyes widened at the sudden ferocity of her gaze. "Tell James to find a way home," she whispered to him urgently. "Tell him I'll be right behind him."

Before Peter could argue, she flew low and faced Cassius with her chin elevated. "I'm the one you want," she said. "I'm the one who stabbed Bluejay."

When Marlene said the boy's name, Cassius's eyes filled with tears. He gritted his teeth. And Marlene could see that he had loved this boy her brother had tried to kill. Although he looked to be about her age, Cassius could have been a hundred years old—a thousand. He had forged his own piece of eternity, of utopia, on his little island across the sea, and now it was forever shattered.

Marlene felt the arrow tear through her flesh before she ever saw it. But just before it made impact, her memories exploded like the jigsaw puzzles she would dump on her bedroom floor.

Stomping in puddles; swinging from the low branch of a tree; James helping her untangle a ball of yarn; her father singing in a low, deep voice early in the mornings as he shaved in the bathroom mirror.

The medley was over as soon as it had begun. The magic and the memories left her at once, and she fell hard against the water.

Though her mind was wide awake, her body was stunned still, and she couldn't swim. She tried to breathe and tasted the copper of blood in the water instead. She saw a shadow swoop down toward her, and for one glorious moment, she thought it was Peter.

But it wasn't.

Only then did she scream, not out of fear but out of outrage that it was all going to end this way. After she had found the paradise she'd been longing for in secret. After she had been promised forever, and finally believed that it could be hers.

Later, when James thought back on this moment, he would see it with a clarity that he didn't possess at the time. He would understand that he had looked out at the water because his sister had called to him. Not with her voice, but with a violent montage of thoughts of him. He would understand that all the memories Never Land had tried to steal from Marlene had flooded her all at once, and done so with such a force that he felt it, too.

But in that moment, without the calm or the wisdom to reflect, James was held captive by his panic and confusion.

He turned to look at the enemy ship just in time to see Cassius wield a bow. His silhouette was confident and bold against the bright circle of the moon behind him. He nocked the arrow and released it. In less than a single heartbeat it pierced through the air and knocked Marlene right out of the sky.

When James screamed, he had no way of knowing that his sister was screaming, too, just below the surface of the sea as she sank.

He tore through brambles and down the hill of jagged rocks that led to the beach below.

The world blurred. He scarcely felt the cuts and scrapes he accumulated in his descent. His blood stained the sand when he finally made it to the beach only to remember that he was trapped by the water. The ship, and Marlene, were dozens of yards away. He'd made some progress with his swimming, but if he tackled such a distance, he was certain he would drown long before he reached her.

The sky was dark with ash. From here, he could barely make out the silhouette of the enemy ship and the distant voices shouting.

She wasn't dead. He refused to believe that she could be dead. He paced madly along the water's edge.

Fire crackled and burned in the forest behind him, but he didn't care. Let this awful place burn down. Let it all turn to nothing. Let Peter lose everything he loved, too. It was only fair.

14

It was nearly dawn when Peter returned to his island. He arrived amid smoldering ashes. The Lost Boys had labored for hours to extinguish the flames caused by the fiery arrows, but the damage was devastating despite their tireless efforts.

Peter descended at the mouth of the cavern where everyone was taking cover. James was on him the moment his feet touched down.

With all his force, James knocked him to the ground and pinned his arms. His eyes were bright with rage, his lips quivering with it. "You left her!" he cried. "You left her to die!"

Fairies attacked him, some scratching with tiny fingers and others using their glowing strands of magic as scourges, stinging his ankles, the back of his neck. They drew blood, but James didn't care. He didn't care if they sliced him to death.

For a moment, Peter lay beneath him, prone and exhausted. But then he snarled and flipped James onto his back. "Your sister is a troublemaker, just like you!" he said. "It's been nothing but chaos since the pair of you arrived."

James struggled and kicked until he gained the advantage again. They rolled through the dirt, snarling like feral wolves, shouting, until James was able to reel back and throw a punch. His fist connected with Peter's jaw, making it crack.

As Peter drew back, James broke free of him and stumbled to his feet. It was fury—not sadness—that filled his eyes with tears. He couldn't be grieving, he reminded himself, because his sister wasn't dead. She couldn't be dead.

He looked up, and all he saw were unfamiliar stars in an unfamiliar sky. These constellations made no sense, and the air smelled strange. He couldn't hear the persistent whispering of the trains from here. He couldn't chart a way home.

Looking for something familiar, he felt around for the pocket watch he had brought with him, only to discover that it was gone.

Just like Marlene.

His sob was loud and ugly, and he despised himself for it.

"You left her," he said again, his voice strained and broken. Of all the things he felt, that was the only one he could put into words. "You left her."

Peter stood, outraged, ready to go again even as he held his jaw with one hand. But when he advanced on James, Sam got between them and said, "That's enough," in that soft, practical way of his. He put an arm around James's shoulder and led him away. "There now, come on," he said.

In that moment, James hated Sam. Hated him for being so patient and so kind. Hated him for being impossible to hate at all.

"You shouldn't have done that," Sam said, once the others were all out of sight.

"You saw it, Sam," James blurted, still in tears. He wiped at his eyes with the backs of his fists. "You saw him leave her."

Sam sat on a log and frowned sympathetically at James. "What I saw was Peter go in and try to save her," Sam said. "As soon as she hit the water, he dove in after her. But Cassius was faster. He just was. Peter had no choice but to let him take her. She would have drowned if Peter had tried to fight him off."

James hadn't seen any of this. When he thought back, all he could remember was Marlene's silhouette falling like dead weight. Panic had taken over then. He remembered his descent down the rocks, and the smell of blood, and looking out over the water for any sign of her.

He barely even remembered how he'd made his way back from the shore. Vaguely, he recalled trying to swim, only to be hauled back by Sam.

Now he slumped forward and buried his face in his hands. "I have to get her back. And don't you dare tell me that she's gone, because I'll throw you out to sea." Not that it would do any good. Sam would only come swimming right back. He was everywhere, always.

"All right," Sam said. There was an edge to his tone. "Tell me how you'd like to do that."

James raised his head from his hands and stared at the boy, uncertain whether he was being sincere.

"Go on," Sam said. "You can't fly. You can barely swim. You've killed one of their men, and now they'll likely impale you with an arrow if they see your face again. Peter is the only one who could possibly help you, and you've just spat in his face. So let's hear your plan."

James clenched his jaw. No words came. James and Marlene had disrupted the blissful paradise of Never Land simply by existing here. Sam was finally angry enough to stand up for himself, and James respected him for it, even if that anger was turned against him.

Sam raised his eyebrows expectantly. "Nothing?" he asked. "Then I suggest you cool your head and then go apologize to Peter. Maybe if he's feeling merciful, he'll be willing to help."

"You know he won't," James muttered. "He doesn't negotiate with them."

"The agreement has always been that we leave them alone, and they leave us alone," Sam said. "We've all broken that agreement now. Peter has many things they want. Marlene may be worth bargaining for."

James was so frustrated that he could have burst. Marlene. A bargaining chip. He shook his head. Whatever it might take to get his sister back, he would not place her life in Peter's hands. "I need something to write with." He looked at Sam. "Don't just stand there. Ink, paper, a bloody pile of leaves, I don't care. Something."

Sam scurried off and returned minutes later with a peculiar black flower that resembled a tulip. But when James got a closer look, he saw that the center of the flower was a dark, inky pool. "Tootles uses these for his doodles," Sam said.

It would have to do. James tore at the stem of a giant leaf and dipped into the makeshift inkwell.

Using a large flat rock as paper, James began to draw. He worked best under pressure, and with all that was at stake now, he worked with a fervor unlike anything he'd experienced before.

Sam aided him in silence, bringing new inky flowers when the one prior was depleted. He didn't ask a single question, although James was sure he must have been curious.

James knew that he would be a good engineer. When he

looked at vehicles, he liked to dismantle them in his head. He could imagine where the hinges and gears might be, and how he would measure the parts to assemble it. He often drew hypothetical vehicles and maps for practice.

But in Never Land, there were no trains or automobiles. On Peter's island, there wasn't even a ship. If one wanted to go far, one needed to fly.

Just as the early bits of sunlight cast gold highlights on his black hair, James swept the last stroke of ink against the rock. He stood back to scrutinize his work in its entirety.

When he saw that James was finished, Sam asked, "What is it?"

Drawn on the rock in delicate, precise lines was a sketch of a human silhouette wearing a great pair of mechanical wings. Bolts and gears were sketched along the sides, meticulously numbered.

"If I don't have whatever magical nonsense it takes to fly," James answered, "then I'm going to make my own magic."

15

The sun was high and hot and buzzing when Marlene opened her eyes. At first, she couldn't understand why her ribs were burning, or why her mouth was so painfully dry. She tried to move, but her body seized up in protest.

"She's awake," an unfamiliar voice said. And for a feverish, delirious moment, Marlene imagined that she was home and in bed. She had the thought that she wouldn't make it to school because she was ill, and she needed to summon the strength to call for James to bring her a glass of water.

But then she at last opened her eyes, and the piercing brightness of the sun reminded her that she was not in her sleepy seaside town in late December. She was very, very far from home.

As she became aware of her surroundings, she saw the outline of two of the dozen or so boys on Cassius's island crouched at her feet. Their eyes were big and fearful, as though she were the one holding them captive.

"Does she know how to speak?" one of them asked.

"Of course I know how to bloody speak," Marlene retorted, and broke into a fit of coughs that sent pain shooting up her side.

"Get Cassius," the other boy said. His companion ran off.

Cassius. The enemy boys' leader. Her stomach twisted with dread. She remembered the anger on his face, and the sudden bite of his arrow piercing into her side. She recalled sinking, sure that she was about to die. And then—darkness.

But she was still very much alive, which was something to be relieved about, if nothing else. She was lying in a ditch, on a soft pile of leaves and long grass, and she could smell the fragrant flowers budding on the surrounding vines. A bird was cawing loudly, and she heard the trickle of running water nearby.

When she'd first approached the enemy island in search of James, she'd gotten an aerial view. It was dense with trees, but she'd seen the lookout post near the shore and managed to evade it. Though it was difficult to gauge the layout through the forest, she had been able to gather that it was similar to Peter's island—filled with dips and valleys and waterfalls.

And now, lying on her back, she could see a series of cables strung between the trees above her. A means of travel? It was clear that these boys had built their island around the idea of survival—lookout posts in the trees, and all of them armed with arrows or daggers or swords. It made her wonder, as she became more and more lucid, what they needed to protect themselves from.

"Leave us," Cassius said to the other boys. She looked up to see him standing with one hand on his hip. His jaw was clenched, and what struck her was how angry he was. He'd arrived so silently that Marlene hadn't even heard his approaching footsteps.

The other boys left Marlene's line of sight, but she suspected they were nearby. Branches rustled in overhead trees, and she couldn't be certain whether it was just the wind. She knew that all the hatred she could feel pouring off Cassius was intended for her and her alone, and she steeled herself. She wouldn't be afraid of this boy, or this island, or this place. She would survive whatever he had in store for her and emerge victorious, and she would return to Peter's island—to James—unscathed.

Well, relatively unscathed. There was still the injury at her side to contend with.

Cassius's gaze bored into her until she was forced to meet

his eyes. For a moment they stared at each other, caught in a peculiar dance of wills.

Marlene betrayed nothing. If Cassius thought she could be intimidated, he had another think coming.

"So you're the one who stabbed Bluejay," he finally said.

"He was going to alert the others and stop me from saving my brother, James," Marlene said. Her strength returned in small doses, and she was able to prop herself up on her elbows. She gritted her teeth at the rush of pain, bearing it until it subsided to a dull throb.

"Brother," Cassius snorted, an almost laugh. "That cowardly little child is your brother, huh? I suppose you do look alike. And you both make fool decisions. But it's clear you're the only one with a spine."

"Leave him be. He has nothing to do with any of this," Marlene said. "You have what you want now. You've won."

"Won." He laughed bitterly. "That would imply you're some sort of prize, rather than a thorn in my side."

Marlene chose to ignore this. She was in enough trouble as it was, injured and at his mercy. If she was going to survive, she would have to play to her strengths and make these boys like her.

Cassius blew out a hard breath, rustling the sandy hair at his forehead. "I didn't believe that a single person could wreak so much chaos for my men, but now that I'm looking at you, I don't doubt you're to blame for all of this."

The pain flared when Marlene tried to push herself fully upright. She sucked in a hard breath and fell back against the dirt and leaves.

Cassius stared at her for a moment. He took one cautious step, then another, and knelt at her side. "Let me see it." When he reached for the hem of her flannel shirt, he was tentative, surprisingly gentle, as he rolled up the fabric to inspect the wound.

Marlene saw for the first time that a makeshift bandage of pale green leaves had been applied to her hip. Her skin was frightfully pale, a shock of white in the daylight, like an unearthed root.

She bit her lip, stifling a cry when Cassius peeled the leaves away. The wound was angry and scarlet red, the surrounding skin pink and inflamed.

"These will draw out the infection," Cassius said. He reached out to pluck more of the large pale leaves from the brambles that grew around the ditch. "Give it a few days and you'll be fine."

"Fine?" Marlene said, taking great care to hide her irritation. "You're not going to kill me, then?"

Cassius slapped a leaf over the wound with more force than was necessary, and then he met her eyes. "That depends on you."

Morning dew had made the leaves soft and malleable, and

they clung easily to her skin. They had a peculiar cooling effect that soothed the angry heat of the injury. She had seen these very leaves growing wild along Peter's island and thought nothing of them. They were dull and unassuming compared to the vibrant flowers and glittering fairies that made up the backdrop.

"Here." Cassius offered her a canteen that appeared to be crudely forged out of scrap metal. "It's spring water."

He put the canteen into her hands, and Marlene didn't realize how thirsty she was until she had her first taste of the cool sweet water. She drank all of it down greedily, and by the time she looked at Cassius again, he had finished plastering leaves over her wound.

"Why are you keeping me alive?" she asked. "After going through all the trouble to shoot me with an arrow."

"About that." He frowned. "I suppose a net would have captured you just fine. The arrow was for what you did to Bluejay. If I wanted the shot to kill you, it would have." He stood and offered a hand to her. "If you're able to walk, I'll show you why you're here."

Marlene wasn't sure she could get up, much less walk anywhere. But she would die of exhaustion before revealing any further weakness to this island of enemy boys.

She let Cassius pull her to her feet, and though she staggered a bit, she began to take halting, tentative steps. The twigs and dirt were hard against her bare feet. She'd left her shoes back on Peter's island, lost somewhere in the tall grass, because the earth had been so lovely and soft that it hadn't mattered.

Although she and Cassius appeared to be alone on the dirt trail they followed, Marlene knew better. She could feel the eyes of his boys hiding up in their lookout posts and in the brambles.

It wouldn't just be a matter of appeasing Cassius, Marlene suspected. She would have to charm the whole lot of them— violent and infuriating as they were. It wasn't only about saving herself, but keeping their sights off Peter's island, where James still resided. Which boy had been the one to attempt to stab Peter, she wondered. And more importantly, *why*?

Cassius was clearly the leader. Marlene could hear the authority in his voice. But it didn't make sense that they would be so loyal—not only to Cassius, but to this island that was so far removed from all else that Never Land had to offer. None of these boys could fly. The fairies didn't even venture to this shore. They would go only so far across the ocean before recoiling.

So what was it that kept Cassius's boys from making amends and returning to the other side of Never Land?

As they walked, Cassius kept his eyes on Marlene—as though she were in any condition to go running off. And although she was brimming with questions, she said nothing.

Not yet. She was still working out what Cassius wanted with her, and how she could fulfill it.

There were two boys standing watch over a hut that had been fashioned out of brightly colored palm fronds—the sharpest purples and yellows and greens she had ever seen. Even without fairies, this side of Never Land shared the strange magic of Peter's island.

Cassius nodded to the boys, who stared hesitantly at Marlene before parting to either side of the entrance.

Cassius entered the hut first, bowing his head so that he would fit. Marlene trailed behind him. As soon as she was inside, the beauty of the vivid colors was lost to her, over-powered instead by the humid stench of sweat and misery.

Lying sprawled in the center of the cramped space, sweating and twitching in a fitful sleep, was Bluejay.

Marlene gasped. She hadn't expected him to be alive, not after what James had done to him. By the looks of it, he was barely clinging to this world, red and flushed with fever, his chest heaving miserably for air.

"Don't look so shocked," Cassius said, deadpan. "Take a look at your handiwork."

This is the boy who held your brother captive, Marlene reminded herself. *This is the boy who held you by the neck.*

Marlene swallowed the lump in her throat. "So he's alive, then."

"Yes, and you're going to make sure he stays that way," Cassius said.

Marlene stared at the boy. Where he wasn't flushed with fever, he was pale as death itself. "Me?"

"You're going to share his fate, whatever that may be. An eye for an eye. That's how we do things here," Cassius said. "If he survives this, so do you."

Tentatively, Marlene moved to stand beside him. She had not anticipated this. Wrath and vengeance, she could have predicted. Cassius trying to kill her, she would have been able to counter. But this?

If she nursed Bluejay back to health, he would gain the strength to speak. He would tell everyone that James, not Marlene, had been the one to do this to him.

It would have been smart of Marlene to let him die. If Cassius wanted someone's head for this crime, better hers than James's.

Dead men told no tales. But the living always did.

16

inker Bell kept an aggressive watch over James all morning. She did little to hide it, fluttering her wings as she trailed behind him but darting behind trees and brambles whenever James turned to look. James had observed that she was Peter's favorite fairy from the way she always hovered around and doted on him, and his particular affection for her. He spoke to her, conferred with her. Her light was often seen hovering beside him when he walked alone.

James ignored her. For hours he labored, sleepless and determined, to build the invention he had sketched on the rock. He only stopped for Sam when the younger boy brought him various tools and forced him to drink sips of water that he gathered from the trickling river.

By late morning, sweat beaded James's brow and his arms ached. He'd spent hours sawing branches and carving small bits of wood into gears. He barely had a prototype to show for his efforts. He'd crafted a frame that spanned the length of his height, and he could strap himself inside it. All the beams were connected by vines that served as rope. The wings bent at his elbows, as though they were an extension of his arms, but they were crooked. The foot pedal groaned loudly on its hinge, and the structure was far too bulky to glide.

He needed something that would let him fly on his own, without any pixie dust. Even if he was able to convince Peter or one of the other boys to help fly him to the island to get Marlene, which seemed unlikely, it was too risky. For all he knew, they'd drop him halfway across the sea. Besides which, James hated to ask for help. He saw it as a weakness, and right now, especially, he needed to be the one in control. The only person he could rely on was Marlene, and she was the one who needed saving.

"I-it looks nice," Sam offered. Those were the first words he'd spoken since construction had begun.

"Nice?" James spat back. "Nice? What am I supposed to do with 'nice'—ouch!" Something pinched the back of his neck. He swatted, and Tinker Bell went flying out of his reach. "Did she just poke me?"

Sam tried not to laugh. "She's a bit protective."

James regarded the wooden pieces laid out on the grass. "I'll have to redesign this whole thing."

Sam knelt beside him. "I think you're being too critical. It will fly." He crinkled his nose. "I—I think. Probably."

James sighed. There they were, the only two on Peter's infernal island who couldn't fly, trying to build a pair of wings.

"Maybe if you use canvas," Sam went on. "It's thin. And it will catch the wind. I could bring you a blanket."

"That might work," James mumbled, distracted. "Maybe then I won't need so many parts."

Sam patted his shoulder sympathetically. "And perhaps a bit of sleep wouldn't kill you, either?"

James shot him a glare, and Sam recoiled. "I'll go find the blanket."

"Yes," James said. "You go do that."

James's vision blurred. A wave of exhaustion pulled at him. His body protested and begged for rest, but he made himself think of Marlene. He couldn't imagine the state she must be in. If her injuries were grave, she needed him at once. And if her injuries were minor, James feared greatly that her spirit and anger would endanger her more than anything else.

Suddenly, Peter's shadow eclipsed the body of the flying device, as though it were wearing the thing. And then Peter landed with his usual grace, a few of his Lost Boys lingering behind him.

"You'd be able to fly without all this"—Peter gestured to James's machine—"if you were more like your sister and could think of just *one* happy thing."

"Yeah, well, I'm nothing like her," James muttered. "Clearly."

Peter sat across from him. "Sam is right, you know. You ought to sleep."

Big surprise that Peter had been listening in, James thought. The boy was somehow everywhere and nowhere at all times.

"You sleep," James said. "I have work to do. I can't rest until I know that my sister isn't being tortured, or bleeding to death, or—whatever else." Saying the words out loud somehow made them easier to manage, as though he were merely talking about a book he'd read.

"Marlene is strong," Peter said. "She'll be all right."

James could have screamed, he hated Peter so much in that moment. All of this was his fault, and here he was pretending to know Marlene. He didn't know anything about her. Not one precious thing.

He rubbed at his exhausted eyes and turned back to his handiwork. Maybe if he sanded down some of the brackets, that would lighten the device. But then, that might weaken the structure.

"Listen," Peter said, lowering his voice and squatting down beside James. "I didn't want the other boys to hear this, but

I'm not going to leave her there. I want to get her back, too."

James looked at him, suspicious. "Why? You were willing to leave Sam and me for dead."

Peter didn't answer, which only worried James all the more. It was no surprise that Peter might like Marlene—everyone did. But he'd made it more than clear that all who crossed the sea were on their own, no matter how he might have felt about them.

Before James could probe further, Sam returned with a bedsheet in his arms. It was pale yellow with blue flower buds printed across it. It was such an ordinary, sensible thing to exist in Never Land that James wondered how Sam came to be in possession of it.

"Will this work?" Sam asked. He laid the bundle before James with great care, and that's when it made sense. Sam must have brought this to Never Land with him. Wherever he'd come from and however long ago it might have been, this was his only piece of his old life.

"I won't need it," James said, making a decision.

"Of course you do," Sam said. "What was the word you used? 'Aerodynamics'?"

James was certain he hadn't used that word, but it heartened him that Sam knew the word nonetheless. Although Sam didn't remember his life before Never Land, James could look at him and see the sort of boy he might have been. Soft-spoken, a bit stout, with a lot of wisdom hidden behind his timid nature. Perhaps if he held on to that bedsheet of his, one day his memories would come back. When James finally rescued Marlene and they went home, Sam could come, too. There would be a place for him in England.

All at once, James felt the weight of having dropped something. The fear of a precious, breakable thing slipping from his fingers and down into the jagged rocks below.

"What is it?" Peter asked. His voice was uncharacteristically gentle, as though he was prepared to offer his condolences.

James only stared at him. Then he turned his gaze out to sea. Marlene was trying to tell him something. It was either this, or his grief at losing her to those enemy boys was making him delusional.

It frightened him how bloody soft Never Land was. There were no feral jungle cats and no tsunamis. But the peacefulness was somehow worse. This place swallowed things up in silence, and no one noticed until long after they were irretrievable.

"I have to go," he said. "Now."

"You'll break your neck," Slightly said. "This thing will never fly."

"I don't care." James slid one arm and then the other into the wings of his wooden device. He'd tinkered, adjusted, scrapped, and fixed as much as he could, and now there was nothing left to do but try. There was a time when he never would have attempted such a thing. He would have stayed on the ground, pacing and muttering while his sister took the lead. But it was precisely Marlene's bravery that had left him with no better option than to be the brave one now.

If only he could conjure up a happy thought, he could fly. But whenever he tried to think of anything at all, he saw only the awful things that were surely happening to Marlene on that island. His mind spun with it. His sister, half-dead and bleeding as Cassius stood over her and laughed. Her body tumbling down and down into the waterfalls, where the churning froth would swallow her up forever.

He couldn't think anymore. He needed to act.

Once James's feet were secured to the wooden pedals, he ran for the cliff's edge and jumped.

"You're not thinking right!" someone shouted. James didn't disagree. Rather than screaming out loud, he felt the sound catching deep within his diaphragm, where it ached and burned.

He squeezed his eyes shut, waited for the slam of his body hitting the sea.

But it didn't come.

Cautiously, he opened one eye and then the other, and discovered that he was gliding—no, flying. He was flying high above the water with the cliffside and the Lost Boys behind him.

The laugh that came out of his mouth was hysterical, giddy, and unrecognizable.

When he ventured a glance over his shoulder, Sam was jumping up and down, sharing his triumph.

Happy thoughts indeed, he thought. Forget about carousels and candy canes. He would navigate Never Land through science and logic.

The wooden device creaked and groaned where the wind pushed against it. After a few seconds, James leaned into the sea breeze and felt himself settle into a smooth glide.

His heart leapt into his throat, and for a moment—in all the madness and despair this place had brought him—James felt as light as the air itself. He laughed as though nothing were wrong at all.

He dipped the left side of his body down, arched the wing on his right arm, and spun into a horseshoe pattern so that he could return to the cliffside.

The boys were all whooping and cheering for him now. All but Peter, who stood with a pensive expression, tapping his chin.

The ground came at him fast when he landed, and James stumbled for several yards as he lost momentum. Sam was the first to run to him, his face alight.

Only then, once he was safely on his feet, could James realize what he had just done. His heart—once light and free—hammered erratically now, and he wheezed to catch his breath. Had he lost his mind? What had he been thinking?

"You'll be able to make it clean across the ocean," Sam said. "I'm sure of it!"

"I've never seen someone fly without magic!" Tootles said.

The boys gathered around James, abandoning the wariness they'd afforded him since he'd arrived in Never Land. James was nothing like his magnanimous sister, and he knew this. From their first day on this strange island, Marlene had begun earning the friendship of these boys. She'd climbed their trees and learned the lyrics to their made-up songs.

But James, as ever, had been quiet, surly, something of which to be suspicious. It was the same in Never Land as it had been on every playground, in every classroom.

And yet now, wielding this wooden flying device like a coat of armor, *he* was the one to whom these other children were drawn.

James allowed himself to smile. He'd done it. He'd flown. Without any magic, and without relenting to his practical anxiety regarding the matter.

But the excitement and congratulations all died down when the boys heard Peter approaching. Peter took slow, thoughtful steps, his hands set upon his hips. The Lost Boys stepped away from James, clearing a path between him and Peter.

Peter stared at him, chin raised just slightly in defiance. Science versus magic.

"I never thought such an unhappy boy could fly," Peter finally said.

Happiness—ha! James thought. But what he said in response was "I'm just trying to get to Marlene."

Peter stared at him for a long time. His brown eyes followed the length of each wing, the foot pedals, and finally, James strapped to the machine's heart.

The silence built up like knots tied on top of knots, so heavy and tangled the air was thick with it. Maybe Peter was scared of these other boys. They had tried to murder him, after all. But more than that, they had rejected his rules.

Finally, Peter said, "They'll be armed with arrows. And if we venture to that side of Never Land, the fairies won't be able to protect us. We'll need weapons."

Despite himself, James felt his heart lift a bit at Peter's words. The boy had said *we*.

17

All day, Marlene was restless. She'd spent the morning fretting over Bluejay, tending to his wounds—and her own—while trying to think up a solution. She hadn't come to Never Land to nurse the wounds of anyone—much less her enemies—but she had to be practical. As long as she was useful to them, she was safe.

He might not survive, and it shamed her to think how convenient that would be. He could succumb to his wounds in the night, and his secrets would die with him. After all, he was too weak to do more than mumble nonsense in his fevered state. If Bluejay died, all she would have to do was talk Cassius out of killing her.

Why did James have to stab you? she thought, mopping the boy's fevered brow. She could predict James's counter to this: *Why did you have to fly over and save me? Why did you bring us to this place at all?*

She stood, arching her back in a stretch. It was positively miserable in this hut. Some fresh spring water, not to mention a bit of food, would do them both some good.

As soon as she peeled back the fronds and stepped outside, Marlene heard the clink of bows being drawn. Two of Cassius's boys stood at either side of her, murder in their eyes.

"That's a bit dramatic, isn't it?" she said. She wouldn't show them a lick of fear, even if the sight of them had made her heart skip a beat.

"Can't let you leave the hut," one of the boys said. "Cassius's orders."

Marlene considered her options. The boys had weapons, but they didn't have the authority to kill her. She saw how they all waited for Cassius to command every move they made. She would wager that if any of them defied their leader, they'd be cast out to sea. And since Peter and the fairies wouldn't have them on the other side of Never Land, they wouldn't have anywhere to go. They would drift and drift away until nobody saw them ever again.

"I'm only going to get some water and fruit for Bluejay," she said. "And for that matter, this flap should stay open. You can't expect him to get better living in a tomb."

She walked forward with a confidence that wasn't entirely authentic. There was always the chance that an arrow would pierce through her spleen.

She ventured a glance over her shoulder. The boys were staring at her in aghast silence. She offered a wan smile and a little wave, but this only seemed to stoke their dismay.

Marlene followed the sound of the trickling stream. The water in Never Land was the clearest she'd ever seen. Nothing at all like the murky waters back home.

Home. The word appeared and then evaporated, like the lingering images after waking from a dream.

"Home," she said aloud to herself. *What is it? Where is it?* She remembered James, of course. Her skittish, nervous brother. He was clear as a bell. But what had Mother and Father looked like? Were they still alive?

Her blood went cold. She searched furiously through her thoughts for any piece of them. Their hair, their smiles.

She was in such a panic that she forgot about her locket until she knelt at the water's edge and it slipped out from the collar of her shirt.

But when she opened it, the man and woman staring back at her were strangers.

Marlene was on her feet the instant she heard leaves rustling behind her. She spun to find Cassius standing high above the ravine, a hand on his sword hilt.

"What are you doing?" he asked.

She held up the canteen, now dripping with spring water. "What does it look like?" she said. "You can't expect Bluejay to get any better lying in that hut. He needs some fresh air, and fresh water."

Cassius cocked an eyebrow. "Are you an expert in medicine now?"

"You better hope I am, for his sake." Marlene dusted the moss and grass from her pajama pants. Bluejay really would die without her. The boys might have cared for him, but they'd left him lying in a pile of soft grass in a baking-hot hut with barely enough water to get him though the morning, much less the day.

She trudged up the embankment, using roots as a makeshift staircase, the pain in her side already duller than it had been earlier. "You can let go of your sword, you know. I'm not going to attack you."

At that, Cassius burst with a laugh. Marlene couldn't help laughing, too. She wasn't even sure what was so funny. The absurdity of Never Land, she supposed. All these children who might have grown up to be lawyers or artists or train conductors, living forever in this wilderness of make-believe.

As Marlene made her way back to Bluejay, Cassius followed a pace behind her. She noted that his hand was still on his sword.

She'd never encountered boys like these, so impulsive and yet impressively organized. Marlene had confirmed that the cables she'd seen above her when she'd first opened her eyes were, in fact, zip lines connecting all the various lookout posts and forts they'd built. Marlene knew better than to try flying away, because that boy with the freckles kept watch over the airspace. And Cassius was at the heart of all of it. She could see why. He had more confidence even than Peter—which was saying something, given that Peter had all the magic on his side.

"Hasn't anyone told you it's rude to stare?" she said, not bothering to turn around. She could feel Cassius's eyes on her.

Cassius stepped on a twig, snapping it in half with a loud crunch. "No." And then, "What's 'rude' mean?"

Marlene scrunched her nose. "You're serious? Rude—as in manners. Or in your case, a lack thereof."

"Never heard of it."

She smirked to herself. "It doesn't matter. I suppose you don't need them in Never Land."

Cassius took a broad step, bridging the gap between them. "You're *really* related to that boy? The one who sank down to his knees and all but cried when I showed him the waterfall?"

Marlene's chest tightened at that, but she didn't let on. "Yes," she said. "I *really* am."

She was angry with Cassius, suddenly. Angry that he had frightened her brother when she wasn't nearby to protect him, and angry that James's fear amused him even now.

But she held that anger—like all else—deep inside where

no one could see. She was the only girl in Never Land, and she understood that there was power in this. In a land of mermaids and fairies and glowing dolphins, she was the rarity, and these Lost Boys could never dream how strong she truly was.

Cassius followed her all the way to the hut, but he stopped at the door. Marlene looked back and saw how pale he went, not only at the sight of Bluejay, but at the stale smell around him.

"I told you," Marlene said, softening just a little. "The boy needs air."

Cassius stood frozen for a beat. And then, coming to his senses, he began barking orders at his men. "Change his wounds, and peel back these walls. Let the breeze in. You heard the girl."

Gently, Marlene lifted Bluejay's head in the crook of her arm, as though he were an infant. She held the canteen to his lips and poured slow bits of water, waiting for him to swallow before tilting the canteen again.

Around her, the boys peeled away the walls of the hut, allowing the late morning breeze to fill the space.

Bluejay's eyebrows furrowed and he let out a pained moan before going silent again.

Marlene leaned over him to inspect his wounds once more, her dark curls spilling around their faces like a curtain. When she looked up, Cassius was studying her with unsettling scrutiny, as though she was the strangest thing he'd ever seen. His eyes were wild and curious. Perhaps it was the care she afforded to this injured boy in her lap. Marlene didn't dare confess she'd learned this sort of gentleness from James. He was the patient one. He brought her tea when she had a cold, and he read her homework assignments aloud when she was too tired and feverish to keep her eyes open so that she wouldn't fall behind when she was forced to miss school.

But as far as Cassius was concerned, Marlene had a motherly side. And he was going to be an obstacle. She knew this. As much as he loathed her brother, Marlene would have to earn his favor with the same degree of intensity.

Cassius took another look at Bluejay and winced. "Leave," he told the other boys.

"But, Cassius—" one of them protested.

"Go," he said. "I need to talk to the girl."

The two boys who had been keeping watch eyed Marlene with ire. She pretended not to feel the heat of their outrage.

Once they were alone, Cassius took a step forward into a beam of sunlight. He hesitated, and then knelt on the other side of Bluejay's prone form.

Cassius didn't speak right away. He was looking at Bluejay the way Marlene might have looked at James. She was never safe, never happy, unless she could look back at her brother and know that he was, as well. Marlene thought of how Peter had acted after Sam and James were taken. He forbade any of his Lost Boys from going after them. Indeed, if he'd had his way, Sam and James would have been dead by now. The many mattered more to him than the few. It seemed Cassius held a different view on protecting his own.

"You're wondering if he'll die," she said at last.

"No one dies in Never Land," Cassius said.

"No one is allowed to commit murder, is what I heard from Peter," Marlene clarified. "Anyone can die."

"Peter." Cassius spat the name out as though it were something sour.

"You wouldn't need me to tend to Bluejay if you weren't worried for him," Marlene fired back. She nodded toward Peter's island, although it wasn't visible from here. "The Lost Boys said that if you die in Never Land, everyone forgets you existed. Is that the truth?"

Her words had upset him. She saw that much in his demeanor. "There used to be more of us," he said. "All of us. Before the fairies split the land into islands and left us here to rot."

Rot was a dramatic way of putting it, Marlene thought but didn't say. This island was every bit as beautiful as Peter's. True, there were no fairies to illuminate it at night, but she had seen the lanterns strung between the trees. They made do.

"What happened?" she asked, making her voice soft, pliant. Her matronly tone had worked on Tootles, who opened her cage the night she flew over to save James and Sam. These boys were desperate for a soft voice, she knew. Someone to tell them nice things and make them imagine what it must feel like to be loved. If she had already all but forgotten her own mother, surely they had long forgotten theirs.

"It was all Peter's fault." Cassius snarled as the words came out. "He didn't create Never Land—no one did—but he made it what it is. He made it so that we all forget."

Marlene crawled closer until she could smell the sun and the sea air on him. "How?" she murmured.

"There was a time when we could leave," Cassius said. "I scarcely remember it now, but we used to fly, all of us, in and out wherever and whenever we pleased. After all, a lifetime in Never Land is only a day out there."

Dread twisted in Marlene's stomach at this. Out there. *Out there.* What had it been like? The thick billows of train smoke. A metal chime outside of a shop window. It left an awful ache in her head when she tried to see it more clearly.

"There was a boy who flew home one day and didn't return," Cassius said. His face was strained, as though it also pained him to find the memories. "Peter sent me to find him, and I did, but it was too late by then."

"Too late?" Marlene echoed. She forgot to be soft, and Cassius visibly startled at her abrupt tone, as though she'd woken him from a dream.

Cassius shook his head. "This has nothing to do with anything."

He moved to stand, but Marlene grabbed his wrist. He froze, still as stone.

"Please," Marlene said. "My brother is over there. I want to bring us home."

"You won't be able to do that," Cassius said. "Soon enough, you won't even remember where home is. It won't matter to you anymore."

Once she was certain he wouldn't run off, Marlene let go of his wrist. She didn't say a word, afraid that she would break this fragile trust that she sensed growing between them.

"I was too late finding the boy because he was dead. His drunk of a father had killed him. He'd gone back. I can't imagine what for. And after that, Peter—he thought he was protecting us. He made it so that we can't remember where we come from. Remembering is the only way to go home."

"But . . . Peter remembers," Marlene said. He seemed to have so much clarity about everything, even as her own had begun to slip. "Why does he get to remember if the rest of us can't? Why does he get to decide the rules of Never Land?"

"It's those damned fairies," Cassius said. "He's always gotten along with them. I think—whatever happened to him before he came here, he finds it easier to connect with them than with people, sometimes."

"I wouldn't say that," Marlene ventured. "He's just . . . sensitive."

"Sensitive," Cassius snorted. "Anyway, the fairies have the power to do everything, and he has them wrapped around his finger."

Marlene's heart sank. "I'll be of no use there," she said. "The fairies hate me."

"Nah, they're just protective, too," Cassius said. "It takes them a while to warm up to new people. Especially pretty ones." Immediately his cheeks burned red. He hadn't meant to say that.

Marlene's blood felt warm, and she looked away. Her heart thudded so loudly that she thought Cassius would hear it, but fortunately he coughed and continued.

"Anyway, the fairies will use their magic however Peter wants, and what he wants is for no one on these islands to remember where they came from, or why, or who they left behind. It isn't fair. Why should Peter get to decide what we remember, or where we go?"

"But *you* remember things," Marlene pointed out. She realized now why Cassius stood out from Peter's Lost Boys. He wasn't as innocent or cheerful, because he had grown up— just a little—just enough—and he couldn't be a child the way that they could.

"I see the images in my head," he told her, and rapped a finger against his temple. "Not just faces, but numbers too. All sorts of things."

"That's incredible," Marlene said. "Maybe you're some sort of genius." Cassius laughed at that, but she meant it. James was the smartest person she knew, but being able to maintain such vivid memory in this peculiar place—it would take an unparalleled intelligence to keep one's mind sharp and discerning here.

"No one else remembers," Cassius said. "If Bluejay dies, he'll be just like those skeletons in the waterfall. I put them down there, you know? To give them a proper water burial. After the bodies were reduced to nothing but bones, I caught two of my men using the ribcages for target practice. It isn't their fault they've forgotten those bones used to belong to someone they knew. Someone they considered a friend."

Marlene looked down at Bluejay, who was still flushed with fever. Every breath he drew was something precious, she realized. If he didn't make it through another night, would she remember that he had ever been here? How would it go? There would be the fleeting sense that she had tended to something fragile. And then—nothing. Not even a thought as the moments passed.

"That's why you wanted to kill Peter," she murmured.

"If Peter dies, maybe the fairies will see reason." Cassius nodded. "Without his orders, maybe they'll give the boys their memories back. Even if our homes are long gone, even if our parents died a hundred years ago, it's still our right to know."

Marlene couldn't remember her own world. The panic she'd initially felt upon realizing this was dull around the edges now, and it didn't frighten her as much as it once had.

"But if Peter dies . . ." Her words trailed.

"There will be no one to lure people into Never Land.

Peter is the only one who seems to know how to get us here," Cassius said. "Anyone could come and go. Our memories of the world outside might change how we do things in here. It might change whether we want to stay young forever."

Marlene considered this, falling silent as she plied Bluejay with another sip of water. Would Never Land still exist if there were no one to believe in its magic?

Before she could form her next question, Cassius was turning away from her. He moved for the exit as though she'd done something to frighten him. "Take care of him," he said, not looking over his shoulder at her. He was trying to bark orders, but his voice lacked the conviction he had when he addressed his soldiers. "Remember, if he dies, you're of no use to me."

18

By nightfall, James had rigged his flying device with weapons. Or what would have to pass as weapons, given that Peter was the only one with an actual sword.

He had labored for hours, and his skin was thick with sweat and dirt. The lack of sleep was clawing at him, making him just delusional enough to believe that his plan would work.

The Lost Boys had forgotten their distaste for James, astonished instead by his engineering. They readily followed his instructions as he blurted them, their extra hands and effort invaluable to the construction work on other pairs of wings.

Peter flitted in and out of James's periphery, and James

hardly bothered to notice. Now, as the sun began to set, James knelt over his flying device and an arsenal of makeshift weapons. Although it had flown a short distance earlier in the day, it still needed to be adjusted if it was going to make it all the way to the other island.

Sam crouched beside him. "James," he whispered, "you really should sleep." He used a fistful of moss to mop at James's sweaty brow.

"I can't," James said. He hated that this process had taken so long. He was adept at making things. He had nimble fingers, he'd been told. He could fashion a raft in under an hour, and repair a broken mast in just as much time. But this infernal flying device had taken all day because there was so much more at stake now. Everything had to be just so.

"Sam is right," Peter said. James flinched. When he looked up, the boy was standing over him, hands on his hips. "We'll fly out when they least expect it. They change lookouts just before sunrise."

James knew better than to ask Peter why he was helping. He was smart enough to understand that he needed Peter's help, much as he distrusted him. When Peter sat before him, James saw how tired his expression was. His eyes—usually mischievous and impish—were dull and glassy. His rosy cheeks had paled just a bit.

Who is she to you? James wanted to ask. It wasn't as though Marlene intended to stay. Once he had her back, they would continue to look for a way out of here. They would sail to the edge of Never Land itself on a fallen log using their hands as paddles if they had to. But they wouldn't stay here. They couldn't.

"The fairies won't be able to help us, you know," Peter said, reiterating what he'd said earlier. "They won't go to that side of Never Land. The boys there will kill them; you've seen it."

"I can get by without fairies," James said. "I've made it this far in life without any magic."

Peter narrowed his eyes. "Listen," he said. "I'm telling you how this needs to go. Those boys might not have any magic, but they're smart. They have a lookout system, and they're a crack shot with arrows. If we aren't just as smart and just as cunning, we'll end up dead, and then nobody gets rescued."

Sam elbowed James. *Listen to him,* the gesture said. Sam, as ever, provided the only reason to be found in this place. It was for him, not Peter, that James kept his mouth shut.

"You'll take the lead," Peter said. "But whoever is spotted first will create a diversion. The rest of us will fly in from all directions—undetected if we can manage it. If we find Marlene right away, there won't need to be any bloodshed."

It was a better plan than anything James had managed to come up with. He nodded, and his lips moved silently as he recited the plan in his head. *Fly in first. Stay undetected. If spotted—ambush.*

"And James—" Peter interrupted his thoughts. "I want to prepare you. We don't know what sort of condition she'll be in."

James picked at a splinter coming up from one of the wings. It peeled away in a smooth curl. "Marlene is all right," he said. He couldn't explain how he was certain of this. As was often the case between him and his sister, he just knew.

Sometime after nightfall, surrounded by the roar of the cicadas, cradled in a bed of moss, James succumbed to sleep. His shoulders and fingers ached from the hours of constant labor, but it was the hollow feeling in his chest that made his rest a fitful one. He thrashed and muttered, rocking and reeling on a sea of senseless images. Faces he didn't recognize, the smell of some faraway sea, and words that didn't come to form.

When he finally broke free and sat up, he was sweaty and gasping. This—this was why he hadn't gone to sleep after Marlene's capture. Vulnerable and unguarded, his brain ran wild and his heart filled up with fear.

Fairy light hovered over him, and beyond that, a brilliant sky of deepening shades of blue.

Was his sister awake and staring up at the same burning stars? Was her head also filled with nightmares?

He closed his eyes again, but sleep wouldn't come. At last he gave up and rose to his feet. All around him, the Lost Boys were sleeping soundly, scattered about and breathing out of rhythm with one another.

James stepped carefully around their prone forms and made his way through the brush and trees. He had the odd sense that something was waiting for him out there.

The premonition brought him to a giant tree growing at a cliff's edge, its thick branches stretching far out over the water below. Perched on one of the low branches, with his knee drawn to his chin, was Peter.

"Oh," James mumbled to himself. "Of course."

Peter laughed humorlessly. "I don't know why you think we're enemies," he said. "I'm not the one that brought you here. You'll have to take that up with that sister of yours."

"Believe me, I intend to," James grumbled. "Once we're home, she'll never be able to make it up to me."

Peter canted his head. "You never talk about your home. Tell me—what is it like?"

James didn't owe Peter a description of his home. That's what he wanted to say. But as he thought back, he realized that he couldn't have given one anyway. He saw fragments of the dream that had roused him just moments before, but his head ached when he tried to picture something more complete.

Mother. A blank space.

Father. A hollow word with no meaning attached.

He stumbled back, his eyes going wide. *Don't show him,* he tried to tell himself. *Don't let Peter see that you can't remember.*

But as ever—as always—Peter seemed to know.

"Would you like to see them?" Peter asked. "Your family."

"You—" James hesitated. "You know where they are?"

Peter hopped down from his branch and landed with a soft thud before James. "Never Land knows everything," he said.

James stuck out his chest. Without Marlene to protect him, he had to prove that he wouldn't be intimidated by this silly boy who boasted so much power. "If you know where they are, I insist you take me to them," he said, imbuing his voice with an authority he very much didn't feel.

Peter softened. "You and Marlene came here for a reason, James. You came here because it's safer. You can be loved here for who you are."

"Safer?" James barked. "What 'safer'? My sister has been kidnapped by a boy who shot her out of the sky with an arrow!"

"It's safer than what's out there!" Peter's sudden intensity made James flinch. Peter swept his arm out to the open sky, as though gesturing to a city far below the palatial cliffside. "There are unspeakable horrors outside of Never Land. And after the world has beaten you down and left you cynical and lost and alone, there's nothing to do but grow old and die.

Then there really is no hope, is there? You go into the ground and you stay there forever."

The words hit James like a slap, but he wouldn't let them in. This boy was not going to override the logic that had carried him this far. He would not be swayed by something so inconsequential as emotion. If the truth existed to be told, then he would hear it. Only then would he decide how to feel.

"If you know where my parents are, I want to see them," James said again.

"Maybe we should wait for Marlene," Peter said.

"Marlene isn't here." James steeled himself against the words. She would want him to do this. Although she never complained about all the ways she looked out for him, James knew what a burden he was. He knew how freeing it would be for her if she didn't have to look over her shoulder for him in crowds and at the schoolyard.

His sister was so clear in his memories now, even as the crowds and the city around her were blurred into nonsense.

Very softly, James said, "Show me."

Peter held out his hand, and it took James several seconds to realize this was his invitation. "I can't make you fly," Peter said. "But I promise not to drop you."

James allowed the boy to grab hold of his wrist. A moment later, they were going up, up. James was dead weight until he felt his ankles lifting up on the night breeze. He looked down and saw Tinker Bell sprinkling him with fairy dust. It didn't make him fly, but it helped make him lighter. Strange, spectacular little things the fairies were.

If Marlene hadn't been held captive across the sea, James would have thought to be frightened now. He hated heights almost as much as he hated the water. And despite the boy's word, he couldn't be certain that Peter wouldn't drop him.

But without Marlene, he found that he was braver. He would survive anything—he had to—so that he could find his way back to her.

He felt it the moment they left Never Land.

Suddenly the sea receded to a rocky shore, and, hanging on to Peter's hand, James could swear that there was something familiar about the smell of this little town spread out below them. Small boats were tied to the docks, and smoke billowed out from the chimneys of tiny houses arranged in a crowded formation.

Peter was flying them down the length of a serpentine river crowded on all sides with buildings. As they approached a city all lit up against the night, a clock belted out a song to mark the hour.

James counted eight chimes, and with each increasing chorus he felt an ache intensifying in his bones. He could almost believe that his parents were the chiming of that enormous clock whose face was glowing high above the rooftops. He felt so certain that he belonged to that sound.

But Peter was on a sure path. "It's just there," he said, nodding to a towering edifice. James was astonished by the beauty of it. An elegant brick building with high arched windows filled with light.

Peter flew them to the top floor, and they came to land on a small wrought-iron balcony outside of a nursery. This was it, James thought. This was his home. It had to be. Even though he couldn't remember it, even though this city was unfamiliar, he felt in his heart that he had always belonged here.

Hope filled him. Once they found Marlene, Peter could fly them both back here. There was another way out of Never Land after all.

When James looked inside the window, he saw two beds with lavish canopies and fluffy white blankets. Which bed was his, he wondered, and which was Marlene's?

The door—ornate, carved with flowers, and painted lavender—creaked open. A woman entered. She was tall and elegant, fashionably dressed with her hair pinned back and neatly curled.

"Mother," James blurted. An epiphany. She had the dark hair and blue eyes he shared with his sister, but beyond that there was something familiar about her. Something he recognized.

When he turned his head, Peter was staring at him, sadly.

The woman turned down the blankets and fluffed the pillows. She lingered as she stood between the beds, lost in her thoughts.

This was definitely his mother. James was sure of it now. How long had he and Marlene been in Never Land? A day? A year? However long it had been, their mother was mourning them. She was entering their bedroom and preparing their beds just in case this was the night that they returned home.

A shriek of laughter lanced his thoughts. The pounding of small feet. Two children came bounding through the door, giggling in their long nightgowns as they leapt into their respective beds.

"I—" James stuttered out a clumsy, meaningless syllable. On the other side of the window, his mother tucked a little golden-haired boy and a little golden-haired girl into their beds. She smiled and kissed their foreheads. And then, drawing up a white rocking chair, she opened a book and began to read.

"I don't understand," James said. Buried deep below his shock, anger began to burn. "She isn't even sad that we're gone."

"If we're going to rescue Marlene, then it can't be for nothing," Peter said. "It can't be just to take her back where she came from. She's the one who came to Never Land, and nobody comes to Never Land unless they're running from something."

James scarcely heard the words. His mother read to the blond children with animated gestures and playful smiles. The children cozied up under their blankets and stared at her with wonder.

"Don't you want to be where you're wanted?" Peter said. "Don't you think Marlene wants that, too?"

James was still watching the woman with his hair and his eyes. She was happy, energetic. "She doesn't even miss us," he said, equal parts wonder, rage, sadness, and resignation. "She doesn't miss us at all."

"She doesn't," Peter said. James's gaze turned stormy.

"Take me back," he told Peter. "We're rescuing Marlene. Now."

19

Marlene lay awake on the floor of the hut, while Bluejay snored softly beside her. The walls to the hut had been reassembled since the nighttime hours had given way to a chill.

Now that she was alone, she could think more about what Cassius had revealed to her. It was strange, Marlene's not remembering where she'd come from. Her entire life had faded away from her as easily as a dream.

"Think," she murmured aloud to herself. "You must be able to remember *something* about home."

Hadn't there been a river? A clock tower? There must have been. *Tower* was a word that didn't exist in Never Land.

Out here, it was all tree houses and huts and makeshift forts. But Marlene knew all sorts of words for buildings—*towers* and *houses* and *manors* and *bakeries*. Surely, one of these things had been her home.

But the more she thought, the more abstract time seemed. How many nights had she spent in Never Land? A dozen? A thousand?

James would surely be keeping track. When she saw him again, she could ask him.

The wound at her hip had healed significantly, which gave Marlene some suggestion of how much time had passed. But injuries seemed to heal quickly in this place. Unless they were especially brutal, like what her brother had done to Bluejay.

As though on cue, Bluejay groaned. Marlene sat upright to check on him. In the waning lantern light, his face was sweaty and fair. His color was no longer a flushed tomato red, and the sweat meant his fever was breaking.

She brought the back of her hand to his forehead. Cooler than the last time she'd checked.

When she rolled up his shirt and peeled back the layers of leaves to assess his wound, she found it to be less angry. The skin around it was healing, no longer pink and inflamed.

"There," she said, and set about replacing the wilted leaves with fresh ones. "I promised you'd live, isn't that right? So you owe me for this, really. It would have been much more convenient if I'd let you die."

She looked up at Bluejay's face and started at the sight of his eyes. They were open now, bright green, and watching her.

"Bluejay?" she ventured, cautious. She couldn't be certain how much he remembered, or even whether he was truly conscious or still trapped in a delirium.

"You—" His voice was hoarse, and he broke into a riot of feeble coughs. Marlene brought the canteen to his lips, but he swatted it away. "You're the girl."

"That's astute." Marlene hoped her cheery tone might mask her fear. "I am indeed a girl."

Bluejay shook his head. His sweaty brown hair fell across his forehead in broken rivers. "You're one of Peter's. What are you doing here?" Then the confusion in his eyes gave way to understanding, and his expression turned aghast. "You were with that boy who stabbed me—"

Marlene lurched forward and clapped her hand over his mouth. Bluejay screamed a muffled protest, but she clamped down tighter and he relented, staring up at her in astonishment.

"Quiet," she rasped. "Listen to me. I'm sorry that my brother tried to kill you. He's not usually so impulsive, but it's this place—anyway, that's not important. What's important is that you're getting better now. You *are* feeling better?"

After a moment of silence, Bluejay gave a nod.

She was leaning over him now, so close that her curls touched his cheek. She moved her hand away from his mouth, and Bluejay swallowed hard, but he didn't shout again.

"I'm here to help you," she went on. *Not that I have much choice in the matter.* "But Cassius thinks I'm the one who did this to you, so that's what you have to tell him."

Bluejay propped himself up on his elbows. This was promising, Marlene thought, even though he winced at the pain. "Why?" he asked.

"Because." Marlene looked over her shoulder. She knew that Cassius had two men keeping watch outside of the hut, but from the measured sound of their breathing, they had fallen asleep. She imagined Cassius wouldn't be happy if he knew about that.

She lowered her voice. "If Cassius finds out it was James who hurt you, I'm worried that he'll kill him. And if he wants to take revenge on someone, well, I can handle myself much better than my brother can."

Bluejay considered this. "Your brother did whimper a lot."

"I have to get him home." Marlene nodded. "He can't make it in a place like Never Land." She looked into Bluejay's eyes, appealing directly. She didn't know a thing about this boy—he'd been unconscious during most of their time here, and before that he'd tried to hold her captive. But Cassius cared about him, and Marlene had to believe there was a reason for that. There was something about him that was worth saving.

"You'll never have to see James again, anyway," she said. "Once he's home, he'll never want to come back here again."

"What about you?" Bluejay asked. "Are you going to come back?"

The question stunned Marlene into silence. *Home* was a hollow word without her memories. For all she knew, back home she was a queen who lived high up in a glittering tower. Or a pauper's daughter, destined for a life of hardship.

What she understood was that Never Land was all around her, vibrant, gorgeous, and strange. In Never Land she could stay young forever. She could do as she pleased. Imagining herself returning home, wherever that was, and growing up and into an adult upset her for some reason she couldn't quite understand.

"I don't know," she answered, accidentally telling him the truth. Before he could comment on it, she said, "Lie back down. Let me take a look at you."

"Where is Cassius?" Bluejay asked, gritting his teeth as she continued to tend to his wounds.

"Sleeping, I assume," Marlene said.

"He never sleeps," Bluejay said.

Nor did Peter, Marlene thought. Maybe that was what made those boys fit to lead their respective islands—they remembered everything and they never seemed to rest.

Bluejay was already starting to fade, exhausted as he was. His eyelids were heavy. He fought it, watching warily as Marlene dressed his wound and then rolled his shirt back into place.

She caught him staring and said, "No, I'm not here to be your mother, so don't ask me to be."

His eyes closed and he let out a defeated, exhausted sigh.

These boys were helpless, Marlene thought. How had they made it this far without anyone to protect them?

She grabbed the canteen and climbed out of the hut. The guards were asleep, just as she'd suspected. They were propped against each other and clutching their bowstrings.

It didn't matter if they couldn't keep awake; Marlene knew there were eyes on her everywhere. It was impossible to know who might have been perched high up in the tree forts.

Marlene was halfway to the ravine to refill the water canteen once more when she sensed it. That unmistakable flutter of magic swimming down from the stars and straight into her chest. It stopped her in her tracks.

Peter.

She chased the presence through the trees, doing her best to avoid twigs and leaves so as to stay silent. Somewhere in the thick of the woods, the presence grew stronger, bright as a light in her mind's eye.

There was a peculiar creak, like gears shifting, and then something—some dark figure—glided down from the sky and stumbled before her.

It couldn't have been Peter. That much was obvious by the lack of grace. But when the figure picked itself up, muttering a curse, it was a voice she would have known anywhere.

"James?" she whispered, incredulous.

In the scraps of moonlight that escaped through the tree branches, she saw her brother's face and she ran to him. She was so glad to see him that she barely noticed he was wearing a gigantic wooden pair of wings.

His eyes were wide when he saw her, and when he gathered her in an embrace she felt the rush of desperation, of worry. He would never say aloud how frightened he was, but she could sense it.

She was frightened, too, though not for the same reasons. "What are you doing here?" she rasped, once he'd finally let go of her.

"What am I doing?" he echoed. "I'm saving you from the bloody lunatics that shot you and left you for dead."

Marlene ventured a glance overhead. There were no zip lines here, thus hopefully no lookout posts. They were in the middle of the island, where there was nothing worth protecting but insects and mossy fallen trees.

"How did you . . ." Her voice trailed. She studied the wooden structure that he was strapped into. She traced her finger over the arch of a wooden beam. "You made wings."

"What else was I supposed to do?" he said. "I can't fly."

Her bewilderment turned to relief, which quickly turned to fear. "You shouldn't be here," she said.

"Obviously," James said. "Neither should you. Come on. We have to go."

He grabbed her wrist, but when he tried to lead the way forward, she didn't budge. She was thinking of Bluejay, still lying in the hut waiting for her to bring him a canteen of water and one of the sweet green fruits from the budding trees because he was hungry.

If she left now, there was no way to ensure that Bluejay wouldn't tell Cassius who had really stabbed him or that he would survive his wound. And if Cassius had been angry enough to shoot Marlene out of the sky that night, there was no telling what he would do to James.

James wouldn't be able to charm Cassius in order to be spared. He didn't know how to make people like him. He didn't know how to play by the rules of these boys.

James, dead.

James, a skeleton in the waterfalls.

James, gone from her memory forever.

"You're white as a ghost," James said. "What is it? What have they done to you? Never mind, tell me once we're off this cursed island—"

"No." She broke free of his grasp.

The surprise and hurt in his eyes lanced through her chest.

"You have to go," Marlene said. "Don't worry about me. I'll escape when it's safe. But they can't find you here."

"What?" James spluttered.

"I'll explain it when there's time," Marlene said. "I haven't forgotten that this is all my fault. I'm going to get us home.

But it has to be when it's safe, with as few enemies as possible, James. You saw what happened when we tried the last time."

"We can't go home," James said. "Mother has already forgotten us. She's found new children to care for."

Marlene took a step back. She thought of the pictures in her locket—the two strangers who resembled her and James. What were their names? What had they been like? "That isn't true," she said automatically. But she wasn't sure.

"She never loved us," James insisted. "That's why you wanted to run away in the first place."

The words felt foreign, and his expression was strange. In the moonlight, Marlene almost didn't recognize her brother. They were fraternal twins—that was the word their doctor had used when they were born. But they might as well have been identical. They had the same heavy black curls, although James kept his much shorter and did his best to manage them. The same blue eyes, although James's were more subdued and distant because he was always thinking.

But in that moment, Marlene didn't see her brother. She saw a Lost Boy of Never Land. She wasn't any different, she supposed. They couldn't remember a thing about home. But even so, Marlene was certain that he was wrong. He had to be.

"I saw her," James said, reading her mind. "Peter took me back home and he showed me what she was up to. She had new children with golden hair and she was reading them a bedtime story. They were in our beds."

Marlene shook her head. "I don't believe you."

"Go on and tell me what you think, then." James's irritation was palpable. "If home was so wonderful and we were so loved, then why did you bring us here to begin with?"

Marlene didn't have an answer for that. She searched through her memories and found only a dull, fading scar across her heart where her life stories used to be. Home was not even a shadow. Her parents were not even silhouettes on a dark night.

It was as though her life had begun the day she emerged in Never Land, dripping with seawater, with her brother at her side.

James's expression turned sympathetic. "We don't have a home anymore," he said, and once again he held out his hand. "We only have each other."

In the daylight, Never Land was lush and beautiful, filled with mystical creatures, lit up by a beaming sun. At night, the stars were glittery and the sky was an unearthly blue. Marlene had been so enchanted by the beauty of it that she had forgotten what a city was like by comparison. She still held the words in her mind: *towers, houses, manors, bakeries*. But the longer she stayed here, the more the words became just meaningless sounds, less intelligible than they had been even hours before.

James opened and closed his fingers, begging her to take his hand.

"Intruder!" a voice cried. James spun around, and his rigid

posture said that he was certain the words were for him. But no one came barreling through the woods for them.

A body sped between the trees—Cassius, on a mission for someone who wasn't James.

"Y-you'll never catch me!" A clumsy, stuttering voice.

"Sam?" Marlene whispered.

"That means we're in danger of being found out." James grabbed her wrist and pulled her into a run, his makeshift contraption folded under his arm to the size of a suitcase. "He's creating a diversion so that we can escape."

As they moved closer to the shore, Marlene heard echoes of Peter's haughty laughter. Her chest filled up with that peculiar warmth Peter's nearness always brought.

"James, wait—" Marlene tried to say, but James had made up his mind. He was almost never so authoritative, but when he was, it spelled trouble. The last time Marlene had seen him so set on a course, he'd stabbed Bluejay. He was going to get himself killed if she couldn't stop him.

"I can fly us out of here, but I'll need a running start," James said. "And you can fly on your own, can't you? Maybe if we go in different directions, they won't catch us."

If Bluejay told Cassius who had really wounded him, James would be in danger. That was what Marlene was thinking as her brother pulled her through the trees.

By the time they made it to the other side of the woods, Marlene could see Peter and the Lost Boys flying over Cassius's ship. Sam was gliding in clumsy circles, flapping giant wooden wings that mirrored the ones James wore. Even from afar, Marlene could see how terrified he looked, and she knew James must have employed him to be a part of this rescue mission.

James stopped and tugged Marlene closer to him. "There," he whispered. "I can run down this trail of land beside the sand. That ought to give me enough momentum, and then the wind will do the rest. We'll have to be quick so they can't shoot us out of the sky."

When he started to run, Marlene was tethered to him by their joined hands. James was thinking only of their escape, but Marlene was thinking of Cassius and his temper and his arrows. She was thinking of Bluejay.

But above all else, she was thinking of James. He was all that she had left in this unpredictable place, and if she lost him the way that she had lost her memories of their mother and father, she would have nothing. She couldn't fathom being so impossibly alone.

The waterline was fast approaching. A sea breeze was pushing forward, and it would be just enough to propel James into flight.

At the instant they reached the edge, James leapt into the wind and flew into the air.

Marlene let go of his hand.

20

It was too late to turn around. There were already arrows flying toward them. James could have shot back, but his painstakingly carved projectiles wouldn't have made a lick of difference; he could see that now.

Marlene stood at the water's edge, clutching the collar of her shirt like some desperate maiden from an old painting sending her husband off to war.

"Fly!" he shouted at her. "Come with me! Now's your chance!"

It wasn't until much later, when he was back on Peter's island, that James realized what Marlene had been mouthing up to him as he flew.

She had been saying, *I'm sorry*.

And only once he realized this did he also realize that their hands hadn't broken apart by the impact of his jump. She had let go.

She'd let go, given up her only chance to escape. After everything. After all he had risked to go and get her. These revelations came to him in small pieces because he couldn't imagine such a betrayal.

"It's okay, James," Slightly said. They were back on Peter's island. The others had returned to the encampment, but Slightly had lingered behind. He came and sat beside James, who was sitting up in the highest tree he could find. From here, he could just see the outline of the enemy island in the distance. An island full of traitors. An island that Marlene had chosen over him.

"Siblings don't make sense anyway," Slightly went on. He frowned as if he couldn't remember where that knowledge had come from.

James wrestled with this idea. It was true that he often couldn't follow Marlene's logic. It was true that she had led them to Never Land in the first place. But even so, there was always a plan underlying her reckless and hasty ideas.

"They shot her with an arrow," James said. "Why on Earth would she stay with them?"

"What's Earth?" Slightly asked.

"Earth," James said. That should have been its own

explanation, but Slightly's blank expression told him otherwise. "You know. The planet."

Slightly shrugged. "This isn't Earth. It's Never Land." He bumped his shoulder against James's. "Come on, you can't spend all day sitting around worrying about it."

James looked at Slightly, really studying him for the first time. He was a peculiar boy—tall and wiry, with ears that were entirely too big for his head. "What's it matter to you?" James asked. "I thought you hated me."

"Yeah." Slightly stretched his arms over his head. "You seemed a bit stuck-up at first. But those wings you designed were pretty great. And you didn't want to leave a man behind. Well—a girl."

A sphere of light hovered over them, and James blew at the fairy until she careened away from his face.

"Don't be mean," Slightly said. "She's only trying to help."

As though in confirmation, the fairy sprinkled glitter over James's head. He sneezed. "Help me do what exactly?"

"Fly," Slightly said. "Everyone has to learn how to fly eventually."

"Sam didn't."

"Sam is a crybaby," Slightly said. "I thought maybe you were, too, but a crybaby wouldn't do what you just did."

"I don't need magic," James insisted as the fairy continued to flutter around him. "I can fly on my own."

James sneezed again as the fine glowing dust swirled

around his nostrils. Happy thoughts and pixie dust. It was such a childish idea. But then again, Never Land was filled with children, and no matter how James dreamed of being an adult one day, he *was* still a child. He knew this because he shared a birthday with Marlene, who had just done something unfathomably childish.

Marlene. Her name felt strange to him now. He'd never been so angry in his life, much less with her. He'd never been so betrayed.

If he hadn't been a twin, none of this would have happened to him. If he had been an only child, there would have been no harebrained sister to drag him to Never Land. He never would have left that grand bedroom on a high floor of that brilliant tower. His mother would be tucking him into bed, and not those golden-haired children.

He would have a warm place by the fire, and his stomach would be full of something delicious and warm—the food wouldn't form in his mind, but he could almost taste it; something sizzling on a hot griddle—and his head would be filled with bedtime stories.

The thoughts were so light that James didn't realize he was floating away until Slightly clapped and whooped and hollered.

When he looked down, he saw the ground far below his feet. Feeling none of the vertigo that heights usually afforded him, James burst out with a giddy laugh.

This was it, then. This was what it was like to be so happy one could fly.

Marlene had seen the hurt in her brother's eyes. Even from the distance that had spread out between them before he turned and realized she wasn't beside him.

When he'd finally understood what was happening, he hadn't circled back to her. He'd flown away.

Good, she'd thought. *That's good, James.*

But the thought was a hollow comfort. It was as though a cord had kept them tied to each other their whole lives, and now it was snapped.

It was for the best. She had to remind herself of this. If Cassius had been willing to kill Peter, then he would think nothing of killing a sensitive easy mark like James. And even though it seemed like Bluejay was going to live, she needed to stay on Cassius's good side just to be sure he wouldn't change his mind about letting her go free.

Marlene stood at the shoreline until she heard footsteps crashing through the forest behind her. Cassius was gasping to catch his breath by the time he stumbled out into the clearing. "I saw—" He stumbled over the words. "I saw him try to take you. I thought he'd done it."

Marlene stared at him for a long while. Here was this boy

who had shot her with an arrow in a fit of rage—this boy from whom she needed to protect her brother at all costs—and she couldn't understand why he seemed so worried about her. Why his face was so much softer than it had been before. Why he was so afraid of losing her.

"You promised to leave my brother alone if I stay and tend to Bluejay," she reminded him.

Cassius met her eyes. In this land of mermaids and fairies and flying boys, he looked at her as though she was the great wonder. He nodded.

"Say it," Marlene demanded, a snap in her otherwise cool tone.

Cassius knew what she wanted to hear without her telling him.

"I promise," he blurted. "I promise to leave him alone as long as you stay."

She swept past him, stomping every branch and dry leaf in her path. Her eyes stung with tears. *Don't you cry,* she thought furiously. *Don't you dare.*

On her way back to the hut, she found the canteen where she'd dropped it upon sensing the flying presence that was James. She picked it up, dusted off the bits of leaves, and kept on her path. She picked two green fruits from one of the trees. They were oblong, almost resembling onions, but she could smell their sweetness even without taking a bite for herself.

When she made it back to the hut, Bluejay was lying on his back, watching her. "What took so long?" he asked.

She threw the fruit at him. "Hey," he said as they rolled across the dirt. They came to a stop on either side of his head.

He was awake, at least, but he still looked positively miserable, and Marlene fought with a fleeting moment of sympathy. Why had he had to grab her that day? Why had he had to make James stab him?

"You should eat" was all she said. "Work on getting your strength back."

"Where are you going?" Bluejay's voice cracked.

"For a walk," Marlene said.

"But you've just come back from a walk."

"For goodness' sake, you're not a baby," she snapped. "You'll be all right for a few minutes."

Minutes. Did anyone in Never Land use a word like *minutes*? *Hours*? *Days*? *Years*?

As she paced through the woods, she felt all the pairs of eyes watching her from lookout posts overhead, like always. She ignored all of them and headed to the waterfalls. She stood at the highest point and looked down. It was so loud here. Water rushed and fell down and down to a pool hundreds of yards below. Behind the curtains of water lay the skeletons of boys whose stories were long gone. Boys who couldn't remember their mothers or where they'd come from, just like her.

"Hey." Cassius had to shout to be heard over all the white noise. "What are you doing all the way out here?"

This boy. He was everywhere. She walked away from the waterfalls and he followed her.

"I'm not going to run away," she said, exasperated. If she wanted to, she could just fly up through the trees, and he would have to shoot her down again if he dared to.

"I know that," he said. "I came to see if you were okay."

"I'm fine." She stopped and spun on her heel to face him. He nearly crashed into her. "If you killed Peter," she said, "do you really think the fairies would let us have our memories back?"

He blinked. "I—" For a leader, he was caught off guard quite often when it came to Marlene. Something about her presence seemed to reduce him to a stuttering schoolboy. "I think so."

"No." Marlene poked him in the chest. "Not *think*. I want to know for sure. If you killed Peter, would you be enough of a leader to get our memories back so that we can all decide for ourselves if we want to go home or stay in Never Land?"

She was so close to him now that she could see the pale freckles scattered across his cheeks. She could see the lashes of his bright and bewildered eyes. In that moment, she sensed the power she had over him, even if she didn't understand where it came from. She understood that she frightened him, for whatever reason. She understood that, as they stood alone in this dense and hallowed place, she was the leader—not him.

"Yes," Cassius said. He regained his composure and stood to his full height, barely an inch taller than she was. "Yes. If we kill Peter, I'll get your memories back."

At his words, a new determination filled Marlene. She had been the one to bring her brother to Never Land, a place that continued to reveal itself to be more and more dangerous the longer they stayed. She had been the start of all this trouble. But just maybe, she could be the one to take them both home. She could be the one to take all of them home.

21

James had never fit in anywhere.

His obsession with numbers and directions left little room for things like games or idle banter. It always seemed as though James could make friends or indulge his interests, but not both. But in Never Land, this didn't seem to be a problem at all. When he flew into their encampment, the Lost Boys peppered James with questions about the wings he'd engineered. Sam boasted about James's raft—which, although not entirely effective, had impressed him greatly—and they all began to debate over what they should build under his tutelage.

They decided to craft a giant slingshot, with a chair and

a track big enough to fit one boy at a time. It would launch them into the air with as much force as a cannon.

For hours, James absorbed himself in his work. Drawing up the plans, delegating tasks. He worked until the ache in his chest began to subside. He worked until he felt almost whole again.

The slingshot was nearly complete by nightfall, at which point Peter put a halt to everything.

"It will still be waiting in the morning," he said.

"Aw, Peter." Tootles sulked, but didn't protest further.

For supper, James used a spear to catch sea trout and Sam gathered heaps of rainbow-colored berries.

"Yuck," Tootles said as James staked the fish on sticks and held them over the fire he'd started.

"You have to put them on a spit so they'll roast evenly," James said.

"Where did you learn that?" Sam asked.

James considered this. He'd performed the actions quickly, without thinking. As he'd waded in the water and looked for fish, he'd felt a vague pang of dread, as though this was a task he had performed to his own chagrin a hundred times before. But he couldn't remember the circumstances.

Peter clapped his hand on James's shoulder and said, "He's just a born fisherman. We should all be more like him."

Despite himself, James smiled. Peter's approval was hard won.

After supper, as the final embers in the firepit began to die, the Lost Boys trudged off to bed.

James rested in his bed of grass under a sky of overly bright stars. Without anything to keep his hands busy, his mind ran wild. He could still recall all the things he knew about himself. That he loved to build things, that he could engineer and sketch and measure with precision. He knew how to stand very still in the shallow water and strike at just the precise moment to catch a fish.

He also knew that he hated everything about fishing. Hated the smell, and the way that the fish wriggled in his hands. But he could endure it, because someone at some point in his life had taught him how.

Lying there in the stillness, with nothing but time to think, James was less sure than ever about who he really was. He couldn't be certain of his own sister anymore, much less himself. He knew Marlene cared for him, but then she had let him go. He had believed he needed to save her, but then she had stood on that enemy island appearing to be in good health, not at all eager to leave it.

Marlene is on my side, he told himself. *Marlene is good.* But all he could recall were ways that she had infuriated him. Abandoned him. Left him wondering who either of them was.

Sam was lying in a bed of moss beside him, and he scooted closer. "It's okay, James," he said, his voice soft. "We're all here for the same reason."

"What reason is that?" James asked dryly.

"Because someone, somewhere, didn't want us."

James closed his eyes, and in the darkness he saw his mother in the nursery, singing two faceless shadows to sleep. And then, slowly, she began to fade.

The days slipped by, and James couldn't count them. He measured the passage of time, instead, by how much higher he could fly without feeling lightheaded from fear. He measured it by his hatred for Peter, and how that hatred slowly faded away until it was something resembling fondness, even loyalty.

Peter didn't mention Marlene again, so neither did James. It was as if Peter had traded all his interest in one sibling for the other. And though he tried to hide it, James basked in the attention.

When he slept, he dreamed of Never Land. Of mermaids and fairies and a clear and glittering sea.

One night—he couldn't be certain how many had passed, exactly—he awoke with a feeling like the air had changed. He sat up, plagued by the remnants of a dream he couldn't remember, but which still held him in a fleeting hold.

The small sound of something ticking was what woke him, he realized. A clock? But where? He'd never seen a clock or a calendar or even so much as a yardstick in Never Land.

Stepping around the sleeping bodies of the Lost Boys, he tried to follow the sound.

He climbed down the jagged rocks along the cliffside, scraping his knees and bare feet along the way. And when he reached the shore below, the sound grew louder.

He dropped to his hands and knees and dug through the damp, soft sand.

Tick — tick — tick.

His heart beat to the rhythm. He dug and dug, and the ticking grew louder. His mouth went dry as sandpaper and his heartbeat grew heavier with each *tick — tick — tick.*

James kept digging until finally he found the source. A pocket watch, rusted shut, still clinging to its severed chain. He pried at the seam, and after a moment it came unclasped. The face was bright and clear as the moon itself. Both the large hand and the small pointed to the 12. The second hand moved forward, forward, forward.

He held the pocket watch in his palm, and something strange twisted deep within his chest, as though a small fish were swimming around his heart.

Marlene awoke with a gasp. Sometime in the night, the heat had turned unbearable, and her skin was clammy with sweat. Her heart beat to a fixed rhythm, like the ticking of a clock.

She looked over to where Bluejay lay, sound asleep with berry juice still staining his mouth and cheeks. As time had passed, he had almost completely healed, but she still kept a close eye on him. The progress of his wound was still the only indication of how long it had been since James had left her to return to Peter's island.

She had spent her days since then doing many of the same things as before, primarily tending to Bluejay. But she had added new activities to her routine, like talking to Cassius about their plans to take down Peter. They spent much of the daytime strategizing how they would get to the other island without being seen, and what they ultimately would do when they arrived.

Cassius had become something unidentifiable to Marlene. He was no longer her enemy, but *friend* also seemed like both too strong and not strong enough of a word for him. The way she felt around him reminded her of how Peter had once made her feel, warm and emboldened. But unlike Peter, whom she had constantly felt the need to impress, Cassius never made her feel as if she needed to do anything but be herself to be worthy of his attention. Where Peter had tried to influence the way she thought, Cassius seemed fascinated by every word that came out of her mouth.

But just this once, Cassius was far from her mind as Marlene crawled for the door of the hut and made her way out into the night.

The air was still. Strange. The stars were twice as bright.

"James?" she whispered, although she knew that he

wouldn't hear her. How long had it been since she'd said his name out loud? He'd been in her thoughts constantly, but she hadn't said as much to Cassius or his men. She wouldn't dare.

She made her way to the edge of the woods and scaled the highest tree she could find.

"What are you doing?" someone said. One of the lookouts—Thomas—stationed in a nearby tree to watch over the island at night.

"Nothing," Marlene said, frustrated. She was never alone in this place. Even when she was sure that she had found the deepest part of the forest. Even when she dove as far down into the water as she would dare, there was always a pair of eyes on her. If only it were safe for her to fly. But she could feel the pixie dust on her starting to fade. Peter said the fairies were banned from this island, and for only a little while, some of their magic lingered on Marlene. But it had taken her as far as it could. She had been there for too long—for how long she wasn't sure—and soon it would be gone.

"Wouldn't be climbing a tree in the middle of the night if it were nothing," the boy said.

Marlene ignored him. She strained her eyes to see Peter's island in the distance. But all she could make out was the dark shadow of it. She couldn't see her brother. She never would.

Tick—tick—tick. Her heart still beat in that peculiar way, stirring up thoughts of dread.

"Marlene?" Cassius's voice made her flinch. She looked

down and saw that he was climbing his way to where she sat. "What is it?"

Nothing happened on this island without grabbing Cassius's attention.

"I don't know," she said, and that was the truth. She could hear the faint *tick—tick—tick*, but from the way Cassius stared up at her, she could tell that he didn't hear it.

"Are there any clocks in Never Land?" she asked.

"If there are, I've never seen one," Cassius said. "Why?"

Marlene wasn't sure she could articulate this feeling of dread that had awoken her, much less whether she could trust him with it. If Cassius cared about Bluejay even a fraction of the way she cared for her brother, then maybe she could explain it.

"Something is wrong," she said. "Over the sea."

"On Peter's island?" Cassius sat on the branch beside her. He was so close that she could feel his breath against her cheek. He reached for an overhead branch to steady himself, and an odd flutter moved through her chest at his nearness.

Cassius stared first at the island, and then at Marlene. His eyes narrowed in thought. "You feel something? Out there?"

Marlene couldn't be certain what was calling to her, but she knew, somehow, that it had to do with James. She knew that he wasn't safe.

"It's time," she finally said, the words she'd been wanting to utter since their conversation about Peter and the fairies bubbling up from deep within her. When she turned to look at him, his eyes were wide and dark and reflecting twin moons. "We have to kill Peter. Now."

Cassius did not question Marlene. He only nodded and walked with her back to camp to rally the others. The boys all got to their feet without hesitation at Cassius's orders, and they boarded their boat like troops deployed for war.

The ship moved, silent and shadowed, on a sea that was dark as ink. They sailed a longer course, avoiding the places where the moon was bright. The boys clutched their bows, ready to draw an arrow at a moment's notice.

Nobody had woken Bluejay. He was still too frail to be of much use, although he'd made tremendous strides. It was Cassius's idea to leave him. He wanted to keep him safe, like he was something tender that Cassius needed to protect, and in that small gesture, Marlene was certain that Cassius loved Bluejay as a brother. But even so, Bluejay was far more possessive of Cassius. Bluejay saw him as his entire family, someone he had to look out for, and he did seem to get quite jealous.

It didn't matter. Bluejay woke up anyway. Perhaps he sensed the silence and the emptiness of the island once the ship raised its anchor. Marlene looked back and saw him stumbling out of the forest and onto the dock. He doubled over to catch his breath, and then Marlene thought that he might dive into the water and try to swim after them.

But he didn't.

He stood, gasping, and watched as they left him behind.

22

James didn't know what the pocket watch meant. But he knew that it was important, regardless. A tiny, fragile thing that he wanted to keep safe.

The Lost Boys had their trinkets—glass bottles and copper pots and threadbare blankets—but they were nothing like this. Nothing that could keep time. Nothing that evoked whatever strange and distant emotion James felt when he held it in his palm.

After tucking the watch in the pocket of his nightshirt for safekeeping, he spent a good amount of time wandering around the island. He flew up the cliffside, stumbling uncertainly. Flying still unnerved him—even though he'd become more practiced at it—especially when there was no one around to catch him if he went crashing to the rocks below. He breathed a sigh of relief when he was again on solid ground, and then he made his way back to the encampment, but he knew that he wouldn't be able to sleep now. Something was ticking inside of him, like the cadence of the clock resting against his chest.

The sound of footsteps made him pause. A voice. A whisper.

His heart and all its ticking rhythm went still. He knew that voice.

In the next instant he was running. Without meaning to, he lifted off into flight, soaring faster than his feet could have managed.

He sensed Marlene before he saw her. A shadow in a part of the forest so dark that the moon didn't even visit. He crashed into her, and both of them went tumbling from the momentum, spilling through the dirt and the leaves with a crash.

Other footsteps followed, and James knew without looking up that they were surrounded by boys from the other island. He didn't care. He sat up, and his eyes were on Marlene. Only her.

"James!" she cried, and threw her arms around him.

He froze in bewilderment. *Now* she was happy to see him?

After she'd let go of his hand? After she'd chosen the enemy over him?

She didn't seem to notice that he wasn't returning the embrace, his arms rigid at his sides.

"What are you doing here?" he asked.

Marlene finally drew back. She took his face in her hands, turned his head one way and then the next as though inspecting him for cracks. "Are you hurt?" she asked.

He broke away from her and rose to his feet. Only then did she seem to register that the air was different between them. "I asked you what you're doing here," he demanded. "Why aren't you back on your own island?"

"James—" Marlene rose to her feet, and Cassius stepped in front of her.

"Out of the way or we'll kill you, too," Cassius said.

"Stop that." Marlene pushed him out of the way. "Don't come between us like that, do you understand? Not ever."

But Cassius had already come between them, James thought. She had already chosen his side of Never Land. And now she was back, as though her choice shouldn't make a difference to him at all.

James could only stare at her, trying to recall how many days it had been. For all he knew, years had passed since the day he'd tried to save her. The mechanical wings that he'd once pinned all his hopes on were lying in the moss and overrun with weeds now, for all the use they'd been to him.

"James." Marlene pressed forward and took his hands. "There's so much I have to tell you, but there's no time to explain now."

Her nearness flooded him with an overwhelming sense of memories he couldn't quite reach. The crackle of a fireplace. The smell of a house whose rooms he couldn't remember. A feeling like being cautious, and curious, and safe.

But if Marlene didn't see James's apprehension, Cassius did. He had been in Never Land for an eternity, and James supposed he knew a thing or two about betrayal, given what had exiled him to the other side of Never Land.

"You need to leave," James said. He didn't know whether he was talking to Cassius or to his sister. "If the fairies catch you, they'll wake Peter and he'll run you back out to sea."

Marlene flinched at the harshness in his voice. In the darkness, she stared at him as though he were a stranger. "James." Her voice was hushed. "I've come to take us back home."

Home. That word again. It hit him like a punch. James staggered back. The cicadas and the grasshoppers sang all around him. Somewhere, there was the gentle trickle of a stream. These were the sounds that lulled him to sleep on these warm summery nights. And in the morning, he would awaken when the sunlight spilled out from the horizon and warmed his skin.

These things were more familiar to him now than anything

he could remember about his life before Never Land. His life with parents or a sister or a house.

"I am home," he said.

Undeterred, Marlene reached into his pocket and grabbed the watch that had been quietly ticking a rhythm against his chest.

"Hey!" James said. "Give that back."

Marlene held it up like an accusation. "I heard this ticking from all the way across the ocean, you idiot," she said. "Can't you see that it's a sign?"

James tried to grab it back, but Marlene extended her arm and held it out of reach. She was only a hair taller than he was, but it was enough.

"A sign of *what*?" he cried, indignant.

"A sign that it's time to go home, James."

"It's only a clock," he said.

"Yes," Marlene replied. "The only clock we've ever seen in Never Land. I think we brought it here. I think it was supposed to be a reminder for us to leave when it was time."

James stared at the face of the clock, glowing white in a moonbeam. It did sound like an idea he might have had—to measure the hours. It shuddered just slightly with the force of the second hand. *Tick—tick—tick.*

"Just listen to me," Marlene said.

"We've wasted enough time on him," Cassius said. "Let's just tie him to a tree so we can get on with killing Peter."

"Killing Peter?" James said, appalled. "I won't let you." He turned on his sister. "Is this the sort of person you want to side with? A murderer?"

"You don't even like Peter," Marlene argued.

"Of course I do," James said. "He's—" James struggled to find the word. "He's my family. Peter, the Lost Boys, Sam. They took me in when I didn't have anywhere else to go. They saved me."

All of Never Land seemed to go still after he'd said it. Marlene sensed it, too. All of the things in the forest went still.

Marlene stared at James in shock, and he knew that he had hurt her.

But no—he wouldn't feel sorry for this. If he hurt her, it was only because she had hurt him first.

"What's happened to you?" she whispered.

Once again, Cassius formed a barrier between the siblings. This time, Marlene didn't stop him.

"If you don't want to help us, that means you're against us," he said.

He was taller than James, and he cut an imposing figure against the moonlight. James had the fleeting sense that he might have feared this boy if they'd met at another place, in another time. But here in this moment, all James felt was anger.

Stumbling ashore in a delirium, flying over the city only to see his mother tucking new children into bed, Marlene's letting go of his hand, the ticking of the clock—all of it flashed before him. Churning and angry like a hurricane, until he thought he would explode with it.

He screamed before he knew that he would. In the next moment, he was up—up—flying above the trees. If happy thoughts were the only way to fly, the thought of revenge filled him with some kind of twisted joy that allowed him to propel upward. "Peter! Sam! Slightly! Wake up!"

Before any of the boys could answer, the fairies did. They swam up from the thick of the leaves where they'd been sleeping, and their light filled the darkness like dancing stars.

It was so bright that James could have looked down and seen his sister's face one last time. But he flew toward the Lost Boys' encampment and didn't look back.

23

"Go!" Cassius was shoving Marlene back in the direction of the ship.

She rooted her heels in the dirt. "We can't!" she cried. "We've come all this way. This will be our only chance."

A sharp blow landed on her neck. Then another and another. Fairies clung to her arms and legs, and she swatted furiously at them. Wretched things. Loyal to a fault. They didn't have mothers or fathers to return to. They didn't know what Peter was costing all of his Lost Boys—costing James—costing her.

"I'm going after him." She wasn't sure whether she meant

her brother or Peter. In that moment, she was angry enough to murder them both.

Cassius shouted an order for his men to follow her, and Marlene was sure she heard him mutter, "You're reckless, girl. Stupidly reckless."

The fairies tore at her skin. They flew around her face, blinding her with their light. They tugged vines and branches in her path to trip her. But Cassius was right—she *was* reckless, and nobody this reckless could be bothered with a little thing like logic.

Somewhere beside her, Cassius waved his knife at the fairies. One gave a tiny cry as he sliced through her.

Marlene felt it, as if he had cut through her instead. Only in that moment did she realize the sheer enormity of what they were doing. They had gone over their plans what felt like a thousand times, but nothing could have prepared her for actually seeing the damage they were now inflicting. She had never killed anyone before—had she? She couldn't be certain.

There was a significant portion of herself—whoever she had been before Never Land—that was so far gone she didn't have enough knowledge to grieve it. Perhaps she had been a saint, or perhaps she had been a murderous criminal. The only thing she knew for certain was that she had always been a twin. James was all she'd ever had, and Never Land wanted to take him away. She couldn't let that happen.

James was flying far ahead of her now. She saw his silhouette and heard him shouting out a warning.

"You take care of Peter," she told Cassius. "I'll stop my brother."

"It isn't safe for you to go alone," Cassius said, breathing hard as he ran beside her. "All of my men are down here. They can back us up."

"None of this is safe," Marlene said. With a quick motion she grabbed one of the small fairies zooming by. The fairy let out a jingle of protest, and Marlene shook her until some pixie dust touched her skin. With the glow of the fairy's magic on her, she launched herself into the sky.

It was a wonder that she could fly. There wasn't a single happy thought in her head. Only death and blood and anger.

No, that wasn't entirely true. *Cassius.* His name floated through her like the barest note of a beautiful song.

James didn't see her coming before she barreled into him. Her arms coiled around him and she clamped her hand over his mouth. He let out an enraged roar, his breath hot against her skin.

They struggled and fought until neither of them could maintain their altitude and dropped to the hillside. James kicked and thrashed, but she pinned his arms at his sides. "Stop it!" she rasped. "You aren't thinking properly. You used to be so sensible!"

She barely recognized this boy before her now. He had

her blue eyes and her heavy black hair, but he snarled at her like a feral dog. "You can't kill him!" There was a whimper and desperation in his words, and Marlene softened. She didn't want to fight James—she wanted to protect him. That was all she had ever wanted. Why couldn't he see that? "You can't kill him!" James insisted. "You'll ruin everything!"

Peter flashed through her mind. His nearness. The way he had stared at her, as though he'd wanted to hypnotize her. As though he could make her love him.

And now he'd done the same to James. It wasn't right. He was too powerful. It wasn't fair.

Still pinning James in place with her knee, she unfurled the rope she'd fastened to her makeshift belt. It had been Cassius's idea, in case they'd needed to take prisoners. She would never have expected her prisoner to be her own brother.

James didn't make it easy. He fought her, and he spat. But however Never Land had transformed him, he still wasn't athletic or solid like Marlene, and she overtook him.

"It's for your own good," she said, as she secured the final knot around James's wrists.

Her fingers moved around the rope expertly, and for just a second, she had a fleeting sense that tying knots was familiar to her. Some distant memory of a faraway sea. The call of gulls overhead, and the smell of an open-air market selling raw fish.

She flinched as though the rope had burned her. Whatever

the memory was, James seemed to sense it, too. He'd stopped fighting, and he lay on his side, staring at her with venom in his eyes.

"I'm going to get our memories back," Marlene told him. "Whether or not you choose to trust me, I'm doing this because I love you."

She didn't stay to hear his reply. She leapt into flight and followed the sound of voices shouting through the trees.

Marlene caught up to Cassius, not because she had seen where he'd gone, but because she could sense him, the way that she had once sensed Peter. There was a peculiar warmth in her chest when Cassius was nearby. And though she could feel Peter calling to her, his presence was faint and she could push it away.

She descended in the middle of a standoff. Peter stood at one side of the clearing, flanked by his Lost Boys. Cassius and his group were at the other, all of them restrained by glowing chains of fairies.

Marlene landed at Cassius's side, her eyes trained on Peter.

"What have you done with James?" Peter asked.

Of all the things he could have asked her. "James is coming with me," Marlene said.

Peter took a step closer, and Cassius snarled. Marlene cast him a sharp glare. *Don't do anything foolish.*

"You can't take James to that island against his will," Peter said. "I won't allow it."

"I don't mean to take him back there," Marlene said. "I mean to take him home."

All of Cassius's men were restrained, but the fairies hadn't come for her. Perhaps it was because Peter hadn't commanded them to. Despite everything, he still believed that there was something in her that he could shape. But she wasn't one of his Lost Boys. Not anymore.

Peter held his hands out in supplication. "Marlene." It was the way he said her name, like a disapproving parent, that angered her. It was not Peter's fault that Never Land existed; once upon a time, he'd stumbled upon it, a lost boy himself. But since then he'd turned it into a playground of his own design. He offered magic and fairy dust and infinite tomorrows. But all of that was to cover up what he took away.

Marlene thought of all the empty gaps in her mind where memories should have been, and the hatred in her own brother's eyes.

She grabbed Cassius's knife from the ground where it had fallen, and she charged forward with a scream.

Peter's eyes widened in shock, but he didn't move. Didn't even hold up a hand to protect himself.

Maybe, just maybe—Marlene thought, in her frenzy—he didn't believe she would do it. But the murderous anger had overtaken everything, and she knew that this was the only way. His life was a lofty price, but so were her memories. So was her only chance at returning home. At getting all the boys home.

She drew back and then plunged the knife forward with all the strength she had.

It took her a moment to realize that she had only swiped at the air. Peter was no longer standing before her. He was up, high above the trees, staring down at her.

She felt the stinging at her neck. One sharp jab, then another, and another. The fairies had latched on to one another and formed a chain around her throat. Their pull tightened until she couldn't breathe.

Desperately, she clawed at them. The knife fell to the soft dirt and made no sound. Her efforts were met with stabs and burns at her fingers. She struggled, and more fairies emerged to grab her wrists, her ankles. They were endless and everywhere. The more she fought, the sharper their wrath.

Cassius was shouting something, demanding and then begging that they let her go.

Her chest burned. Her vision clouded. All she could see was Peter, his face flickering in and out of sight like a dying lantern.

She was going to be a skeleton. A name that nobody remembered. Her eyes filled with tears from the strain, but through the blur she didn't take her gaze off him. If he was going to murder her, then she would be sure that he always remembered. Her eyes would haunt him every time he tried to sleep.

And then the angry, indistinct jingles of the fairies turned into screams. Small and tinny, like the warped notes from a broken music box. Blood splattered her face, and only then did she realize that Cassius had managed to break free, that he was killing the fairies who were strangling her even as they coiled around him, too.

"That's enough!" Peter shouted.

Air rushed back into her lungs with a loud, inhuman gasp. She spilled to her hands and knees, retching, clawing at the dirt. Her muscles throbbed from the violent force of life rushing back through her body. The night returned with jarring clarity, and all around her were the tiny still-glowing limbs of the fairies Cassius had destroyed.

"Get her," someone was saying. Arms hoisted her up as though from the depths of the sea.

"You're okay." Cassius's voice was a warm low sound that eased the pain shooting through her. "I've got you. I've got you."

Dazed, Marlene stared back up at Peter. The remaining fairies circled at his feet, lighting up all the sharp angles of his face, making him strange.

"You have no idea what you've just done," Peter said, his voice eerily calm. "If you come back here, I swear on everything, you'll regret it."

24

The distant scream cut through James's chest. He struggled where he lay in a soft bed of moss, his wrists and ankles bound.

He had a horrible sense that something grave had changed with that sound.

Off in the distance, a heavy branch cracked and then fell from its tree.

James lay very still. He held his breath and strained to hear what might come next, but nothing did for a long time. And then—there was the crackle of thunder. A bolt of lightning stretched across the sky, rendering it purple and red.

James struggled to free himself of the rope, but the more he pulled, the tighter the knots became, until his skin was pinched and his muscles ached from the struggle.

"James!" someone called out just as the first droplets of rain began to fall.

"Sam!" he cried. "Sam! Over here!"

Good Sam; faithful Sam; brilliant Sam. James already felt lighter when he heard the boy's heavy footsteps crashing through the foliage.

They shouted each other's name until at last Sam emerged, gasping. "What in the world happened to you?" he asked, kneeling to inspect the ropes.

Only then—alone in the darkness and the rain—did James feel the realization that had been hiding deep within him all along.

Marlene had left him. Marlene was gone. Marlene was a traitor.

His eyes burned with tears, and as much as he tried to hold them back, they spilled out into the rain and streaked through the mud already coating his cheeks.

Sam loosened the ropes just enough to free James's wrists. "There," he said. His voice was gentle. "You're all free now."

James sat up, and they stared at each other, soaked through with rain, hair plastered to their faces.

Sam was inspecting him for wounds, but his expression

changed when he saw the look on James's face. He wouldn't find broken bones or bruises or blood, but even he could see that something had broken James.

"She's betrayed me, Sam," James croaked.

Sam nodded. "She tried to kill Peter." He stood and extended his hand to pull James to his feet. "Come on. You're all right now. Let's get you back home."

Sam threw an arm around James's shoulder. And as James stumbled through the forest in the rain with the sky growling overhead, he was confused by how weak and exhausted he felt. He was positive he wasn't carrying any injuries, and yet it was as though some vital organ had been scooped from his body.

By the time they made it back to the encampment, James had swallowed the last of his tears. If Sam had noticed them, he didn't say. They followed the firelight glowing from the mouth of the cave, and as soon as they entered, they were greeted by Peter and his Lost Boys.

Tootles ran up and hugged him. "We were worried about you!"

Slightly patted him on the back.

But James was focused on Peter, who leaned against the cave wall just beyond the fire's glow in the dancing shadows.

He was unharmed, that much was clear. But he stared at the ground before him with a scowl James had never seen before. Not the vengeful look of a boy who had just been nearly murdered for the second time, but disappointment, like a child who hadn't gotten his way.

"Peter?" James said, forcing his voice to project. He couldn't afford to be the timid mouse he used to be in his sister's shadow.

"Are you hurt?" Peter asked. Finally he looked at him.

James was stunned into silence. Peter's eyes were bleary, and James knew that he had been crying—even if he wasn't supposed to see it, he did.

"No," he finally managed. And then, "I wouldn't have gone with her. I didn't know she was going to do any of this. I couldn't make her see reason."

Reason. What a peculiar and meaningless word in Never Land.

Peter nodded, but he didn't meet James's eyes. He ventured a glance at them only once and then averted his gaze. James suspected that Peter couldn't bear how much James resembled her; it was a sentiment James understood.

Marlene had always been a bit wild, he knew. Unpredictable. But there was a core of reason and logic behind everything she plotted, and even if James didn't always understand, he had respected it. He couldn't respect that his own sister had plotted such a horrible thing.

That night, all the Lost Boys slept huddled together in the cave like puppies. James curled up in the shadows alone. He even brushed away Sam when the boy tried to sit with him.

Lying on a bed of dirt and listening to the riotous applause of the thunder and rain, it took James a while to realize that something else had changed in the midst of the night's unexpected events. He dug into his pocket and extracted the watch he'd unearthed earlier in the evening.

It had stopped ticking.

25

Marlene was furious. She paced the length of the deck as they sailed away.

Cassius grabbed her arm. She tried to tear herself away, but his grip tightened.

She wanted to fly out of this ship. Back up into the storm. Into the lightning and the rain. But whenever she tried, her body felt heavy and weak, and her frustration only grew.

When she tried again to fly after the fairies attacked her, she discovered that Peter had somehow taken that, too. He'd taken her brother. Peter had taken everything in the world that mattered.

When they reached land, Cassius guided her down the

ladder, practically carrying her most of the way. "It's done," she heard him saying over the aggressive rainfall.

She hadn't counted on the fairies being so strong, but looking back now, she saw that this was her mistake. They had always hated her. A human girl who'd captured Peter's attention and disrupted their entire way of life.

The fairies had torn through her skin. Her wrists and throat were bleeding, bruised, raw. The rain stung where it hit her injuries.

But these wounds would mend.

She let Cassius lead her back to the hut where she had been sleeping each night, keeping vigil over Bluejay.

It was empty now, half-flooded from the rains with mud on one side. Distantly, she wondered where Bluejay had gotten off to. He was much stronger now. Maybe he'd woken up and gone looking for food.

Cassius lit the hanging lantern and drew up some of the giant leaves that were stacked against the wall for bedding. "Sit," he told her.

Marlene did, but only because there was nowhere else to go. She had nothing but this moment and this space.

She could not recall ever hearing such angry rain and wind. The next clap of thunder shook her deep within her marrow.

Cassius sat across from her. His fingers probed against her neck, taking extra care with the bruises that were starting to bloom.

"I've had worse," Marlene said, and flattened her gaze. "You shot me with an arrow, remember? These are just some tiny fairy scratches."

"Those 'tiny fairies' could have killed you," Cassius fired back. "You'll do well to remember what they're capable of."

"You shouldn't have gone after them," Marlene said. "Peter will have revenge, you know. That was foolish."

When Cassius met her gaze, his eyes were dark in a way she'd never seen. "When I saw what they were doing to you, I—" His voice hitched, and Marlene watched him intently. "I don't care if Peter is in charge of Never Land or king of the damned universe. I would have burned this whole place down before I'd let anything happen to you."

His hand had moved to her cheek, and Marlene took it in her own. She ought to have argued with him, reminded him again what a powerful enemy he'd made in Peter. She should have pushed him away, called him an impulsive child, and reminded him that she couldn't stay in Never Land forever. She should have told him that she didn't need his protection in any case, and that she would have found some way to outsmart Peter before he'd taken her out.

But when she opened her mouth, all that came out was "Thank you."

"Marlene," Cassius murmured. "I—"

The next clap of thunder interrupted them and made her heart skip a beat.

Cassius drew away from her like he was waking from a dream. He frowned at the mud puddle that was spreading across the floor. "It's not safe to be up in the tree houses, but we'll spend the night up there if this thunder lets up."

"Has it ever rained like this in Never Land?" Marlene asked.

"Rarely." He positioned the lantern between them. "Look at me," he said.

She did. His cheeks were flushed, his hair heavy and clinging to his cheeks, curling at the edges.

"You have to let your brother go," he said.

Marlene balked. "I can't do that. You don't know James like I do. He's—" *Sensitive. Soft. In need of protecting.* But the James she'd just seen was none of those things. He was angry and violent. He was almost a stranger. These were the words she couldn't say. Not if she wanted to keep him safe.

She settled on "He's reasonable. I just have to remind him of that."

"I have no doubt that he's reasonable," Cassius said dryly. "It's you I've always wondered about." He grabbed her wrist, but gently, to steady her as he tended to her injuries.

Scowling, Marlene sat still.

As her temper began to subside, the rain pattered down to a gentler rhythm.

"How am I going to go home if I can't take James with me?" she asked.

"Marlene." The way Cassius said her name had always startled her. Especially now, here, alone in this hut with nothing but the wind to hear them.

She would never understand this boy. He had come to expect her to be as strong as any of his men. He tasked her with carrying heavy pails of water up the ladders so the lookouts didn't have to leave their posts to bathe and drink. He taught her to use the zip lines, and he followed her across the sea to murder the boy who held Never Land in his palms.

But then he said her name as though she were something fragile and rare and small.

She returned his stare with a sour expression.

"James won't be leaving, but neither will you," he said. "If you can't remember where you've come from, then it shouldn't matter anymore."

"What are you talking about?" Marlene said. "Of course it matters."

"It doesn't," Cassius said. "James is already home, and so are you."

He reached forward and put a hand on her shoulder. After all the violence of this night—violent fairies, violent words, violent thoughts—he was a rock in the tempest.

She held him with a curious gaze, and then she reached out and touched the damp hair that curled as it fell over one of his cheeks. It was softer than she'd expected, like feathers. Like the look in his eyes.

She brought her face closer to his, and as she did, Cassius held his hands up at his sides. He was surrendering to her. He was letting her inspect him, bring herself near to him. He was telling her that she could have him if she wanted him. She leaned forward.

His lips were rough and full and warm when she kissed him. He tasted like salt and the rain that had fallen all over them just moments earlier.

The warmth that stirred in her stomach was a curious thing. She had little memory left of the world outside of Never Land. The faces of her classmates and friends had long since blurred into senseless shapes, and Marlene was not sure if any of them had captured her interest in such a way. If any of them had touched her hand, or kissed her.

But in this moment, it didn't matter. Cassius's breath was gentle and sweet, and the sound of it filled her. His fingertips traced the slope of her cheek, and the boy who commanded a makeshift army, who shouted orders and fired weapons, was so careful with her.

"Marlene," he whispered when she drew back to look at him. Somehow, her hands had found his, their fingers tangling together. He canted his head to look at her like she was the only beautiful thing in this world of beautiful things. He opened his mouth to speak, but Marlene cut him off. She already knew what he was going to say.

"Don't," she said quietly.

"Stay in Never Land." Cassius said it anyway. "You can—"

One of the leaf panels that made up the door peeled back. Marlene turned her head, and she could just make out the outline of someone before whoever it was disappeared. Boys everywhere on this bloody island. There was no such thing as privacy.

She pulled her hands out of Cassius's, and she saw the hurt on his face when she made her own expression cold. "This isn't my home," she said. "This is just a stupid island in the middle of nowhere, and this isn't over. Not by far."

It hurt her to say the words. It hurt not to push forward and kiss him again.

But if she stayed, if she let herself forget, then all hope was lost. She and James would be trapped here forever.

Cassius didn't try to argue. Instead, he stood and turned for the exit. Suddenly he couldn't move away from her fast enough. Marlene saw his eyes for just a moment before he turned away. They were shining with fresh tears.

"I'm sorry, Marlene," he said, his back to her. "That this place isn't what you want. I wish I knew how to change it."

In the way he said her name, she knew what she had long begun to suspect. He felt the same confusing thing that she did. He could have been born a hundred years ago, or even a thousand. In Never Land, there was no way to tell. But still, here they were, suspended, forever, in this moment in time. And some part of her was grateful—the same part of her that wanted to tell him to stay, and to kiss him again. She felt a new rage toward Peter for giving her brother a reason to stay in Never Land, and for being the reason they needed to leave.

It was hours before the rain stopped. Marlene lay alone in the hut, unable to sleep, steeped in the humidity. The storm left her with an uneasy feeling. She thought of Cassius. She thought of home. She thought of what a foolish chore it was to have a heart at all.

When the door to the hut was peeled back, she reached for the lantern and held it up.

"It's just me," Bluejay said.

"Where have you been?" She lay back against her makeshift bed. "I was wondering if you'd gotten eaten by a mountain lion."

There was still a limp to his gait, but he was getting better each day. Marlene had suspected for a while that he no longer needed her to tend to him but was enjoying the company. On an island of nothing but boys, with nobody to offer him any compassion, he was soaking up every bit that he could get.

"I was hiding in a cave waiting for the rain to stop," Bluejay said. "I've never seen a storm like that. Like the whole sky was angry at us." He drew up some leaves and made a bed for himself, much closer to her than usual to avoid the flooding.

They lay in silence for a while, and then Marlene said, "Something has changed in Never Land."

From the weight of Bluejay's silence, she knew that he felt it, too.

"It's my fault, isn't it?" she said. "Me and James. We changed something by coming here."

After a pause, Bluejay said, "Not by coming here. By trying to leave. No one leaves Never Land."

Marlene listened to the crickets that had already resumed their chirping now that the air was still again. "Maybe."

"Is that what you were doing when you sailed over there?" Bluejay asked. "Trying to leave Never Land?"

"Cassius says there's no way," Marlene said. "We need to get our memories back."

"Cassius thinks he knows everything," Bluejay said, and there was an edge of bitterness to the words. "Always telling us what's best for us. *Don't sail out too far. It's your turn to be lookout.*"

Marlene looked toward him, but the lantern had gone out, and she couldn't see anything but darkness. "He really cares about his men too much, doesn't he?" Marlene said. "On Peter's island, the Lost Boys act like Peter is their king. But Cassius isn't like that. To everyone here, he's more like a parent."

From the day she had been dragged to this side of Never Land, she had been able to sense that Bluejay was Cassius's favorite. He had gone to such lengths to make sure this boy survived.

"He never goes to Peter's island." Bluejay shook his head. "But he did tonight. Because of you."

The words were quiet, but Marlene felt the accusation behind them, even though the words were said without malice. She *had* changed Never Land. These boys were capable of waking up if they wanted to. Really wanted to. At times, their oblivion frustrated her. How silly of them to flit around without a care. But other times, she envied them. She saw how easy it would be to get lost here. And it frightened her.

"I just want to go home," she said. "If James won't come with me, then—then I'll go myself. I'll remember where we came from, and then I can return and make him understand." James wasn't lost to her. He couldn't be. Somewhere in there was the logical, practical brother he'd always been; he required evidence. She would come back with something—a trinket from their house, or some memory that they'd forgotten in this place, and then he would snap out of it.

"How?" Bluejay asked.

"If I can't kill Peter, there must be another way. The ocean, maybe," she said. "I think that worked before. My brother and I were able to leave by diving into the water at first. That was how we got here to begin with."

Bluejay considered this. They had spent days sharing this tiny hut, possibly even weeks—Marlene couldn't be certain of the time. He'd proven to be the most soft-spoken on the island. He would have fared better on Peter's island, flying from the treetops, blessed by fairy dust.

But he was observant. And he was smart, which made him useful. Brute strength could only account for so much.

"I'll help you," he said. "I know a way."

26

James dreamed of a city whose windows were made of gold. Bells in the distance made the most haunting and beautiful song. A train whistled its hello as it rushed along crowded streets into bright green hillsides.

In his sleep, James found the place that he called home.

When he opened his eyes, though, he was lying in a shallow pool of mud.

The morning sun was relentless and buzzing. The air was humid and hot. His mouth felt dry as sandpaper, and there was something—what was it?—that he needed to remember.

Oh. The thought came sourly. *Marlene.*

He rolled over. The cave was empty now, with only the charred remains of a campfire to remind him that anyone else had ever been there.

As James stepped out into the daylight, the insects and birds gave softer calls, as though all of Never Land had been startled by the storm.

He heard voices in the distance. Laughter and the crackle of another campfire as the Lost Boys cooked breakfast. They had taken to James's method of catching fish.

James didn't join them. He couldn't bear the idea of company just then. He headed for his makeshift work area instead. It was a neat pile of newly chopped trees and roughly hewn tools. Partially completed projects were laid out in organized formation, dampened by rain.

The water had made the wood fragrant and heady. James breathed it in, and some frustratingly vague memory haunted him. The heft of an axe. Sawdust in his hair. *What is it? Was this something I used to do?*

"Go away," he said aloud to the memories. If they weren't going to reveal themselves in full, then he didn't want them. He didn't want the tall buildings with the golden windows, or the meddlesome sister, or the faraway idea of a mother's love.

He set about doing the only thing he ever knew to do when he felt powerless. He picked up a board, swiped away the dampened leaves, and began to work.

"I was looking for you." Sam was standing over James when he looked up. He was holding hunks of roasted trout on a stick. "I brought some breakfast."

Despite himself, James smiled at that. The trout looked awful—charred on one side, too pale on the other. But he was grateful nonetheless.

"What are you making?" Sam asked.

"A ship," James said. "That's the one thing we don't have, isn't it? It doesn't seem fair that our enemies have one."

"We don't need ships. We have pixie dust," Sam said.

"A lot of good that's done you," James said through a mouthful of trout. "You can't even fly."

This shut Sam up immediately, and James felt guilty.

"I'm sorry," James said. "It's just—if even *I* was able to do it, you certainly should be able to." Sam was skittish, yes, but he was an optimist to a fault. He surely had a hundred happy thoughts in that head of his. A thousand.

Sam looked over his shoulder. They were entirely alone in the clearing, save for the birds that were busily chattering overhead. His expression was uncharacteristically somber, and it gave James pause; he stood. "What is it?" he asked in a low voice.

"I—i-it's nothing," Sam said.

"Don't play me for a fool, Sam," James said. And then he opted for a softer approach. "You know everything about me by now. Why keep secrets?"

Sam looked at him, and in the midmorning light his eyes were determined. It was as though he'd become a different boy entirely. Making a decision, he grabbed James by the hand. "Follow me."

James did as Sam instructed, not daring to utter a single question lest he cause Sam to change his mind. Sam led him through the trees and past the waterfall that sang out a quiet song as water rushed through its boulders. They stepped over a stream and down an embankment and then to a place that was so nondescript, so ordinary, that James began to question Sam's sanity.

Sam looked over his shoulder again. It was quiet here. Even the fairies didn't bother to hover over a place so mundane and dull.

Sam knelt in the dirt and began clearing away mounds of dry leaves. James helped him, and his fingers brushed against something metal and cold. He drew back. It looked like something he had seen before—something outside of Never Land. His mind fought for a memory and gave him some distant notion of a cobblestone street flooded with a summer rain. The street had iron circles just like these.

James raised his eyes to Sam, who was gnawing on his lip. "You—you can't tell Peter. You can't tell anyone."

"What is it?" James asked.

"A manhole cover," Sam said. "I found it a long time ago. Long before you or even Slightly got here." He reached forward, and with a grunt for the effort, he pushed the manhole cover aside, revealing a narrow dark tunnel beneath it.

James's throat went dry. If there was anything he hated as much as heights, it was dark spaces. "Don't tell me you've gone down there."

"I can't explain it," Sam said. "I can only show you."

James balked. Sam. Timid, mousy Sam, who couldn't fly and had covered his ears during last night's thunderstorm, could gather enough bravado to squeeze down into that endless tunnel of dirt.

James stared at it, and his heart kicked up a frenzy. Heights, water, tiny spaces—how long was he going to let fear dictate his life? There had been a time when he'd feared being without his sister's protection, and he was managing just fine without her, wasn't he?

"I—I don't have to show you," Sam said. When he looked up, the boys locked eyes. "I've never told anyone about it before, and I—I want you to see it. But I can't force you."

"Why haven't you told the others?" James asked. "Slightly? Nibs? Cubby?"

"Because." Sam clenched a fist around the hem of his tattered shirt. "You're the first friend I've had in Never Land."

James would never admit how profoundly those words reached him. Instead, he cleared his throat and puffed out his chest. "All right, then," he said. "If you promise we won't be buried alive—lead the way."

Sam dropped into the tunnel first, scaling his way down through the darkness using roots and rocks as footholds. James studied the way down before climbing after him, slower and less sure-footed than his friend.

His throat felt tight, and his palms were slick with sweat, but he made himself move. *There's nothing to be scared of,* he told himself. *It's only Never Land.*

The tunnel seemed to stretch on forever, though James reasoned that it had been only a few seconds. At last, his feet touched the earth, and he let out a breath of relief in the damp, stale air.

"Just give me a second," Sam murmured from somewhere in the blackness. "I know I left a lantern down here somewhere."

James worked to keep himself calm, though the darkness was a vise crushing him. *Marlene isn't here to protect you anymore. You must be braver,* he told himself.

There was the click of an oil lantern, and then light entered the space—small at first, and then broader, illuminating everything around them.

The space was much larger than James had anticipated. Large enough to be a house. The walls were lined with shelves carved directly into the dirt, overtaken by roots and half-buried rocks. On those shelves were strange things. After all this time in Never Land, James had grown accustomed to the nature around him. Peter and the Lost Boys lived off the land because they had no choice. There were no cities, no shops. They didn't even sleep in proper beds.

But here—James saw an object he immediately recognized as a gramophone. It had a copper horn that connected to a small wooden box, and although James couldn't recall a single song from his life before Never Land, he still remembered that this item should play music.

He spun around to look at everything. Glass bottles; a music box upon which a tiny girl who danced—a ballerina, his mind shouted, it was a ballerina—pirouetted endlessly; worn penny loafers; a rusted pram; a threadbare umbrella.

"What is this place?" he rasped.

His eyes spotted a metal hook about the size of his hand. He picked it up, carrying its weight in his palm. His warped reflection stared back at him. Something about it sent a shiver through him.

Sam's eyes were big and nervous in the lantern's glow. In his expression, James could see that he truly hadn't trusted this place to anyone else before.

"They're memories," he said. "I find them sometimes."

"Whose memories?" James asked.

"All of ours," Sam said. His voice was hushed, as though anyone could hear them all the way down here. They were so far below the earth that even the fairies—those meddlesome things—would never think to look for them here.

"Your bedsheet." James came to the revelation as soon as

he'd said it. "The one you offered me to build my wings. That has a memory attached to it."

"Tootles has a teddy bear. Nibs has an old fisherman's hat," Sam said. "Little things like that."

"But these go deeper, don't they?" James brushed his fingertips against a rocking horse whose paint was chipped and faded down to practically nothing. He turned to Sam, a realization hitting him. "You know more than the others. It's just the way you are. That's why you can't fly."

Sam hung the lantern from a root that stretched out across the dirt ceiling.

"Not everything," he said. "But I still remember little things, like my name. N-nobody called me Sam before Never Land. It was always Samuel. Samuel Smiegel."

"Smiegel," James repeated. "That's an unusual name."

"The kids in the s-schoolyard called me Smee."

James squinted curiously. What a clever one he was, to have kept this all a secret. "Smee," he said, tasting the unfamiliar word on his tongue.

"None of the other boys have a last name. No one knows what they used to be called in the real world before they came here. I suppose that's got something to do with why they can fly and I can't."

"Because they've let go of everything," James said, understanding. "Even their names."

Sam nodded.

"And Peter doesn't know about any of this? You're certain."

Sam nodded again. "I've been collecting them forever," he said. "I find them. In—in the sand or the grass." He fidgeted anxiously with his shirt hem. "I know that Peter would destroy them if he knew. After he b-banished Cassius and those other boys to the other side of Never Land, he started to hate memories."

"Why?" James asked. The rocking horse creaked as he gave it a nudge. "They're just toys. What could be wrong with that?"

"If the Lost Boys remember where they're from, they might leave," Sam said. "Go back out there where it isn't s-safe. Grow old. Die."

A dull ache had started to form at James's left temple. The air was so stale in here.

"I remember things," Sam said. He was looking expectantly at James, as though he might lash out at him. "Lots of things. I wish I d-didn't remember some of them. But every time I try to fly—the thoughts just take over."

James placed the hook down and paced the length of the space. His fingers left a trail through the dust that coated a glass vase. Under the dull residue, there was a brilliant green glaze. The pain in his temple grew sharp, and for a bright burst of an instant, he saw a shop window on a busy sidewalk. There was a mannequin dressed in a smart burgundy dress with a ruffled hem. He was a child, clinging to someone's hand. *Come along, James,* a woman was telling him. *We're already running late.*

He drew back sharply, and the vase tipped and rocked on its ledge.

London. The city was called London.

Sam was watching him, and his expression had turned guilty. "We should go back up," he said.

"You can't turn into a scaredy-cat on me now," James said. "Not after showing me all of this." His eyes fixed on something that glinted in the lantern light. "Wait," he murmured, and paced toward it.

Sam was still as a statue now, the shadows making his face look strange. He didn't say anything as James picked up the item that had caught his attention, but the air shifted in some inexplicable way.

James gathered up the tiny gold pin. It was unclasped, its sharp point sticking out and slightly bent. The front was shaped like a sea bass with its mouth wide open, surrounded by ocean waves.

"I—" James stuttered. He brushed his fingertip across the gills, and each tiny bump embossed on its surface hit him like the beat of a drum. "I know this."

"Are you certain?" Sam asked. "There are plenty of things here that never belonged to me, but I can s-still remember something because of them. Carousels, parks, wishing wells . . ."

James held up the pin as though it were an accusation. A memory of watching the gold pin sink into the sea came back to him. "Where did you find it?"

"O-on the beach," Sam said. "I find a lot of the smaller things there."

The same place where his pocket watch had been.

A small round table in a modest kitchen. The smell of fish stew. A birthday. James clenched his fist around the pin and sucked in a breath when the object bit into his fingertip. A perfect sphere of blood appeared over the spot.

"I remember," he whispered. Not to Sam. Not even to himself. The words just came out. "The day we came here for the very first time. It was our birthday."

James closed his eyes, and once again he saw the city over which he and Peter had flown that final night. Now he knew what it had been. *London.* The word surged up in his heart along with all the great affection he felt for that place. That beautiful, busy place that smelled like rain and train steam and warm dough wafting out from bakery doors as people came and went.

The Chapman Holmes mansion block stood at the heart of it. High up in the palatial flat, James remembered pressing his face against the glass and staring down at the city below. He had been so much smaller back then. Marlene fidgeted restlessly beside him.

"Both of you behave," his mother said, turning them around to face her. "You sit here and don't touch anything."

Once she'd gone, Marlene wrinkled her nose. "Why does Mother want a job nannying some rich lady's children, anyway?"

"Quiet," James whispered, not because he wanted his mother to get the job, but because he wanted to pretend that he lived here. He had never seen wallpaper so elegant, glinting like silk in the warm lighting.

He and Marlene were dressed the part. They'd gone a month with scraps for supper so that their mother could afford James's small suit and Marlene's ruffled lavender dress. It wouldn't last. James knew that. These clothes were not for them. They were for show, and as soon as the interview was over, his mother would return them to the shop.

Marlene scratched at her lace collar irritably. "I hate this bloody place," she said.

"Stop." James grabbed her wrist. "You're going to ruin it."

"So? What do you care?"

He should have known better than to reason with her. Beautiful things were lost on Marlene. Unless they were written in the pages of one of her silly bedtime stories.

She didn't understand. Marlene had the luxury of a wild imagination that could take her anywhere. Before they fell asleep she would whisper to him in the dark about boys who lived among the animals in the wilderness, or girls who solved murders. If she didn't like their ramshackle house with its leaky roof, she could build a giant bridge in her own head that would take her anywhere.

But James had no such imagination. Sitting in London's most esteemed housing, dressed in someone else's clothes, was the first time he had ever felt that he belonged.

James emerged from the memory with a gasp, like waking from a dream.

"What did you see?" Sam asked.

James looked down at the pin. He could see his father's face through a smog. He was docking his modest fishing boat, calling for James to come and help him haul the net to the market. James remembered now that he never went out to sea with his father; he vomited whenever the waves jostled them, was terrified of falling in and drowning, and still his father had hoped to give him the family business.

"My mother hasn't replaced us," James said, slowly realizing. "Peter took me to the window and I saw her tucking children into their beds, but those were her charges." He looked at Sam, as though Sam could possibly know the sudden fury he felt. The desperation. "Marlene was right. I have to find her. We have to go home."

27

arlene stood at the base of the waterfalls, at the point where they all formed a circle that went down into endless depths.

"This is the deepest pool in Never Land," Bluejay said. "Nobody has ever been able to swim all the way to the bottom."

Marlene strained to see in the froth of all the jostling waters far below. "You can't be serious. You want me to jump down there?"

"There's something about this place," Bluejay said. "Anyone will tell you. We all hear whispers. Cassius says it's the other side. The way out of Never Land."

The water was loud and angry, and it was no mystery to

Marlene that someone might hear voices in the white noise. "It's just the water," she said.

"No." Bluejay shook his head. "If you listen long enough, you'll hear that something is out there."

Marlene was wary, but Bluejay's certainty was disarming. He was sidled up beside her, so close that their shoulders touched. In the time they'd spent together, he hadn't been the sort to make up wild stories, or even tell simple white lies. He was honest to a fault. The only one Cassius himself seemed to really trust.

"Why doesn't Cassius jump, then?" she asked. But what she was really thinking was: *Why didn't he tell me? Why did he let me try to kill Peter if he knew I could find my memories this way?*

"Because it's dangerous," Bluejay said.

"The jump?"

"Going back." He looked at her. His eyes were wide and bright, and he looked so much like a child. It made Marlene remember that Never Land was full of children. Cassius called them his men, but they would never be anything more than children, even if they lived to be a thousand years old.

"Have you ever wanted to do it?" she asked.

Bluejay shook his head. "I've been in Never Land long enough to know that there's nothing left for me out there. Whatever sort of life I had, it's long gone by now."

Long gone. Marlene turned the words over in her head. What if she found her way outside of Never Land only to discover that a hundred years had passed? What if nothing was recognizable and everyone who had ever loved her was dead?

"Cassius will be mad I told you," Bluejay said. "He might want us to get our memories back, but he also doesn't want us to remember things that might hurt us. I don't know—maybe it's better that we don't. But you're not like us, are you? You don't want to be protected."

Protected. If she stayed here and let her memories die, that was all she could ever be.

"If I survive this, I'll see you later," she said. Before she could allow herself to see reason, she jumped.

Her body shot a clean line between the waterfalls like a bullet, down and down, until she wasn't sure whether it had been a lifetime or only a single second.

And then, with a crash, she hit the water. It slapped at her skin, and her body stung from the force. A vibration that reached her bones.

It was impossibly bright—the froth of the water. And then there was nothing but darkness.

Somewhere in the depths of the water, Marlene opened her eyes and realized that she was breathing.

Dumbfounded, she held out her arms, but she couldn't see anything in the blackness. She descended gently, floating until her body broke free of the water. Her feet landed on cobblestones, slick and damp.

A sun was rising in the distance, illuminating the peculiar space with threads of gold and pink.

Marlene looked up and saw the water hovering above her like a glass sky. She had fallen through the bottom of the lake itself. She jumped and tried to swim back toward it, up into the current, but she fell just a hair short.

She spun around, curious and not quite fearful. The air felt different. It was colder. Not the cool sea breezes to which she'd grown accustomed in Never Land, but instead a bitter chill that cut through the flannel of her pajamas.

It was familiar, in that same infuriating way she could never seem to identify.

"Hello?" she called out. Her own voice echoed back.

She began to walk, and as she did, she wondered at Bluejay's motivation in sending her down here. It couldn't be that he only wanted to get rid of her for a while because he was angry with her for leaving him behind the night before, or for taking up so much of Cassius's attention since she'd arrived on the island.

Could it?

The thought hit her, and Marlene realized she had been wondering these things already. He'd acted strangely all morning. He'd made sure no one saw where they were going. What if he'd tricked her out of resentment? Out of spite?

She broke into a run. The sun was rising higher now, and the farther she went, the more the horizon materialized. She could hear seagulls, a tide turning, voices.

The North Sea.

The River Thames.

The narrow two-story house beside the fish market where her father sold his morning catch.

Her father! She remembered him now—a tall man with tired, kind eyes, so much older now than the portrait in her locket. James was named for him, expected to inherit the family fishing business, only he didn't want it. He wanted to cross the River Thames and live in London and do something with numbers.

And Mother. Her mother was displaced in this harbor town. She was distressed to have a daughter so uninterested in pretty things. She worked in the city, and she made herself look beautiful, made herself look like she belonged among her wealthy charges.

Marlene remembered. She remembered all of it. Her heart was racing when she ran up the steps and opened the door.

The house was silent. Cold. Sunlight flitted in through the cracks in the shutters. She was always the one to open them in the mornings. She would stoke the fire in the stove and get breakfast started while James slept until the last possible minute.

"Hello?" she called. Her steps slowed as she made her

way inside, frightened of disturbing such a fragile place. She might have been dreaming, after all, and she didn't want to wake herself just yet. Not until she had everything she'd come back to remember.

"Mother? Father?" No sense calling James. If he was here, she would truly know that this was a dream. He was back in Never Land, hating the thought of her, cursing all mention of her name.

She was halfway up the staircase when she heard the creak of a door. She stopped moving. Held her breath to listen.

A figure emerged from the shadows behind the banister on the landing. The house was so dark that it was barely recognizable. The figure took one step forward, and then another. A woman in her nightgown with dark, sleep-tangled hair.

They stared at each other, each trying to measure whether or not she was dreaming. They realized at the same moment that they were quite awake, and ran to close the distance between them.

"Mother!"

"Marlene," her mother gasped, and only once Marlene was in her arms did she realize that her mother was sobbing. "Marlene, Marlene. Where have you been?"

Marlene didn't answer, but that didn't seem to matter. Her mother grabbed her shoulders and held her at arm's length, inspecting her for damage as though she were a precious stone. She touched her cheek, her sand-crusted hair.

Her mother looked as though she hadn't slept for weeks. Her eyes were dulled over by grief, cheeks stained by old tears.

The sight overtook Marlene, and her legs felt rubbery and numb. After all these weeks—months, perhaps years—of not remembering where she'd come from, she felt all the homesickness hit her like a wave. She had never dared to believe her mother would miss her this much. Her mother, who hadn't wanted a second child after all the hours it had taken to push her brother out into the world. Her mother, who spent all her days caring for the children of wealthy parents in the city.

"I'm sorry," Marlene blurted, struggling not to cry. Sorry for being away so long. Sorry for dragging James into Never Land. Sorry for not realizing how much she was wanted here.

She couldn't tell Mother and Father about Never Land. They already thought that she was delirious enough.

Marlene lay in her bed, wrapped in a blanket and nursing a cup of hot cocoa. In Never Land, it had been an infinite number of days. But back home, it turned out it had only been three.

Three days had still been more than enough to work her parents into a panic. Her father was pacing the hallway, his shoes making hard sounds that filled the house with its own sort of thunder. Her mother was at the bottom of the stairs, talking with the doctor in a soft voice.

"Give her time to tell you what's happened," the doctor was saying. "Forcing it out of her will only make it worse."

The doctor had taken her temperature, appraised the bruises at her throat. He would never have believed that they'd been caused by fairies. The idea was wilder even than the stories Marlene read in the books stacked in her closet. He hadn't asked a single question, and Marlene knew what he must have been thinking. Here in the land of logic and reason, when children disappeared, they had to end up somewhere. Usually because something terrible had happened to them.

Worse still was when one twin came back and the other was still gone.

As her father paced the hallway for the hundredth time, Marlene unwound herself from the blankets and peeked around the doorframe. "Father?" she said, speaking gently so as not to startle him. She couldn't bear the sound of his footsteps anymore, each little pound boring into her guilt for having come back alone.

He stopped and looked at her. His eyes were sunken and dark, and they regarded her as though she had come back from the dead.

"Just tell me." Her father looked down the staircase to be sure his wife hadn't heard him. She hadn't, locked in rapt conversation as she was with the doctor. "Just tell me if he's alive."

It's my fault. The words spun around and around in her head, but she could never say them. It *was* her fault that James hadn't come home with her. She should have fought harder that night on Peter's island. She should have dragged him, bloody and screaming if she had to.

There was something about that place, something she could only see when she was away from its too-sweet fruit and too-bright sun. She and James had been hypnotized so slowly by all of it that they didn't realize what was happening until it was too late.

She wouldn't have known how to explain this to her parents. One could only understand if they'd been there and seen Never Land for themselves. All she could do to comfort her father now was nod.

Hope and then confusion appeared on her father's face. James would have been astonished to see how much their father loved him. Marlene could hardly wait to tell him. That fact alone would make him forgive her for this misadventure. It would make him jump down into the depths of Never Land's highest waterfalls to come back.

"I'm going to bring him home," Marlene said. "I promise."

She had found a way out of Never Land. She had done what Peter and Cassius had said was impossible. She would go back to do it all over again, and this time she would bring her brother with her.

And Cassius. The name felt so faraway and strange to her

now that she was here, surrounded by her familiar, ordinary things. Like a prince from one of her fantasy novels, only he'd been real. She could still feel the gentle way he'd tended to her bruises after the fairies tried to kill her. She could still remember their kiss, and the taste of rain.

When she returned to Never Land, she didn't know how she would tell him goodbye. She already knew she wouldn't ask him to come back with her. He couldn't abandon his soldiers. It wouldn't be fair to ask him to spend a few fleeting years with her in this ordinary world when he had the chance to spend an eternity in Never Land.

He would remember her when the others forgot. In that way, a part of her would live forever, too.

28

James climbed out of the tunnel as fast as he could, and as soon as he made it to the surface, he leapt into flight. Sam stumbled below, trailing him on foot. "Where are you going?"

"To find my sister," James said.

"Your sister!" Sam cried. "But she's on the other side of Never Land. You can't go there."

James pressed his arms to his sides, propelling himself faster.

"The fairies will s-stop you," Sam said. "Be reasonable."

"Reason—ha!" James held the pin in his fist as though his life depended on it. It very well might have. "What reason? There is no reason in Never Land."

Sam jumped, pitifully trying to grab at James's ankles to pull him back down. "You know it will never work," he said. "You'll never make it out there. Even if you make it past the fairies, Cassius and his men will shoot you down on sight."

At that, James slowed to a hover. "What do you suggest I do, then?"

Sam was huffing to catch his breath. "I—I don't know," he said. "Please come down."

James slowly glided back to the earth. He held up the pin so that Sam could see it again. "My father gave this to me for my birthday," he said. "Marlene got a dress. She hated it about as much as I hated this pin." He took a step forward, his voice low and angry. "We were spoiled, ungrateful children. That's how we got here, Sam. We thought we could find something better, and now we're trapped here, my sister and me."

Sam lowered his gaze. "So that's it, then?" he said. "You're going to find a way out and leave here forever."

"Come with us, Sam," James said. "This place was never for you. We both know it."

Sam's cheeks flushed, and he arched his shoulders timidly. "This place is all I know."

"That isn't true," James said. "You know lots of things. I've always seen that, from the very first day."

"T-truly?" Sam asked.

"Of course. You've gone along with all of my ideas, and

that says a lot," James told him. "You're clever and you have a head for numbers like I do."

"I can repair rips in clothing," Sam offered up, gaining a small surge of confidence. "And I'm good with a compass."

"There, see?" James clapped a hand on his shoulder. "And most important, you still remember. You can still go back, Sam. You don't have to stay here."

"All right." Sam gave him a wry smile. "But we'll have to come up with a logical plan to leave Never Land if that's the case."

James nodded. "First, we have to figure out a way back to Marlene."

"Maybe not," Sam said. "If you can find a way back home first, perhaps you can lure her out from there."

"How?" James asked. "She doesn't have her memories. She doesn't know where home is, or how to get there."

"*You* remember," Sam said. "And Marlene remembers you."

James turned to look at the trees. There was a peaceful thrum to all the living things here, and he would miss it. But not nearly so much as he had missed his memories. Not nearly so much as he had missed the tiny house in its harbor town that he'd spent his entire childhood longing to leave.

Dearest Mother and Father,

I wish I could explain. One day I'll do my best to try if you'll promise to do your best to believe me.

I've gone to fetch James. We'll both see you soon.

She started to write *"Sincerely,"* the way she'd been taught to always end a letter, but then thought better of it:

Love,
Marlene

By late afternoon it had begun to rain. Father and Mother were talking in soft voices in the kitchen. They thought she was asleep, and Marlene knew this was going to be her only opportunity to sneak away.

Marlene took great care when climbing down the tree outside her bedroom window. It was with extreme guilt that she left home yet again after giving her parents such a scare the first time, but it was for the best. Even if her parents did love her more than she had realized, she was only half of a set. Until James was home and safe, her own return would bring little relief to them.

The sea was angry and thrashing as the wind picked up. It seemed to know what she was planning.

Marlene ran through a crowded sidewalk, keeping her head down and her face covered by the collar of her wool coat so as not to be recognized. She found her father's rowboat, tied to the pier and bobbing on the raucous waves.

It had taken the deepest lake in Never Land for her to return home this time, and now she understood. The shallows didn't work like they once had. Perhaps Peter was angry with her, or perhaps Never Land had been so easy to reach because she and James had gone together, and Never Land had called to both of them. Maybe Never Land needed her to prove how much she wanted to leave by venturing so far below. Regardless of the reasons, she knew in her heart that if she was going to make it back to Never Land, she would have to row out to where the water was deep.

Marlene burst through the surface of the water with a gasp. The sudden calm and the cerulean blue of the rising dawn told her that she was back in Never Land. And this time, she'd brought her father's fishing boat with her. The rope was knotted securely around her wrist, her knuckles white from her grip.

She wouldn't forget where she had come from. She refused to. She hoisted herself back onto the boat; her father had taught her how to balance her own weight so that the boat wouldn't capsize when she climbed up. *You'll need to know this,* he'd said. *One day, you may be out on the water by yourself with nobody to pull you back up.*

The memories ached now, like stretching a muscle that had been lying dormant for too long. Her father was patient and quiet, and she'd come to know him especially well during their quiet mornings fishing at sea.

He'd held her forearms steady as she cast her first line. Guided her when she hooked her first fish. Taught her how to preserve and scale and cook her catch. He'd done all of this even as he'd known that she wouldn't inherit the family business, either; that one day she would leave just as James intended to.

And she knew that her mother loved her, too, even if she didn't quite know what to do with her. They were both spirited in their own ways. Her mother wanted a life in the city, and she'd found a way to attain it. When the time came, when Marlene was old enough to set out and live her own dreams, maybe then her mother would see that they weren't so different.

If Never Land made her forget, then returning home made her remember with a newer clarity. This place might have had the brightest skies and the most dazzling wonders, but as much as she could have brought herself to love Never Land, it could never love her back.

It was early dawn now; Marlene wondered how many days had passed in Never Land while she had spent only a few hours back in England. She wondered if James was still angry with her.

From where she drifted on the sea, she was equidistant to each island. The squabble all seemed so silly from here. Two faded islands, purple on the horizon, like halves of a locket torn apart.

This place should have been paradise. Peter and his Lost Boys and Cassius and his men had all the time in the universe to do whatever their hearts desired. And all they could do was fight.

I'm no better, she thought. Back in England, she never would have dreamed of killing a boy, but here in Never Land she'd wanted Peter dead if it was the only way to have what she wanted.

"It's for the best we're leaving," she told herself, and began to row toward Peter's island. She and James had never before had such ugliness between them. Their arguments dissolved by bedtime. They had to spend their days together, doing chores, eating dinner in a house that was often empty of their parents. That all reminded them that, when it came down to it, they had only each other for true, unconditional friendship.

Peter's island was quiet at its beach where she arrived. The Lost Boys would be deep in the woods this time of day, flying about, playing war games.

This time, when she found James, she wouldn't be so aggressive about bringing him home. She would start with an apology. She had already rehearsed it in her head as she'd lain in bed listening to her mother talk to the doctor in hushed tones.

I'm sorry that I brought you to Never Land, she was going

to say. *And I'm sorry that I wasn't content with our existence back home. No more adventures for us, no more wishing my life was like the pages in one of my books. Mother and Father love us, and we belong to them.*

The words were smoothed over in her head now, like a stone polished by a hundred years of tides.

This was a nice place to visit, but we really must be leaving.

She would be kind but firm. This time, James would listen to her.

She dragged her boat ashore, bringing it far inland so that the rising tides wouldn't steal it away, and then she trudged up the dune, toward the distant sounds of laughter deep in the trees.

Peter swooped down before her, as though he had manifested from the air itself. His hands were on his hips. His eyes—round and boyish—were stern.

Marlene's throat went dry. She had expected to run into him but had hoped that she would have found her brother first.

"I told you not to come back here," Peter said.

Anger swelled within her at that. How arrogant of him to think Marlene's return had anything to do with him or his dominion. She wanted none of it. She only wanted to leave with the one thing she'd brought here in the first place.

"I've come back for James," she said. "You can't keep him from me."

Peter raised a brow. "I don't have to," he said. "James has made his choice."

"James is a confused, scared child, and he's forgotten who he is," Marlene said. The same went for herself, which was why she could manage this with such certainty.

"But you remember." Mustering up her bravado, she poked a finger hard against Peter's chest, sending him back a step. "You know exactly who he is. You're the one who convinced him that our parents don't love us."

"I'm not the one who brought him here!" Peter advanced, forcing Marlene backward in an angry dance. "That was *you*, Marlene. *You* wanted something better. *You* brought him here because *you* needed *me*!"

They were face to face now, so close that Marlene could feel the heat and the anger radiating through his skin.

Who was he? This boy. Peter knew everyone's story. He made sure all his Lost Boys were just that—lost. Adrift, without any place but Never Land to call home. He told himself—and the boys—that he was protecting them, and maybe some part of him truly believed that, but Marlene saw through it now. He was protecting himself. So long as Never Land was full of laughter and cheery voices, Peter could hide in it forever.

"I dreamed of running away," she admitted, clenching her fists at her sides, stiffening her posture. "Isn't that what all children do? It was a whim. A fleeting, silly little whim, and thanks to you I'll regret it for the rest of my life."

"The rest of your life." Peter sneered. His laugh was cruel and sour and ugly.

Marlene wavered then. Her outrage replaced by surprise, then fear. Marlene could see that Peter didn't realize himself what he was going to do until he was already advancing on her. All at once he'd made some kind of a decision. *How dare you?* She could hear his silent raging at her: *I've given you everything—everything—and you've thrown it back in my face.*

"James!" Marlene screamed for her brother. He must have been nearby. He needed her, after all, and he made sure that she was always in his line of sight when they were back home.

But they weren't home. And there was no one to answer, not even the fairies.

Peter's hands dug into her shoulders as he shoved her down onto her back. She kicked, screamed again for her brother. She gathered up a fistful of sand and threw it in Peter's face.

"You could have lived forever," Peter growled. Dimly, she registered a note of sadness in his voice. Of confusion. "I offered you forever."

When Marlene opened her mouth again to scream, it flooded with water. Somehow they'd struggled their way down the shoreline and he was holding her just below the surface, just inches from the air her body was desperate for.

She fought him, and for one glorious second she broke through the surface and gasped and spluttered. But then she was under again. James would come. The Lost Boys would come. The fairies hated her, but not the Lost Boys.

She looked for them through the crystal clear surface of the sea. But all she saw was Peter, and the fire in his gaze.

29

Cassius hadn't slept. He'd paced the length of his island twice already, his mind a fury of thoughts spinning too fast for him to catch.

"Something is wrong," he finally allowed himself to admit aloud. The sun was starting to rise, and Marlene was nowhere. Peter had done something—lured her over there and locked her in a bloody cage. Who knew what. He had to assemble his men. He had to go over there and find her.

Bluejay hung back several paces, worrying the hem of his shirt. He was sick with guilt, which he hadn't anticipated. The girl had been kind to him, but she'd proved to be too much of a distraction. Nothing good could come of Cassius letting his guard down.

"Cassius?" He finally dared to speak.

Cassius spun on his heels. "Where the hell did you come from?" he demanded, causing Bluejay to shrink back. "Don't come out of nowhere like that."

"I just—maybe you should rest," Bluejay ventured. He cleared his throat and tried to sound less like a timid little mouse. "You haven't eaten all day. You should keep your strength—"

"Where could she have gone?" Cassius interrupted as though he hadn't heard a word. "She can't fly anymore, Peter made sure of that. Besides, I've got lookouts on every side of this rock, and nobody saw a thing." His eyes flashed with a beam of moonlight as he stepped closer. "You don't suppose she fell down a ravine? No—" He shook his head. "She's too smart for that. Get a crew together. We have to go and search for her. Peter is behind this, I just know it."

Bluejay had never seen Cassius like this. All because of a girl. A stupid, meddlesome girl who had only been here for a little while but had already hoarded all his attention.

The bitterness swelled in his stomach, and Bluejay hated himself for it. He had known that if he showed Marlene a way out, she wouldn't want to come back. She came from some-place nice, he could tell. Someplace with hot meals and a warm bed and someone to tell her nice things before she fell asleep. That's why she wanted to remember.

What he hadn't anticipated was how Cassius would latch on to her. Or how much Bluejay had come to like her himself.

"I think—maybe . . ." Bluejay lost his nerve. "Sir, would it be so terrible if she just went home?"

"She couldn't have done that," Cassius fired back. "She doesn't know the way."

The air went silent between them. So silent that they could hear the breeze rolling through the trees. And after that, the faraway rush of the waterfalls.

Cassius turned in the direction of the falls, even though they weren't visible from here. The realization was palpable. Bluejay felt a knot forming in his throat.

Slowly, Cassius turned his head to look at him. "What did you do?" His voice was a low rasp.

Bluejay took a step backward, but Cassius grasped his shirt and dragged him forward with so much force that Bluejay's feet left the ground. He whimpered.

"What did you do!" Cassius roared.

But Bluejay couldn't speak. He had no answer. All the reasons that had made so much sense to him just a moment ago—reasons that felt full and just and even kind—faded away to ash. All that remained was the ugly core of a truth, which was that he was jealous. Cassius was a brother to him. A best friend. He didn't want Never Land to have Marlene if it meant things would change. Besides which, Marlene had her own brother, her own family. Who was she to take his?

Cassius shook him by the collar again, and Bluejay whimpered a timid "I'm s-sorry, sir." And he was sorry to see his best friend's heart so broken, but not for the rest of it. This was for the best, and one day Cassius would see.

Cassius opened his mouth to speak, but when a scream echoed across the skies of Never Land itself, the sound hadn't come from him. Short and sharp, it stung the air like a blade.

James awoke with a gasp. Something had torn through his chest. He'd felt the rip of his skin. Felt the warmth of his own blood spilling out.

He bolted upright, clutching at his shirt. It was soaked through, but as he came to his senses, he realized that it was sweat that had dampened the flannel, not blood.

Frantic, he patted down his arms, his abdomen, trying to find the source of that unbearable pain. But the more he came to consciousness, the more the pain subsided, until he slowly realized that it had been some sort of dream. It had been only a day since Sam showed him his grotto of memories, and nothing had felt quite real ever since.

"Sam," he whispered. "Sam, did you hear that scream?"

Sam was asleep beside him, hugging his tattered and treasured blanket. He mumbled and turned away.

Something was wrong, James thought. The air was heavy and hot, the way the weather turned before a tornado appeared on the horizon.

He rose to his feet, tiptoeing around the bodies of the Lost Boys, none of whom seemed bothered by this inexplicable change.

There was an old memory somewhere deep in his mind, blurred and fading at the edges. The memory of waking up in an empty house. Of cold rooms and a barren fireplace. It wasn't unusual for his parents to be gone all day, but Marlene was always awake before he was. She always lit the stove and boiled the water for the tea.

Even here in Never Land, which was filled with Lost Boys and fairies and more magic than the stars themselves could hold, he remembered that much. He missed it.

When he made it to the beach, he saw the rowboat in the moonlight, dragged ashore and half-buried by sand and seaweed.

There on the side, in chipped yellow paint, was the same emblem as the gold pin he'd fastened to his flannel shirt. He recognized the vessel. His father's fishing boat. How on earth would it have gotten here?

Marlene. Never Land always called to her so strongly,

much more strongly than it had ever called to him. Perhaps Never Land had been so eager to reclaim her that it had sucked her back onto its shores, fishing boat and all.

"James!"

At the sound of her scream, James's head snapped upward to where Marlene was flying overhead. No, not flying. Dangling like a spider ensnared in someone else's web. Her figure lurched forward, and Peter emerged from the shadows of the overhead trees. He held Marlene in a vise grip.

"What are you doing?" James cried. "Let her down!" It was clear from Marlene's struggling that she had lost her ability to fly. There wasn't a fairy in sight to give her the dust she'd need, and they hated her besides.

"Peter!" Marlene screamed. "He's trying to take me to the volcano—he's going to throw me in!"

Frantic, James stumbled across the shore to where Peter and his sister hovered. As he did so, the sky began to darken even as the sun rose. Clouds obstructed the sky, and a single drop of rain fell on his nose.

Peter had a wild look in his eyes. He was the coming storm itself. An otherworldly rage that could exist only in a place so full of magic. "She's a traitor," Peter roared. "She's a threat."

"She's my sister," James cried.

Marlene grasped Peter's wrist and began attempting to climb his arm like a rope. Grunting, she clamped her hand over his face, blocking his vision. He dipped low, flailing at her, and when they were close enough to the ground, James grabbed his sister by the hem of her nightgown and pulled.

She was the subject of a violent game of tug-of-war, clawing and scratching at Peter's face even as he spat and vowed to kill her.

With a hard yank, James tore his sister free of Peter's grasp, and she and he went tumbling backward onto the sand.

"You wretched, awful girl," Peter cried, advancing on her.

Marlene was already picking herself up, but for once, James was faster. He leapt to his feet, his arms outstretched. "Enough!" he said, though his own anger was nothing in the face of Peter's almighty hatred.

Marlene was behind him, gasping to catch her breath, for once too frightened to fire off a retort that would only make their situation worse.

James put more distance between Peter and Marlene by taking a step forward, his arms still outstretched, palms open. "Nobody is throwing anyone into a volcano," he said. "Nobody dies in Never Land, isn't that the rule?"

"Half of my bloody fairies are dead," Peter growled. "That night your sister came to my island and tied you up, she came to kill me. Didn't she tell you that?"

Marlene started to speak, but James shot her a glare and she thought better of it.

"She's not here to create more trouble," James said. "Neither of us ever was." He knew his sister, and in that moment, he understood her more than he ever had. To Peter, she was unpredictable and even feral, which was how their mother and instructors sometimes saw her.

But James knew. She was just looking for a place where she could belong, where she didn't have to dull her shine in order to be accepted. He only wished he'd said this to her much sooner, before they came to this place. Maybe then she wouldn't have needed so badly to fit in.

"She's here to destroy everything," Peter said. "To tear apart everything I've built, to take my Lost Boys away. Do you know what that world would do to them? It would destroy them. They couldn't handle all the heartache they'd find there. I have to keep them safe. Safe from the world and safe from her."

Marlene spat a mouthful of blood in the sand, and that was when James noticed how bruised and scratched both she and Peter were from their fight. "No, I'm not," she said, still breathing hard. "I've just come to take my brother home."

"He is home," Peter said.

"This isn't my home." James squared his shoulders. "Marlene is right. We don't belong here." Even without turning to look, he knew his sister smiled at that.

Up at the top of the sand dune, James saw Sam looking at him with such sadness. Sam was smarter than anyone in this place gave him credit for. Brilliant, even. He knew things he was too kind to say. He carried the burden of all of those memories in his grotto. *I'm sorry, Sam,* James thought. Sorry he couldn't stay, and that Sam might never find another friend who understood him so.

Peter took a step toward James, his face a conflicted mess of emotions. It was unlike him to be so caught off guard, but Marlene's presence had clearly rattled him. "You don't know how hard I've worked to keep Never Land safe," he said. And for one hypnotic, startling moment, James *did* know. It was as though Peter was projecting his memories into James's mind, memories long kept hidden away pouring out for the first time.

James saw Peter as a lonely, timid boy in a London townhouse, his wealthy parents neglecting him, scolding him, telling him that he would need to grow up and make something of himself and that he must not be too loud, must not waste his time being silly and playing with the other boys. The sadness was overwhelming. The misery of it. But then, late one night, there was a light at his bedroom window. Tinker Bell, who had felt his distress and come to save him.

In a flash, next James saw Marlene touching Peter's hand as they sat in a great tree high above the water, sensed the overwhelming love he felt for her. Through Peter's eyes, Marlene was a friend, unlike any he'd had before. He felt a love for Marlene that she could never have returned, because she was not like him. She was not alone in the world the way that he had been.

All that love turned into a jealous hatred now, and James took a step back. He shielded his sister and whispered for her to get the boat.

"I can't let her leave now," Peter said. "She's too dangerous." He spoke the words calmly, and behind him, a bolt of lightning flashed.

As though they had been summoned, dozens and dozens of fairies emerged from the forest and surrounded them. Some delivered a bow and quiver of brightly fletched arrows to Peter.

"James," Marlene whimpered. For once, she was the frightened one. They stood back to back, and she scrabbled for his hand as the fairies made a rope around her.

At first, James thought the fairies meant to tie him and his sister together and hold them captive, but, too late, he realized that they were only taking Marlene. The glowing vines coiled around her wrists, her waist, her throat.

"Marlene!" He clung to her hand as she was tugged skyward. He tried to make himself heavier, to drop all of his weight to his feet so that he could act as a human anchor. The wild terror in her eyes was unlike anything he'd ever seen, and he knew that if he let her go, if he failed her, she'd be gone forever.

"Let go," Peter ordered him, but James did not, even as the fairies shrieked and poked and pinched him. Even as he bled. Even as his feet dragged inches above the ground. He tried to fly, but couldn't; it wouldn't have surprised him if this was somehow Peter's doing, as the fairies always bent to his whims.

"Let go," Peter said again. "In a few days you'll forget all about her. It's happened before, hasn't it? Once she's gone from your mind, you'll feel much better. Never Land can be everything you've ever wanted."

"I don't want bloody Never Land," James said through gritted teeth. "I want to go home!"

Home. Home. Home. The word echoed across the sky, and the rain began to pour.

A figure came barreling down the dune, bull-rushing Peter and taking him by surprise.

"Sam?" Peter rasped.

Docile, sweet, obedient Sam was fighting for the first time in his entire life.

"L-let them go," Sam cried, and his voice was heavy with tears. "They don't want to be here. Let them go."

A moment later, Sam was beside James, prying at the fairies that were binding Marlene. Despite everything, he was gentle with them, mindful not to cause them harm even as he fought them off.

Marlene was less gentle, swatting, snarling, and fighting for her life. Peter wouldn't *really* kill her, James tried to tell himself. Surely he wouldn't. But his sister's fear told him that this was real and that she'd finally gotten herself into true danger.

James didn't dare release his grip on Marlene's hand, his knuckles white with strain, his heels leaving tracks in the sand as he was dragged. "James!" There were tears in her eyes. "James, don't let them take me."

Later, he would be cross with her. Not for making the birthday wish that led them here—he understood that—but for finding a way out of Never Land and coming back to rescue him. Why had she returned when she had been safe at home with their parents? Why had she risked her life to retrieve him after he'd been so horrible to her? She should have let him go. It was what he'd deserved.

An arm clamped around James's waist. Peter held him with unnatural strength, and glittering fairy dust rustled and fell from his skin. The fairies dragged Marlene in one direction, and Peter tugged James in another.

Marlene's hand slipped from his, and all around them the storm turned violent, their screams lost in an enraged roar of thunder. James struggled in Peter's iron grip, elbowing him, kicking, grunting even as he exhausted himself.

It was no use. Marlene was being carried up and ever farther away, toward a volcano that James had never paid much mind to. It blended so seamlessly with the purpled mountains in the distance.

His heart sank. Marlene was going to die, and she was going to die alone, so far from the rest of Never Land that no one would even hear her scream.

A flaming arrow shot across the sky with a sudden *whoosh!* It landed in a tree at the edge of the shoreline, right where the forest began. Cassius stood tall at the bow of his ship as it emerged on the horizon. He shot another arrow with sharp precision, and it landed in the same tree, setting it ablaze despite the rain. "Release her," he shouted, and even from where he stood, James could see the hatred in the boy's eyes. "Or I swear on everything, I'll burn this whole place to the ground and then I'll kill whatever's left."

The fairies wavered, though Peter's vise grip on James didn't. Marlene dangled high above the sea now, still fighting, trying to pry their glowing vines from her arms only for another one to coil around her throat.

"Go back to your miserable little island," Peter shouted back. "Take your boys with you. This doesn't concern you."

"Marlene is one of us," Cassius said. Beside him, Bluejay was striking the flint and lighting a spark for a fresh arrow. "And the girl's brother," Cassius said. "He's with us, too."

"Let them go," Sam told Peter. Tears stained his cheeks, but to his credit, he didn't waver, didn't even move a hand to wipe them away. "You know it's the right thing to do."

James felt the shock roiling off Peter. The loss and betrayal. James stopped fighting when he felt Peter's grip loosen, and James turned to face him.

"Why can't you just listen?" Peter asked. "I could make

it so easy. You know that your sister is dangerous. She'll ruin everything."

"She won't," James said. "We just want to go home." But even as he said it, he couldn't be certain that it was the truth. He'd never been able to control his sister, and he'd never wanted to. Even as her energy exasperated him, even as he scolded her for always being in a hurry and for acting so impulsively, the truth was that he wouldn't change a thing about her.

Peter couldn't possibly understand, and so James didn't try to explain. Peter had his own idea of perfect, and he couldn't fathom that anyone might want something different.

"It won't hurt for very long," Peter said. "You'll forget her. You'll stop missing her. You all will."

Marlene had stopped screaming for help. In the corner of his vision, James saw her squaring her shoulders, bracing herself to take whatever Peter threw at her with that foolish pride of hers. And in this, James could see why Peter had loved her, and why Marlene could never love him back.

Another arrow shot past them. The Lost Boys were gathering at the forest's edge to put out the fire, but even with the rain, it was spreading quickly. They called to Peter, asking what was going on and imploring the fairies for help, but Peter ignored them, his expression pained. He didn't even regard Sam. He stared at James, only James.

"Maybe I will forget," James said. "But I'll remember again. It's already happened once. Never Land is strong, but some things are stronger."

A flash of lightning blazed behind Peter as though he were controlling it. Maybe he was. If Never Land had a consciousness, it surely favored him. The fairies and the magic and the eternity of this place were his—he commanded it all. James and Marlene were just two children who had not been as lost as they'd seemed, and letting them go was such a small price for Peter to pay.

Finally, after a long, tense pause, Peter looked to the fairies and nodded for them to let go.

30

Marlene fell faster than she could scream. Her body hit the water hard, stunning her, knocking the air from her chest.

The blue was so endless and dark that she thought she'd fallen straight through Never Land once more, and that she would emerge in the waters of her sleepy port town. She thought—dazed as she was—that this all had been a dream. She would wake up an hour before her brother, the way she always did, and she would get dressed and go downstairs to stoke the fire. When James came downstairs to join her, she would tell him about this strange dream she'd had.

But her lungs burned, and she understood that she would die if she couldn't get herself to the surface. *Don't panic.* Her body found its buoyancy and she allowed herself to float until at last she broke through the surface with a gasp.

Her lungs and nostrils were filled with the overpowering stench of kelp and brine, but beyond that, she could smell that Never Land was burning. Cassius's arrows had taken, and even in the storm the forest was on fire.

James was swimming toward her, his arms moving in broad, sweeping strokes. She wanted to tell him to turn back; he wasn't a strong enough swimmer, and the sea had turned choppy as the storm picked up. But her lungs still burned and water filled her mouth as a wave crashed into her.

It wasn't safe to swim back to shore where Peter was. Not for either of them.

"Marlene!"

Cassius tossed her a ring tied to a rope, and she clung to it gratefully. "We have to get James," she managed to cough out as he reeled her in. Once she was close enough, he grabbed her by the arms and hoisted her the rest of the way. She was shaking, and not from the cold wind that blew the wet hair from her face.

Cassius touched her shoulders, the sides of her neck, inspecting her. "You're okay?" he asked. "They didn't hurt you?"

She shook her head, even as he wiped a bit of blood from

her cheek. "The bastards were stabbing me all over," she said. "But James—"

"He's coming," Bluejay called from the stern pulpit. "I'm moving us to meet him halfway, but we can't get too close."

Marlene ran to the bow, grasping the wooden railing and leaning over the edge. "James!"

He was still afloat, miraculously, and making his way. But he looked so small out there, with so much distance still between himself and the ship.

One of the boys tossed him the life ring, and only when Marlene saw James grasp it did her muscles relax.

She turned to Cassius, just as soaked as she was from the rain. She took his face in her hands, and in that moment they both understood that this was goodbye. The storm would settle. She would return to her world. He would stay in his. And in many years, she would grow old, turn frail and unrecognizable, her hair all white, but he wouldn't have aged a day.

"I won't forget," she said. Her words were nearly lost in the squall, but the heartache in his face told her that he'd heard them.

He wrapped her wet hair around his hand. With the water to weigh it down, it was longer, the curls all flattened out. "I won't, either," he told her.

She pushed forward to kiss him, and she knew that it was selfish of her. She should have said something practical, or something cruel that would make him miss her less, that would make him want to forget her. But when his lips touched hers and his arms went around her back, she sighed in relief. In gratitude that he was here and he was real.

When he pulled away from her, there was a sudden pain. She looked at him, not understanding. The warmth was gone from his eyes, and they had gone wide with a terror that frightened her and made the pain in her chest bloom into something that paralyzed her. There was shouting, suddenly, and torrential rain, but none of it made sense. She didn't understand even as she looked down and saw Peter's arrow sticking out of her stomach.

"No." That was the word Cassius was saying, over and over. "No, no." He caught her when she fell, both of them sliding to the ground.

She tried to speak, but her mouth tasted of blood and she couldn't catch her breath. James was lunging over the edge of the ship, but it was as though he were miles away. He was shouting orders—to whom, Marlene didn't know. Cassius, the other boys. "Snap off the arrow's head," he was saying. "Get the shaft. Plug the wound." James, ever practical, would know what to do. He would be able to explain why Peter had done this. Later, when all of this was behind them.

"Marlene." Cassius was holding her in his lap. He was covered in blood, and Marlene couldn't make herself understand where all of it was coming from. "Marlene, look at me. Look at my eyes." She wanted to. How to tell him that? Her lips wouldn't move, her body wouldn't respond. He took her chin in his hand. "Marlene." His voice grew softer each time he said it, like he was floating away.

More clouds gathered overhead, black and opaque, until all of Never Land went black. It swallowed all sight, all sound, until she could only hear someone calling her name, far and small and fading like a bird being swallowed by the sky.

A thousand yards east, a bolt of lightning struck down and split Peter's favorite tree clean down the middle. Peter felt it from where he crouched in the sand with his head in his hands, his eyes filled with tears.

31

By the time the ship reached Cassius's island, Marlene had gone still. James knew this, in some practical part of himself, but he ignored reason. He screamed for the boys to tear scraps from their shirts to stop her bleeding, to stop gaping and move. Marlene could not be dead. He wouldn't entertain the idea, and so he could keep it away from them.

Her chest didn't rise and fall. When he pressed for a pulse, all he felt was the unnatural coldness of her skin.

But it wasn't until Cassius said, "James," in that ugly, sobering way that it hit him.

He shook his head. "We can save her." His voice was too

high, his words too fast. "We—we just need pixie dust, or—or that waterfall of yours. If I could get her back home—"

The storm had settled, and as the boys docked the ship, the sun emerged from the clouds. The sudden brightness was wretched. It was worse than the storm that had nearly drowned him when he swam from the island. There couldn't be a day without his twin.

Logic, that thing that had always comforted him, was his enemy now. James hated it. He stared at Marlene's too-pale face, her eyes that weren't quite closed all the way, the old blood that had trailed from the sides of her mouth.

Cassius was kneeling beside her, and he fell forward onto his hands, his head bowed. He was shaking.

Marlene wasn't here. She wasn't anywhere, James realized. He'd been too late. He'd failed. This knowledge was worse than forgetting.

James said nothing. If he opened his mouth, he knew that he would start screaming and that he would never be able to stop. Now was not the time to weep, to kneel and lay a pretty row of stones as Cassius was doing. He had to keep his wits about him so that he could plan his revenge, because even if it took the rest of his life, he would kill Peter for this.

They did not give Marlene's body to the waterfall like the others who had died in Never Land. Becoming a nameless skeleton had been her worst fear.

They buried her at the highest peak of the island, at a spot that had a view of Never Land from all sides. They laid her in the dirt and then covered her with it. Bluejay had the idea to throw down flower seeds so that something would grow to mark the spot.

Later that morning, Sam arrived. For a moment, James forgot his grief to stare in wonder as his friend's silhouette flew clumsily for the island. He had never flown unaided before that James knew of, and he took great dips and flapped his way comically back up like a wounded seagull. But he made it close enough that Cassius's lookouts nocked their arrows.

"Don't shoot him, you idiots," James said. "Can't you see he couldn't hurt an ant if he tried?"

The lookouts paid no mind to James and instead turned their attention to Cassius. He was alone in a tree beside their post, in the spot where he'd spent the night staring blankly at the water. He raised his head now, blinking dazedly. "Lower your weapons. That boy's all right."

As soon as Sam landed, he threw his arms around James in an emotional display that made James go rigid. He had vowed not to waste his time now on feelings. He had a lot of thinking and planning to do.

Still, something within him trembled and he wanted to cry.

He shoved Sam away from him, ignoring the hurt on his friend's face. "I thought you couldn't fly."

"I'd never found a thought that made me happy enough, I guess," Sam said, in that bumbling, uncertain way that made him appear so much weaker than he was. "I remember too many things."

"What's to be happy about?" James snapped. "Now, of all times, you're just thrilled to bits?"

"N-no," Sam said, holding his hands up in supplication. "There's pixie dust everywhere from all the magic they used to put out the fire yesterday. So much of it." He shook out his hair, and bits of glitter fell away and dissolved before they landed. "And I just—I thought of you, and how I didn't want you to be alone, and next thing I knew I was in the air."

James had vowed to make himself unreachable. He needed a heart that was as steely and ice-cold as Marlene's body below the earth. But Sam's words reached him anyway, and he turned away so that no one would see the pained look on his face. Curse Sam and his gentle soul. Curse this place and all its beauty. Curse the arrow that shot Marlene through. All of it had ruined him.

Sam waited patiently, and after a few seconds, he put a hand on James's shoulder. "I know you want revenge," he said.

"You can't talk me out of it." James's voice was tight.

"No," Sam said. He hesitated. "Marlene shouldn't have tried to kill him. She—"

"She thought it was the only way to get me back," James said, pushing down the wave of anger that Sam's words prompted.

"I know." There was no judgment in Sam's words. He took a deep breath. "Peter always tried to do what was best for us. I knew he wasn't perfect, but I thought—I thought he meant well. I even thought Marlene had changed him, provoked him." Before James could start shouting at him, he added, "But she didn't. Marlene just showed us what was always there. That he has too much power."

Traitorous tears filled James's eyes and he squeezed them shut as Never Land blurred. Would his sister's name ever stop hurting?

"He needs to be stopped." The pain was plain in Sam's voice. "I know you want to stop him. You want to make sure this never happens again. I want to help."

James shook his head. "You're too weak," he said, but this wasn't the truth. Sam could be a valuable ally, but James didn't want to put him in danger anymore. "Go on back home."

Before Sam could object, James broke into a run. He ignored Sam calling after him, and the gentle song of morning birds who cared nothing for his sadness. He ran until he thought he was lost, but then he heard the rushing of the waterfall and realized he had been coming here to this place that frightened him when he first arrived. He'd been a silly child then, afraid of some water.

It didn't scare him now. He'd spent his whole life being afraid of trivial problems like beestings, having his abacus broken by a schoolyard bully, being late, or having to live out his father's dreams for him. But all the while he'd never entertained the worst thing that could have happened to him. He couldn't have braced for it.

He fell to his knees and let out a feral, ravaged scream. The tears were too heavy behind his eyes, and he didn't realize they'd come until he felt them falling onto the backs of his hands.

"I'll kill you," he rasped, a promise. "I hate you. I'll kill you."

It was a long time before James heard the footsteps approaching up the trail, snapping twigs as they went. By then, James had finished his weeping, and he was exhausted. He sat at the edge of the cliff with his feet dangling below him. "What do you want?" He shielded his eyes to look up at Bluejay, who was standing over him.

"I can help you," Bluejay said, taking a step forward. His chin was canted in that cocky way he'd had before James stabbed him, but he seemed subdued somehow, like something was eating away at him. He'd been Marlene's friend; James had been distantly aware of that. Even if Bluejay hated him, maybe that friendship was enough for him to forgive James for stabbing him. "I showed Marlene how to leave Never Land, and I can show you, too."

"Why would I leave?" James asked.

"Because you want revenge," Cassius said, appearing behind Bluejay with a bleary-eyed Sam. "And if you stay here, you'll forget her."

James opened his mouth to argue, to be angry at Cassius for suggesting such a horrible thing. But he knew that he was right. He had already forgotten his sister once. He'd forgotten the entire life he'd had before coming here.

He studied the other boys. The sadness in Sam's eyes confused James, but the heartbreak written all over Cassius's face nearly broke his own heart anew. It had not occurred to him that he was not alone in his grief. He wasn't the only one who missed her and had been robbed of a thousand happier tomorrows.

"How do I get back?" he asked Bluejay.

Bluejay nodded his head toward the woods. The four of them headed through the forest down to the pool of water where the waterfalls all converged. "You have to take a running jump, make your body straight, and shoot through the water like a torpedo. That's how your sister did it."

Of course she had. It was exactly the sort of dangerous, foolish thing she'd attempt. But as James stared down into the endless depths, he wasn't scared of hurting himself, or of drowning. He was scared to face his parents and to tell them that Marlene was gone. Maybe he wouldn't, he thought. Maybe he would run away while he formulated his revenge, and let them think their children might both be alive. Better to worry and have hope than to know the truth.

"You'll come with me?" he asked Cassius.

"I can't leave my crew; I'm all they have," Cassius said. "But I'll remember her. I swear it. And when you come back, whether it's in a thousand years or just a day, you'll have an ally in me. I'll lend you my ship, my soldiers, anything you need. You'll always have a friend on this side of Never Land."

Sam stepped forward. "I'll go with you," he said.

"I don't know how long I'll be gone," James told him. "A week or twenty years. However long it takes for me to come up with a plan." He wanted to stay here. He wanted to work with Cassius and have his soldiers and his resources at his disposal, but he knew that Marlene would begin to fade no matter how much he tried to hold on to her.

He stood, meeting Sam's eyes. "When we return, it could be as grown men."

Sam didn't waver. He stepped forward, the spray from the waterfalls splashing onto his boyish cheeks.

"Come on, then," James sighed. "Looks like I'll be stuck

with you." He was grateful that Sam saw right through his meanness, saw that he was thankful to not be all alone in this world.

James and Sam trudged a few paces back to give themselves a running start. "This isn't goodbye," he told Cassius and Bluejay. "I'll be back. Count on it."

Cassius saluted in that effortless and yet confident way that must have drawn Marlene to him. They were so very much alike.

James ran for the waterfalls with Sam at his side. A cloud moved away from the sun, making Never Land bright and wild and full of sharp-edged flowers. And then James jumped, and left it all behind.

Love the Dark Ascension series? Turn the page for a sneak
peek of Jafar's thrilling origin story in . . .

DISNEP

A DARK ASCENSION NOVEL

The Wishless Ones

#1 *New York Times* best-selling author

HAFSAH FAIZAL

DISNEP **PRESS**

LOS ANGELES · NEW YORK

1

– Before –

JAFAR

There were days when Jafar thought his wishes would destroy him. He might have been only eight years of age, but he knew in his heart of hearts that he was destined for more.

And yet today, he was zigzagging through the bustling bazaar, a sack of fresh vegetables clutched in one hand, his little brother's fist sticky in the other. Shouts from angry merchants nipped at their heels because they hadn't brought a single coin in their tattered pockets. But this was their routine: sneaking from the house at the cusp of dawn, darting through the stalls, snatching what they could when the merchants looked elsewhere.

Rohan was sobbing and falling behind. Jafar sighed. He had to do all the work, and it was starting to annoy him as he turned a sharp right and squeezed between two massive carts, pulling Rohan into the shadows with him. And now there was sand in his sandals. While Rohan was trying hard not to cry out of fear, Jafar was trying hard not to cry out of frustration.

Being the eldest son of parents who were poor in more ways than one gave a child little time to *be* a child.

"Are we going to be safe?" Rohan asked, his tears drenching the small leather pouch he had been tasked with carrying.

They were chased every other day. This was nothing new.

Rohan was weak. He was six years of age and behaved like a baby, but he was also Jafar's brother, and Jafar would do anything for him.

"Of course we are," Jafar said, pulling him tight against his side and kissing his forehead just as Mama would do to ease him. He tapped the pouch in Rohan's hands. "I'll keep us safe, but you need to keep this safe for Mama, understand?"

Rohan looked down at the pouch and nodded, successfully distracted.

From the gap between the worn wood of the carts where they hid, Jafar watched with bated breath as the merchants ran past their hiding spot. He waited until the sand settled in the lonely street. Far ahead, a falcon cried as its shadow swooped over them. In the distance, someone strummed a sitar, children laughed with their father, and a camel protested against its owner.

"Now let's get you home, eh?" Jafar asked, rising with caution. Rohan nodded solemnly, picking up the neatly wrapped, painfully sweet malban that had slipped from the pouch to the dusty ground.

The walk back home was quiet, the streets outside of the bazaar still shaking off the dregs of last night's slumber. A rare sandstorm had just swept through, and villagers were either scrambling for provisions or huddling in their homes and counting blessings.

Jafar and Rohan's parents were doing neither of those things.

He heard the yelling before he even reached the house, but Rohan was oblivious, throwing open the door before Jafar could stop him. Sound ceased with the creaking hinges. Jafar should have been used to it by now, but his parents' fighting still sparked his nerves like lightning in a one of the few thunderstorms he'd witnessed. He looked from Mama to Baba and, unsure of what to do, set the vegetables on the table between them.

"This is what I mean," Baba spat. "He is a thieving street rat yet struts around like a peacock."

Jafar said nothing, though he took a step forward to put his brother behind him.

"And now we will have something to fill our bellies,"

Mama said, before a series of horrible coughs racked through her. Concern flashed across Baba's face, there and gone. It should have relieved Jafar that Baba loved Mama, even when they fought, but Jafar couldn't deny the truth of what that meant: Baba didn't like *him*. His eldest child, his son who was doing more for their family than he was himself. And as much as Baba loved Mama, it sometimes appeared as though Mama loved her boys more.

She pulled Jafar close while Rohan slipped under her other arm, and Baba stormed past the curtain to his room.

Rohan swallowed. Jafar bit the inside of his already raw cheek.

Mama looked between the two of them, a thousand and one emotions swimming in her eyes the color of smothered embers. Her skin was a little duller than it had been yesterday, her hair thinner. She finally settled her expression in a pained smile and picked up a pot, the hem of her gown flaring with her spry movements. "Did I ever tell you the story of the golden scarab?"

So began a new tale, Mama's usual method for distracting her boys from the world and its troubles. Jafar had found comfort in the stories, once. But they did nothing to change their reality, only made it go away for a while, and Jafar didn't think he was a little boy anymore.

And he might have stolen the food they would eat tonight,

and had eaten every night for the past however long, but it was still more than his father had done.

Jafar was worth more than the disgust curling Baba's lips. If only he could make Baba see that. If only he could control Baba the way Baba tried to control everything.

"It is said that an ancient enchanter created the golden scarab as a compass," Mama said, slicing through his angry thoughts.

"A bug?" Rohan asked, making a face. "That's not a compass."

"It was made to find something that didn't want to be found," Mama said, "and so, its creation required years and years of studying, scouring accounts on history, lore, and"— she leaned closer to Jafar, sensing his disinterest—"alchemy."

Jafar felt the hairs on the back of his neck rise at the word *alchemy*, along with his interest. Alchemy, Mama had once told him, was the study of something as close to magic as reality allowed. And being that Jafar wasn't fond of his reality, it fascinated him.

"Did he study alchemy in the House of Wisdom?" Jafar asked.

"Oh, but Jafar, all great men do," Mama replied with a smile. "He was, however, unaware of the powerful treasure the scarab could lead its owner toward, of the genie that could grant his master three wishes. When he learned of the potential power that no one person should ever possess, he split the scarab in two and hid each half far, far away from the other."

Rohan gasped. Jafar's gaze had strayed to the curtain at the end of the hall that led to Baba's bedroom.

"And then what happened, Mama?" Rohan asked. He was still full of wonder, still rife with the awe that only a younger child could keep alive.

"The two halves remain divided, and for whoever gathers both pieces and joins them together once more, a great reward awaits. Do you see, Jafar?" Mama asked, slicing an eggplant into neat circles.

"What?" Jafar asked, only to indulge her. He gathered the slices in a bowl before pulling out her basket of spices.

Mama smiled. "My little helper. They are two halves of a whole—"

"Like me and Jafar!" Rohan exclaimed.

Mama laughed. "Indeed. Good catch, my daffodil. Together, you are both as powerful as the golden scarab. You can do anything and stand up to anyone, remain strong against adversity."

"And summon a genie?" Rohan asked. "I already know what I'd wish for." He was looking at the small pile of sweets on the counter.

Mama's laugh grew. "Yes, even summon a genie who will grant wishes beyond your wildest dreams."

Jafar wished he could dream. Jafar wished he could control the world around him. He wished he had clung to his mother's stories more. Appreciated the distractions for what they were: little morsels of escape from the reality of life in this village. He wished he had better shown her how much he loved her.

Because it wasn't even three days later when her body was cold and the sands were smoothed over her grave.

2

– Current Day –

ROHAN

It had been eleven years since Rohan had learned of the genie in a lamp, and he was still enamored of the tale. Perhaps because its telling was soon punctuated by a pivotal time in his life. Or because it seemed almost implausible, which made him wish for it even more.

When Mama had told Jafar and him the story, Rohan had known exactly what he would wish for: money that didn't need to be returned, food that didn't need to be stolen, a house that wasn't crumbling at every turn.

He also remembered distinctly what Jafar had wanted even if he had never voiced it aloud. Rohan had seen it in the way Jafar's gaze had darkened and strayed to Baba's room at the back of the hall. Rohan shuddered at the memory now, barely moving out of the way when a maid hurried past.

He hadn't needed a genie after all.

Now, they had coins in abundance, food stocked by servants, a house that was several times the size of their old hovel, clothes no longer stiff with patches. Rohan regarded it all with a deep, troubled sense of guilt. He remembered wanting that lamp so deeply, so desperately, that when his wishes came true after Mama's death, it almost felt as though he'd traded her for them.

And now, their house was so large that the emptiness was almost tangible—even if it was masked by the servants bustling down the halls, scribes rushing out the door, and a parrot's squawk rising above the hubbub. No piece of Mama remained, not her few treasured necklaces, not her old shawl that always hung on the back of the chair, not even her books.

If Rohan *did* have a genie, he would use one wish to bring his mother back, one to make his father a better man, and the last to eradicate the shadow in his brother's eyes.

When Mama had told them the story of the golden scarab, she had really been telling Rohan to watch over Jafar, to keep the family together. Which was why, though Rohan was aware there would be no wishes left for him, he would be content—because he'd be *doing* the wishing, and that made him feel, in a way, almost as powerful as Baba.

He crossed the hall to the dining room, where the low

table was laden with food: pots of labne surrounded by color-ful platters of roasted vegetables, like beets and carrots and eggplants beside more eggplants, all seasoned to perfection and bright with garnishes from crunchy nuts to tangy sumac. At the table's center was a roasted leg of lamb, glistening and fragrant, while steam rose from a fresh stack of blistered flatbread.

Jafar was already there. He was a wisp of shadow, tower-ing above the food with clothes as dark as his hair. His jaw was sharp enough to cut, his nose long and slender. Jafar had always looked effortlessly handsome, striking and command-ing, a contrast to Rohan who could look in the mirror and still be confused by what stared back.

When Rohan's greeting went unanswered, he followed Jafar's gaze to the four different dishes of eggplant, and he knew his brother was no longer here in this room, waiting for their father to sit before a feast fit for a nobleman. No, in his mind, he was back in their decrepit kitchen from a decade before, gathering eggplant in a bowl, helping Mama season it, tracking everything they didn't have and everything he wanted to give them.

Against the backdrop of their father's approaching foot-falls, the two of them sat down, Rohan on his knees, Jafar with his legs crossed. The rug beneath them was a vibrant crimson, with a multitude of colors woven to tell a story of beauty.

"Relax," Jafar said softly.

Rohan's brow furrowed. "I am."

"You're sitting like you might have to flee," Jafar said, quickly matching Rohan's silence as Baba sat on a cushion across from them. The gold edging on their father's ebony-dark cloak caught the sunlight slanting through the window. His attar was heavy with black musk and saffron, his lips pressed thin. He leaned into the light, and shadows crowded in the fine lines of his brow and around his mouth.

"Did I not tell the cook I was tired of lamb?" Baba asked.

Rohan tensed. Only their father could look at something so lusciously alluring and complain. Rohan slid a glance at Jafar, always worried that the latest words out of their father's mouth would make him finally snap. His father wasn't like them; he didn't remember how difficult it had once been, how scarce food used to be. And Rohan couldn't blame Baba for choosing to block out a time when his wife was still alive.

"Barkat *is* getting older," Jafar said about the cook, and Rohan exhaled in relief at both his brother's choice of words and his calm tone. "He either didn't hear or forgot."

Baba grunted in reply, tearing into the lamb with a piece of flatbread. It wasn't clear whether *Baba* hadn't heard or had forgotten how to be civil, but Rohan was too famished to care. He snatched up his own flatbread, warm and still dusted in gritty grains, and dug in.

"Either way, his cooking is still as delicious as ever," Rohan remarked as flavor burst across his tongue. He loved sumac; the tang and the texture. He'd add it to everything if he could.

Jafar, adversely, barely touched the food. He poured himself water, then tilted his glass to and fro in a ray of afternoon light, deep in thought. Some days, Rohan thought Jafar ate less than the parrot the two of them had gifted Baba, the thing that did nothing but mimic anyone and anything all day long.

"Have you"—Jafar's voice caught for the barest instant, imperceptible to anyone but Rohan—"heard from any messengers today?"

Baba finished chewing, and then put more food in his mouth, letting Jafar's question hang in the air between them for no reason at all. Jafar pretended not to care. Rohan wished they could have a nice meal for once.

"About?" Baba asked, a notch colder, no doubt anticipating that Jafar would ask about his newest trade route or his latest agreement with yet another tribe. Once Mama died, Baba had thrown himself into his business, pushing himself to great lengths to become the merchant that he was today.

Jafar had a great deal of opinionated input about every aspect of it, some of which Rohan had overheard and thought made very good sense, but Baba was, well, Baba. He was one of those people who believed wisdom only came with age, and thought being older was synonymous with being an elder.

In short, he wasn't fond of Jafar's ideas.

"My scholarship," Jafar said at last, with a cautious glance at Baba.

Fortunately, it seemed Jafar wasn't interested in discussing business—and having a fight—today.

But Baba wasn't paying him any attention, still chewing away while eyeing the spread around them with far more interest than an ordinary lunch warranted.

He finally swallowed, his mouth dipping into a slight frown: the barest display of concern. "I don't believe so."

The concern was gone in an instant, leaving one to wonder if Baba had ever cared to begin with. And when Rohan looked at Jafar, he paused. Perhaps it was the glare of the sun through the window making it hard to see, but Rohan thought he saw that same darkness in his brother again. A darkness that made Jafar look cold, distant, almost evil.

That expression was partly the reason why Rohan had his own qualms about Jafar's scholarship, but he felt for his brother just then. It was maddening to witness a fractured relationship that could so easily sing with perfection—for Jafar never asked for much, nor had Mama. Rohan *himself* never asked for much.

"I see," Jafar said, disappointment wrapped in the terse delivery of the words.

Baba was set in his ways, and slowly, Jafar was cementing his own. Rohan would simply do what he could before it was too late.

"I must say this lamb is perfectly"—Rohan began cheerily but faltered when Jafar set his glass down with a resounding thud—"tender."

"Baba?" Jafar said. Rohan recognized that tone and braced himself. "Isn't your meeting about that new deal happening today?"

The words were bait, and Rohan swallowed, knowing Baba could not resist. Jafar never expressed genuine concern for Baba's work. What Jafar wanted to know, he found out himself. Self-regard was heavy in this household.

"It is," Baba replied, oozing with pride. "I'll be securing a new trade route and a new line of coin by the next moon."

"It's between you and the son of the Bani Jari chief, isn't it?" Jafar asked, a level calm settling over his voice. The Bani Jari tribe, Rohan racked his brain to remember, was as unforgiving and relentless as the desert heat.

"The son?" Baba scoffed. "Why, were you hoping to school me in the fact the son is immovable and hates every part of this? I know. Just as I know that the father is too senile and too tired to do anything but agree with our terms. It's especially helpful, as the proposal can only be touched by the chief and me and is soon to be signed for posterity."

"I never school you, Baba," Jafar said softly. A stranger might have mistaken his tone for chagrin, but Rohan knew better. It was gentle. Almost pitiful.

Baba knew better, too. His nostrils flared, his right eye twitched.

Jafar's strength lived and breathed in his brain, which was evident in the way he'd helped route trade lines, how he'd suggested a strategy cleverer than brute force during a skirmish, how he'd formulated a way to keep perishable goods cool for longer periods of time by hanging damp reeds. Baba's business could never have grown to what it was without Jafar, and Baba's sin was that he never once appreciated Jafar's insight.

Jafar didn't give Baba time to explode. "I read the proposal, Baba. I've never seen anything more inclined to fail."

Baba recoiled as if Jafar had slapped him.

"It's riddled with holes, the largest of which is the fact that the chief of the Bani Jari and his son share the same name, so the moment the elder dies, the son will renege on your deal and you'll be left to pick up the pieces.

"Your men should have seen that," Jafar continued, "because now you won't be securing anything. I wouldn't be surprised to learn that the son took matters into his own hands and buried his father already." Jafar leaned back and tossed a cube of halloumi into his mouth, unfazed by Baba's temper quickly shifting from its usual simmer well nigh to boiling. "You'll have to be more careful, Baba. Sons can be deadly sometimes."

The Story You Didn't Know
A Disney PRINCE NOVEL

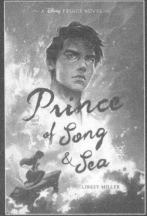

9781368069113

9781368069120

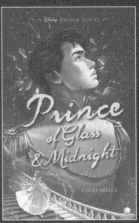

9781368085489

Discover the Queen's Council series:
All-new stories featuring beloved Disney Princesses!

THE QUEEN'S COUNCIL

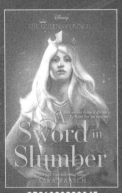

9781368092845

9781368048217

9781368053426

9781368095969

Available wherever print, eBook, and audiobooks are sold